"It's hard to believe you've been gone so long," Chas said.

"Fifteen years," Allison said softly.

"A long time."

"Whatever was between us, Chas, is in the past. And that past is fifteen years old."

She leveled a look at him that would have reduced a lesser man to jelly. She'd had heads of state cower beneath such a hard look.

Not Chas. And somehow, in some indefinable way, he'd turned the tables on her and taken control of the situation. She didn't want to touch him, yet she wanted nothing more than to place her hand in that broad, callused palm, to feel his fingers wrap around hers once again....

★ ★ ★ ★

Don't miss book #3 of ALMOST, TEXAS: Where a hazard-free happily ever-after is *almost* always guaranteed!

Dear Reader,

This is it, the final month of our wonderful three-month celebration of Intimate Moments' fifteenth anniversary. It's been quite a ride, but it's not over yet. For one thing, look who's leading off the month: Rachel Lee, with *Cowboy Comes Home,* the latest fabulous title in her irresistible CONARD COUNTY miniseries. This one has everything you could possibly want in a book, including all the deep emotion Rachel is known for. Don't miss it.

And the rest of the month lives up to that wonderful beginning, with books from both old favorites and new names sure to become favorites. Merline Lovelace's *Return to Sender* will have you longing to work at the post office (I'm not kidding!), while Marilyn Tracy returns to the wonderful (but fictional, darn it!) town of Almost, Texas, with *Almost Remembered.* Look for our TRY TO REMEMBER flash to guide you to Leann Harris's *Trusting a Texan,* a terrific amnesia book, and the EXPECTANTLY YOURS flash marking Raina Lynn's second book, *Partners in Parenthood.* And finally, don't miss *A Hard-Hearted Man,* by brand-new author Melanie Craft. *Your* heart will melt—guaranteed.

And that's not all. Because we're not stopping with the fifteen years behind us. There are that many—and more!—in our future, and I know you'll want to be here for every one. So come back next month, when the excitement and the passion continue, right here in Silhouette Intimate Moments.

Yours,

Leslie Wainger

Leslie J. Wainger
Executive Senior Editor

Please address questions and book requests to:
Silhouette Reader Service
U.S.: 3010 Walden Ave., P.O. Box 1325, Buffalo, NY 14269
Canadian: P.O. Box 609, Fort Erie, Ont. L2A 5X3

ALMOST REMEMBERED

MARILYN TRACY

Published by Silhouette Books

America's Publisher of Contemporary Romance

SILHOUETTE BOOKS

ISBN 0-373-07867-6

ALMOST REMEMBERED

Copyright © 1998 by Tracy LeCocq

Printed in U.S.A.

Books by Marilyn Tracy

Silhouette Intimate Moments

Silhouette Shadows

MARILYN TRACY

lives in Portales, New Mexico, in a ramshackle turn-of-the-century house with her son, two dogs, three cats and a poltergeist. Between remodeling the house to its original Victorian-cum-Deco state, writing full-time and finishing a forty-foot cement dragon in the backyard, Marilyn composes full soundtracks to go with each of her novels.

After having lived in both Tel Aviv and Moscow in conjunction with the U.S. State Department, Marilyn enjoys writing about the cultures she's explored and the people she's grown to love. She likes to hear from people who enjoy her books and always has a pot of coffee on or a glass of wine ready for anyone dropping by, especially if they don't mind chaos and know how to wield a paintbrush.

To Melissa Jeglinski,
for all her help and faith in this series.

Prologue

If you haven't visited Almost, Texas, before, you'll probably be struck by how well kept the town appears. In this desert-dry section of the Panhandle, in this time of drought and wind, most towns appear as dried-up as the shriveled crops. Not in Almost. Every house sports freshly painted porches, neatly trimmed yards and gardens, newly scrubbed mailboxes and, as often as not, recently swept sidewalks. Almost's pristine condition is due to a set of triplets performing "community service."

And now, if you're searching for any of the people in Almost, look for a big two-story Midwest-style house with the yellow trim and the broad front porch. That's Taylor Leary Smithton's house—soon to be known as the Kessler place. Just walk on up the steps and ring the bell. It'll seem like the whole town's there—Homer Chalmers, Delbert Franklin, Steve Kessler, Carolyn, Taylor, the girls, the triplets, Alva Lu Harrigan, Fredda Schooler and Marilyn Huber from over at the alternative school in Pep—and you can sip some iced tea or lemonade while rocking in one of Taylor's back-porch chairs.

You'll probably feel the excitement of Taylor's soon-to-be wedding. And you'll probably also feel the tension in the air because, after fifteen years, Allison Leary is coming back to Almost.

Chapter 1

Though the date on Allison Leary's tickets read February, the light afternoon breeze in the Texas Panhandle city spelled late spring. A clear, pale blue sky arced from horizon to horizon, and the few skyscrapers in Lubbock, a full five miles away, stood in sharp relief against the skyline to the southeast.

Allison drew a deep breath of air and tasted west Texas on her tongue, a flavor she would have thought she'd forgotten in fifteen years. Suddenly all the nuances of the Panhandle came rushing back to her—cattle, cars, tractors, milo, dust, baking asphalt, oil and gas wells and miles and miles of dry grasses.

Occasionally, hurrying down an avenue in New York City, she would pass a specialty shop and stop a few paces away, snared by a memory of west Texas, unable to understand why her hometown of Almost suddenly came to mind. Now, outside the Lubbock Airport, swallowing the ash-dry Texas air, she knew what had captured her on those busy streets: a faint memory of home.

Allison blinked.

Outside the terminal, she counted less than ten squinting people making for cars, casually searching for vehicles. Allison cautiously made her way across the loading-zone street and found her rental car without any difficulty. Her suitcase felt heavier than usual and seemed unnaturally loud as it rolled and jolted beside her across the macadam. Her right leg ached a little, a reminder of why she'd chosen this of all times to come home. Something in nearly dying made her feel a keen awareness of the fifteen years of time lost, of too many words left unspoken.

That, and the growing fear she was losing her mind and shortly wouldn't be able to remember even her childhood.

She pressed on the rental-car signature key ring several times, waiting for the dual-toned beep signaling the unlocking of the rental Buick, and when nothing happened, she realized the car didn't have an automatic-safety-lock feature. It had been years since she'd been near a car without such devices. It had been a couple of months since she'd been this near to driving a car at all.

She loaded her suitcase and carryall into the trunk of the car. After arching her travel-stiffened back, she withdrew her pocket telephone and punched in the code for her answering machine without bothering to glance at the number pad. She'd called it so often her fingers knew the pattern.

Two messages played back for her, both from co-workers and both wishing her a good holiday and a quick recovery.

As she replaced the phone into her handbag, she wondered if she wasn't feeling out of kilter because the messages had wished her a happy holiday. Not vacation, as most Americans would say, but a *holiday*. Christmas,

Thanksgiving, Hanukkah. Not the standard two weeks of paid time off granted most salaried people.

The last holiday had been Christmas. Had it been that long since she checked her phone mail? The thought sent a shiver of primal fear down her spine. She was going crazy.

Once inside the Buick, she checked the car thoroughly before gripping the steering wheel with a white-knuckled clutch. It had been two months since her near fatal car accident. And this was the first time she'd been behind the wheel of any car. Her insurance company had sold her own demolished vehicle to a wrecking yard for scrap metal. Though she'd never wished to see it again, for a brief second, she longed for the familiar grooves and curves of that old and reliable companion.

What if she suffered one of her "attacks" while behind the wheel of a car? Wasn't she being criminal even driving the vehicle? Friends Don't Let Friends Drive Drunk. What about friends letting friends drive while going crazy?

Except she didn't have very many friends, did she? Not anymore. She used to. Colleagues, co-workers, people she met through *Timeline*. She frowned, trying to remember the last time she'd seen any of those friends. She sighed struggling to recall anything that made any sense in the past two months.

As she slowly reversed, shifted gears and accelerated infinitesimally toward the parking-lot fee booth, she was grateful to realize that her subconscious still remembered how to maneuver a car and, moreover, she felt relieved that she'd delayed so long that few other drivers were trying to exit the lot. This dual realization allowed her to relax, albeit marginally.

"I'm Allison Leary. I'm a reporter for *Timeline*, five-time Associated Press award winner. I live in New York

City. I'm thirty-three years old. I was born on December 20 in Lubbock, Texas.''

She followed another departing passenger to the automated exit gate. She continued whispering her careful litany of facts. She'd read that early-Alzheimer's victims could remain focused for far longer if they repeated simple facts on a daily basis.

"Last night I packed my bags to come to Almost. I watched *Timeline*. I...and I...'' Her voice trailed away, and the silence in the car seemed preternaturally loud as if someone waited for her to continue. Someone who would tell her what she really had done.

She watched the driver of the car ahead of her. The man's jerseyed arm arced across to the machine's slot and released the mechanism. He pointed back at her, signaling her that she was free to move forward.

She seemed to be seeing the scene played in slow motion. Nearly in stop-frame animation. She had trouble catching her breath. A familiar sensation of panic threaded its way through her body.

Not now, she silently begged. "Not now," she murmured aloud. Not here, not in a car. But the sensation of being sealed off, of the world fading from view, pressed on with relentless speed.

The man ahead of her inserted his rental waiver and smoothly exited the gate while she sat still, her foot jammed against the brake, her heart suddenly pounding in furious rhythm. A voice in her mind seemed to be screaming for her to run, to escape the car.

Many times in the past two months, she'd given in to the raging, panicked voice. Strangely the panic and the need to run stayed with her while so much else seemed to evaporate. Several times, without knowing why, she'd heeded the instinct to turn blindly from whatever she was doing, whomever she'd been talking with, and dash mindlessly away from…something. Some unknown terror.

She had the door partially open and was all set to jump from the car when the curious demand relaxed its grip on her and she knew she no longer needed to flee.

After a few seconds, she pulled the door closed, forced her foot from the brake, let the car creep forward and used her own waiver to release the gate. By the time the bar rose, she'd regained some semblance of rationality. Her heartbeat felt steadier, though her hands still trembled but were strong enough to grip the wheel with authority. She told herself there was nothing to be frightened of. Not here in west Texas.

The road leading from the Lubbock Airport seemed new to her. She felt certain no such elegantly curved and multilaned stretch of highway had existed fifteen years ago. Surely her recent lapses of memory didn't extend so far back. And hopefully, these episodes of amnesia wouldn't throw her into another panic attack as had happened with such alarming frequency lately. As it had nearly occurred only moments ago at the gate.

Allison, is something troubling you?

Who had asked her that? John Townsend, her boss? Her doctor…Dr. Cross? Dr. Knoss. Her psychiatrist…what was his name?

She shook her head. She didn't have a psychiatrist, did she?

A low sob escaped her. Everything she'd worked so hard to create for so many years was crumbling around her. What was wrong with her?

She soon found herself on the slender, two-laned farm-to-market roads that would eventually land her in Almost…and *home*.

"For you, Taylor," she murmured aloud, forcing herself

not to seize the steering wheel when a massive grain truck roared past her at the new Texas speed limit of seventy miles per hour. A glance at the speedometer let her know how skittish she really felt, and she caught her lower lip between her teeth as she purposefully depressed the accelerator pedal before she was pulled over for driving too slowly.

"Not for my sister," she corrected herself, gritting her teeth. "For *me*." For the lapses of time, for the indecision and confusion. And for the years of wondering and longing.

Maybe you should take some time off, Allison.

Have a great holiday, Allison.

Hey, Allison, don't forget to log in the love story before you get away.

When had those things been said to her? She recognized the voices, could put names to them. But when had they spoken to her? Yesterday? A month ago? Two months ago?

A sob tore at her throat, but she swallowed it furiously, trying desperately just to think clearly. The way she'd always thought in the past.

...no evidence of brain damage, Miss Leary.

Maybe a rest will help you straighten this out, Allison.

The empty roads, the yellow plains stretching out to either side of the pavement, Reba MacIntyre's unique and lilting voice on the radio all conspired to weave a spell that seemed to defy time. Hadn't she driven down this exact road in a similar car in another springlike February, another year, another lifetime, listening to Reba then, too?

No...she'd been a passenger then, riding in an old, battered pickup, and Tammy Wynette had been singing some sad love song. And Chas had turned his shaggy head to look at her with that hint of a smile and a raw, blazing warmth in his brown eyes.

Allison shook her head. Those kind of memories she

could do without. She'd left home fifteen years ago to avoid them. And she had managed to successfully escape them for most of that time.

She thought how her co-workers at *Timeline* would stare if they could hear that the indomitable Allison Leary was actually afraid of something. Most would probably just laugh and brush the thought away like some half-seen flying pest. A few, those few she was closest to, might frown and consider the notion, only to shake their heads in disbelief.

Or they would have. Once.

It was just the concussion, honey, you'll be all right in no time.

Two months wasn't "no time"; it was an extended holiday in Hell.

She could remember the day of the accident clearly. Every moment of it. Despite her fear of another panic attack.

She glared at the road, drawing several deep breaths and reassuring herself that she could handle any situation, no matter how dire. She was surprised to learn she could look at the road as it was, could see it without seeing her recent accident. And without that damnable sense of panic.

Though it brought no comfort, she told herself that her current panic had to do with seeing Dr. Charles Jamison again after all this time. Chas, who had married someone else, who had raised a son with that someone. Good old Chas, who had unknowingly and cruelly ruined her life.

Allison felt a deep well of anger rising in her. Anger she'd never allowed to be aired. She welcomed the ire, nurtured it carefully, conjuring up other memories of Chas's mountain of hurts. As long as she remembered the past, as long as she focused her thoughts on the days long ago, she had none of that dizzying vertigo, no panic. Just simple anger.

But what if she had to see him again? How would she handle that, especially in her current condition? If she'd met him again while mind-whole, she could have disdainfully told him he was less than belly lint.

But now, when she was so terribly vulnerable? How would she be able to cope with her anger at him, her years of longing for him?

Was this trip home—ostensibly for her sister's wedding—yet another in a seemingly endless stream of mistakes? Because without a single doubt, she would be forced to face Chas. She would be forced to meet his wife. His son. And she would, by sheer upbringing alone, be forced to put her hand in his and pretend she'd half forgotten his face, had nearly lost the memory of his name.

But she'd be lying. She still sometimes woke to the echoes of his name being cried aloud, aching from the memory of his lips on hers.

A horned lark flitted out from the side of the road, its little black Batman hat visible above its yellow neck and brown-and-white-striped body, its wings swooped back as it dived for her. Two more larks followed swiftly behind their leader, darting at the insects slipstreamed by the wake of the car.

Allison realized her swerving to avoid the birds was unnecessary even as she stomped on the brake and dragged the wheel sharply to the left. The birds scattered, and the car tires screeched as rubber ground into the pavement.

Instead of the flash of wings and the glint of light ricocheting across the windshield, Allison saw a truck crowding her from the left, a Suburban bearing hard from behind and the white Chevy Nova in front of her. The Nova's plates were customized, and even before the impact she found an irony in their soon-to-be-destroyed message: 4GET-U.

Allison remembered screaming. She covered her head and burrowed down into the driver's seat.

Well versed in the way of cars, the undamaged horned larks swooped over the stalled vehicle, singing and seemingly frolicking only to drift back down to their hunting posts alongside the road, wholly ignoring the woman hunched and crying softly behind the steering wheel of a rental car in the middle of their road.

The man with the wire-rimmed glasses and short, neatly trimmed blond hair felt a rush of adrenaline shoot through him. Allison Leary was right ahead of him.

He frowned heavily. As before, she hadn't recognized him. Didn't *know* him. He ground his teeth to keep from swearing aloud. Or shouting his frustration and triumph to the bright clear skies.

She meant *everything* to him. And yet she didn't know him. They had been so close, had shared some of the most intense moments human beings could ever experience. Now her eyes passed over him as if he were a virtual stranger.

And yet, hadn't she stopped when collecting her bags at the luggage carousel in Lubbock? Hadn't she glanced over her shoulder, combing the crowd for a familiar face?

His heart had jolted when she looked directly at him, and jolted anew when she continued scanning the sparse crowd. He meant nothing to her. She would pay for that, he thought. Oh, yes, she would most definitely pay.

She would remember him then. He'd make sure she didn't forget him a second time. And there wouldn't be any time after that. No time at all. At least, not for Allison.

"Oh, and hang on to your britches, Charles...*Allison*'s coming," Sammie Jo said, pushing his change across the counter.

Chas's fingers, stretching for the pennies and nickels, seemed to numb slightly.

"We see her on TV and everything—big-time reporter on *Timeline* and all, but it's not the same, you know? Hard to imagine what she's like now," Sammie Jo said. "My youngest niece."

Chas thought her voice sounded wistful. He wished he could lift his eyes from the dancing coins to look at Sammie Jo. Her lizard-dry face, sparkling blue eyes and outrageous wig might serve to ground him again. But he was more than half afraid of what he might read in her expression.

"It'll be good to see her again," Chas mumbled, lying through his teeth. His voice sounded strained and felt far worse. If one of the horses he treated sounded that gruff, he'd probably prescribe clindimycin for an abscess.

"Just to see her in real life, won't that be a treat?" Sammie Jo said, and pushed a couple of the pennies a mite closer to his fingers. "Remember how she used to follow you around?"

"Yeah," he acknowledged, trying *not* to remember.

"Lord, but that girl loved the country. She was such a pistol. All these years away. Still, it's always been hard to picture Allison living in a big city and all."

Finally he grabbed the coins and stuffed them into his jeans pocket. Then Chas forced himself to meet Sammie Jo's eyes and was immediately sorry. In hers, he could read a world of family and loss.

He could see her battle with breast cancer and her long-time struggle to come to grips with the death of her daughter, Susie. And he sensed that she knew why Allison had shadowed him fifteen years ago. Worst of all, he could see she understood why he'd let her tag along.

Suddenly, Sammie Jo reached out a sunbaked hand and patted his arm. "Things change, Charles. *People* change. Heck...sometimes dreams we have when we're young are the best dreams."

He didn't know what to say to Sammie Jo, the only person left in the world who occasionally called him by his real name. It had been Allison who had nicknamed him Chas. Allison who had marked him permanently by naming him.

"It's okay, Charles. Don't look so scared. And don't you mind me, I'm just a little fey from all the chemo treatments they're giving me up in Lubbock."

"When is she coming?" he asked.

Sammie Jo's hand on his hadn't pulled the question from him; her frailty had. She owned the market on "life's too short for lies." Meeting her eyes, he knew he owed her nothing less than honesty in return.

Sammie Jo smiled. Chas could see the family resemblance between her and Allison. After all those years, he still recognized Allison's blue gaze. Could still feel the sting of the contempt in them the day she rejected him, though he'd done his finest to reject her only a day or two after that.

"This afternoon, hon. Our Allison's coming back to us today."

He should have known, he thought. He should have felt something this momentous. *Allison was coming home.* The grass should have bent to the east; the clouds should have been filled with rain. Birds should have flown upside down and backward.

"I didn't know," was all he said.

"Well, now you do," Sammie Jo replied. She slid her thin, dry fingers into his palm and grasped his hand with a surprisingly strong grip. "And Charles..."

He tried to smile and felt it slide askew when he saw tears shimmer in her eyes.

He'd known Sammie Jo for nearly seventeen years. As the town veterinarian and makeshift doctor to most of the folk living within twenty miles of Almost, he'd seen Sammie Jo in nearly every catastrophic situation that had come down the proverbial pike. Invariably she was on hand at a funeral, a birthing, a crisis, a homecoming, a wedding or a barn raising. He'd even been there when her daughter, Susie, was buried in the little cemetery on the outskirts of Almost.

"Hey," he said, "talk to me, Sammie Jo. What's wrong?"

She closed her eyes for a long moment, then opened them again, her incredible Leary eyes awash with tears. "I want you to do me a favor, Charles."

"Name it, Sammie Jo," he said promptly, giving her fingers a warm squeeze in return.

"Keep her here, Charles."

"What?"

"I mean it. I don't care what you have to do. You promise me, okay? You keep her home."

"Sammie Jo—"

"Promise me, Charles!"

"But—"

"Goats butt. *Promise me.*"

"This is blackmail, Sammie Jo," Chas said.

The older woman chuckled, but a tear sneaked onto her leathered cheek. "I'm entitled."

Chas raised a shaking hand to brush the streak away from her face and felt the truth torn from him. "I can't promise you to keep Allison here, darling. You know I can't do that." Strangely, at that moment, promising her to do just that was all he wanted to do. That was all he'd wanted to do for the past fifteen years. "She—"

"She'll stay if you ask her to," Sammie Jo said. Her words were sharp, her grip sharper.

Chas gave a whispered chuckle, more a sigh than anything else. "You can't say that, Sammie Jo. She has a life. A career. She's a somebody and—"

"And you're what? Just promise me you'll ask her."

Chas gave up. "Fifteen years is a long, long time, Sammie Jo."

She shook her head, her outrageous wig swaying with her movement. "Fifteen years is less than a grain of sand in the desert, Charles." She didn't let loose of his hand.

"So, what's going on in that head of yours, Sammie Jo Leary? You picturing a romance? The old vet and the pretty TV star?"

"I've heard of stranger combinations," she answered promptly.

"Not this time, darling. There's too much water under that bridge."

She looked over his shoulder, either at the stand of used books or out the broad, dusty window in front of her store. "If I can't have Susie back...I want Allison," she said steadily, despite the two new and unchecked tears racing down her cheeks.

Chas felt as if a fist clenched his heart. "Oh, God, Sammie Jo. What about Taylor?"

Sammie Jo waved her free hand and nodded, as if only partway acknowledging her eldest niece, Taylor.

"And Carolyn?"

Again Sammie Jo waved her hand and nodded, giving only a partial credence to Carolyn, her niece by marriage, as though he knew she loved both Carolyn and Taylor with all her heart.

"Allison and Susie were like twins," Sammie Jo said, pressing his hand, still not looking at him, tears continuing to fall from her blue eyes.

Chas had the fleeting thought that no two human beings could have been more dissimilar than Susie and Allison. Susie had been like Taylor, as sweet as pure honey and as innocent as a newborn calf. Whereas Allison, a long-legged, skittish colt, filled with all the wrong sorts of trust, determination and grit, raced through each day like a thoroughbred, heedless of everything but the need to run.

Sammie Jo cleared her throat, and her fingers tightened on his hand. "I want to get to know her again. I want to know what's going on in that pretty head of hers. I want to know why she stayed away from us so long. I've got to know, Charles."

Chas felt starkly ambivalent. On the one hand, he wanted the same things Sammie Jo did, and on the other, he was dead certain his life would be much easier and his heart much safer if he didn't know at all. Ever. "Sammie Jo—"

Her telephone rang, and she gave it a quick glance. "So, it's settled," she said, and withdrew her weathered hand from his. She gave his knuckles a quick pat. She reached for the telephone. "Minimart, what can I do for you?"

Chas stood perfectly still, his hand still outstretched and hanging in midair. Nothing was settled, he thought.

Her eyes met his. He shook his head at her, slowly, even sadly, trying to convey his unwillingness to be drawn into her schemes for Allison. For her. For him.

She nodded again, as if in response to whoever talked to her over the telephone. But Chas could see that the tears weren't completely gone from her eyes. As if in answer, she pointed a finger at him and mouthed the words, "Keep her here."

He hadn't been able to do that fifteen years ago when it

was the one thing he'd wanted above all things on earth. How in the hell was he supposed to do it now, when he didn't even know how he felt about seeing her again?

He opened the door to the Minimart and stepped out into the glare of the midday sun.

A car passed slowly down the street, a woman gripping the wheel with both hands, her face pale, her blond hair tousled as if she'd run her hands through it many times. Just the way she had when she was younger. A million years ago.

Allison.

Chapter 2

On the far side of the west Texas town, home to some six hundred people, Allison pulled the car onto a narrow strip of wintered yellow grass but made no move to exit the car. She stared through the passenger's window at the two-story house with its bright yellow trim and broad front porch.

It was hard to picture Taylor living here. To Allison, it was still the Porter place. She'd been in the same grade as the youngest Porter girl…Jenny? Janey? They'd spent several warm afternoons sprawled on the rails of the front porch drinking sodas and dreaming about where they would be in ten years, twenty, thirty. One thing they'd never imagined was that the Porters would lose their farm and be forced to move to Arkansas to live with family and that one day Taylor would buy their house and raise her family inside those familiar walls.

Staring at the house gave Allison that same sensation of misplaced time and space as had seized her all too frequently since her car accident. The feeling was much like that of a particularly vivid dream, but one that couldn't possibly have really happened.

Her doctor had told her not to dwell too much on the odd sensations; some residual effects of her accident and the attendant concussion were bound to linger. If they didn't disappear as time worked its healing magic, then he'd run a few new tests to see what might show up.

But Allison was terribly afraid no tests would ever reveal what was really wrong with her. She remembered interviewing a famous movie star once. The woman had described a strange decline her career had taken several years before. "I think I was soul sick," the star had said.

That's what Allison felt now: soul sick. Too aware of missing elements in her life, her love, even her well-established, now possibly crumbling career. And she had the distinct impression that the peculiar soul sickness had started before finding herself folded between a Chevy Nova and a Suburban. The subsequent memory lapses and panic attacks were only an extension of a strange strain of empty-life syndrome.

Suddenly the carved oak door of Taylor's house opened as if in slow motion. Allison found herself holding her breath.

The slow-motion effect ceased abruptly as three identical boys catapulted through the door's gap as if thrown out, arms waving, legs flying, thick blond hair dancing from what appeared to be sheer energy.

She'd known her sister had triplets, but knowing hadn't prepared her for the reality of three Leary look-alikes. They ran across the yard, yelling like wild creatures, and sailed over the low fence as if professional high jumpers.

They circled the car and came to a skidding halt outside the driver's door only to stand, mouths agape, staring at her through the tinted glass. In awe? In confusion? Or was it simply a sudden attack of shyness at seeing the aunt they'd never met before?

The years of absence had never felt so solid to Allison as they did at that moment, sitting inside a rental car studying her three nephews. How old were they? Eleven, twelve? How dreadful, she thought, that she didn't even know.

She could see Taylor in the boys. And Taylor's lost husband, Doug—whom Allison still thought of as Taylor's "boyfriend." And when the three of them raised identical sets of eyebrows, she knew she could see her brother, Craig. And herself. And Aunt Sammie Jo. And Susie. And…Daddy.

I should have never come back, she thought with sharp panic.

"Boys!" Allison heard Taylor call, using the exact intonation their mother had used to call her three wayward children in from the barn.

She dragged her gaze from the boys to the woman crossing the broad porch. She felt as if she'd been hit in the chest. Her heart ached, and her fingers clutched at her handbag with frantic need to cling to something.

Taylor. She'd have recognized her anywhere, anytime. She'd even caught glimpses of that particular shade of blond hair or a hint of her heart-shaped face a thousand different times in crowds waiting at subway stations or bus stops. But this was the real thing. Her only sister.

She mouthed Taylor's name, remembering the girl who had always looked out for her younger sister. She felt her eyes sting as Taylor hesitated at the base of the porch steps, as if uncertain how to proceed.

Allison hadn't wholly turned her back on her family fifteen years ago. She'd sent the occasional Christmas card, received and answered the odd letter. She even had a few photographs of the boys in their infant years. But they hadn't chatted on the phone, hadn't poured their hearts out over the Internet, hadn't seen each other one-on-one any time during those fifteen years. Not because Taylor hadn't wanted it, but because Allison couldn't face it.

Her older sister was a woman now, fully grown and lovely. *Oh, Taylor...I've missed you.* She wondered what that graceful woman saw when looking at her younger but not-so-little sister.

All her hard-won years of sophistication and poise, expertise and knowledge melted away. She felt more vulnerable now than she did after one of her panic attacks. Why? Because what Taylor thought mattered.

Allison might have stayed in the car forever, frozen in place, had the boys not taken the matter out of her hands by opening the car door.

"You're *her*, aren't you?"

"Aunt *Allison?*"

"Doofus. Who'd you think she was?"

"Aren't you gonna get out of the car?"

It seemed like a thousand somewhat grimy hands reached for her. She wondered if they noticed her own hand was shaking as she dropped it into one damp, warm, slightly gritty grasp. A set of strong, broken-nailed, stubby fingers wrapped around her hand. The sensation took her back almost twenty-five years to the memory of her brother's hand clasping hers.

Come on, Allison, hurry up!

"She wants you to help her out of the car, doofus."

"Oh, yeah."

"Cool."

She didn't know which of her nephews' hands she clung to as though holding on to a single log in hurricane-churned waters. She issued a faint smile at all three boys and gave a minimal nod. The hand around hers tightened abruptly while its controller gave a mighty tug and roared as if she weighed something close to three thousand pounds instead of her slim 120 pounds.

She shot from the car like a clown from a circus canon.

"Josh! For heaven's sake!" Taylor reprimanded her son, then said to Allison, "Are you all right?"

Still unsteady on her worrisome leg, Allison gratefully accepted the hands her sister held out to her. Had she not been yanked from the car so precipitously, she might have felt some awkwardness about touching her sister for the first time in fifteen years.

But the moment her hands were enveloped in a blessedly familiar warmth, she felt the ticklish moment evaporate. "Taylor..." she murmured thickly, holding her sister's hands tightly in her own.

"It's about time," Taylor said, pulling her in for a lengthy and long-awaited hug. "Oh, honey, it's so good to see you home."

Allison rested her head on her sister's shoulder and knew she wasn't *home*. And she wasn't all that certain it was really good to be there. But she felt an absolute conviction that it was pure heaven to be held in Taylor's arms and called "honey," again.

The man in the wire-frame glasses and neatly trimmed blond hair pulled over to the side of the road in a town not much bigger than his living room in New York. He studied the few cars parked outside a small, flea-bitten café, then pulled out a briefcase, strung a camera around his neck, ruffled his hair a bit and strolled across the street and crossed into the hot-oil-scented café and its equally redolent customers.

All eyes turned to stare at him, and he forced a Hollywood smile to his lips. "Hello, there. Mind if I snap a few pictures of this place?"

All of the seven people in the café exchanged glances.

"What do you want to take pictures of the café for?" a woman holding a coffeepot in each hand asked in a nasal twang.

He forced his grin to a broader, more friendly smile. "Oh, just scouting around."

He set down the briefcase at an empty but uncleared table and lifted his camera. He popped the lens cap free, held the camera to his face and snapped a picture of the waitress.

He turned and snapped a couple of shots of the men sitting around two tables imperfectly pushed together.

One of them frowned. "Hey!"

The men turned, and he snapped four or five quick pictures of the shabby walls, the crooked and faded prints hanging without any seeming concept of design by single nails and a bit of wire. "By the way, can anyone tell me who owns that fifties Ford pickup parked out front?"

Three of the seven people in the café asked why he wanted to know.

He lowered his camera and turned back around to face them. "My name is Michaels. I'm part of the advance team for the picture."

"What picture?"

He chuckled a little. "That's a good one," he said, nodding at the man who'd asked. He started to lift his camera again.

"What's a good one?" another man asked.

The man with the wire-frame glasses allowed a small frown to furrow his brow and his grin to fade a little as his camera lowered. "*Lubbock Dust*. You know, the movie we're making out here?"

"Somebody's making a movie out here?" the waitress asked.

"You weren't kidding me? You really didn't know about the picture? I just figured everybody knew by now. We're shooting parts of *Lubbock Dust* right here in Anton."

"In *Anton?*" one of the men at the table exclaimed. "What on earth for?"

"Well, we looked around and couldn't come up with anything that looked like Lubbock did about thirty years ago. But the architecture in Anton lends itself perfectly to the concept of the film."

"We say it 'Ant'n,'" one of the other men said. "Not 'An-tahn.'"

The others chuckled a little. But the blond man grinned a little. "Ant'n it is. Anyway, about that Ford pickup outside...?"

"Which one?" asked one of the men, pushing to his feet to walk to the window. "They's at least three of 'em parked out front."

"The red one."

The man at the window gave a snort of laughter. "Well, it mighta been red one day. About twenty years back, I guess. Whaddya want with my pickup?"

"I want to buy it."

The grin faded from the other man's ruddy face. "You wanna what?"

"I want to buy it. For the film. The script calls for the star to be driving a—"

"How much?"

"Well, sir, how much would you like for it?"

"I don't know," the man said, too honestly. "I can't afford to get a different pickup."

"Well, then, what about that Mercury Cougar parked across the street?"

"Whaddya mean?"

"An even trade. My car for yours."

"What kind of deal is this?" the man asked.

"You happen to have the exact make, model and color of truck I need for the film. I can get a new Mercury this afternoon in Lubbock. And I'm willing to bet I can find another make and model somewhere else, given time. I'd just rather not take that time. You got me?"

Five minutes later, the men from the café carried his belongings from the car to the pickup for him. He snapped their pictures a couple more times, then climbed up into the incredible filth of the cab.

He started the vehicle on the third try and backed it from its slantwise slot and headed the car not east and south as they had expected, but west. Toward another little town. One named Almost.

About halfway there, he pulled over again. He carefully removed his wire-frame glasses, tugged off the neatly trimmed blond hair and threw both bits of camouflage into a small plastic bag and stuffed them far beneath the seat of the battered truck, back in a recess already filled with empty food wrappers, beer cans and moldy pools of tobacco juice.

He stripped out of his chinos and oxford cloth shirt and pulled on a pair of stained and battered pants and a filthy shirt that sported a small brownish stain with a smaller, nearly invisible rip right beside the torn breast pocket.

He didn't bother to hide this exchange of clothing. If anyone tried to stop him or even came along at all, he would deal with them as he had the owner of his present outfit of disgusting clothes.

He climbed back into the pickup, sweating slightly in the strangely summerlike February sun. He glanced in the mirror. His gray eyes stared back at him from under dark eyebrows. His jet black hair looked oily and lank after the hours beneath the tight wig. He ran his hand down his face, leaving a streak of black he'd acquired from his disguise hiding beneath the seat of the pickup. He didn't try to wipe the mark away. Instead, he smeared it in, adding more.

He had a part to play, and the added grime would only make his job all the easier.

Allison must be in Almost by now, enfolded in the arms of her long abandoned family.

She remembered *them*, all right. No doubts about that. And because of her memories about them, he knew them also. Every single seemingly insignificant detail.

Again he suffered mixed emotions, sorrow and fury.

She would pay, all right. They would *all* pay.

And they would all pay very dearly.

Allison sank into one of Taylor's rockers on the back porch, exhaustion sapping every bit of energy from her already tired body. Her leg had ached all afternoon with such unrelenting intensity that she'd finally managed to conjure a headache to countermand its incessant reminders of the need for elevation.

The unrelieved landscape seen from Taylor's back porch didn't soothe her jangled nerves. The sun was scarcely setting on the distant horizon, sending out a roseate glow across the sky. In New York, she thought, it would already be dark. And yet one never felt this lonely, no matter how alone.

At least not until two months ago. Since the car accident, *all* she'd felt was lonely. And confused.

She'd once ridden horseback across the seemingly endless expanse outside Taylor's yard, as at home beneath the perfect dome of a sky as in her studio apartment in New York. Gazing out at those miles and miles of grass, she understood how ancient man had believed the earth flat.

She had the dizzying impression that if she tried walking across that field, she would reach the end of the world and simply fall off.

She drew a deep breath, held it and let it go as if releasing it would relieve the tension of the evening. From the moment she'd pulled back from Taylor's welcoming embrace and limped beside her to the front porch, she'd undergone a barrage of family, old friends, acquaintances and total strangers. She'd scarcely recognized some of them, while others seemed wholly unmarked by time.

Each of them had seen her on TV, and each had a different "favorite" story she'd reported.

She remembered all the stories they recounted...except those done in the past couple of months. Those, she recognized only vaguely.

Have a good holiday, Allison.

They touched her too much, clinging to her hands, stroking her face, her hair. They had crowded her, jostled her, nudged her...and *loved* her.

But while all of them spoke with the soft west Texas drawl, eagerly, achingly accepting her back into their fold, every one of them—even Taylor—seemed like a stranger to her.

She didn't need to remember the past, she needed to get a handle on the present. And yet, in Almost, the present was mutable, infinite. It stretched to the horizon beyond Taylor's back porch, unbroken and uncontained.

Hardest of all the people to deal with that afternoon had been Aunt Sammie Jo. Susie's mother. Her own second mother. She found she couldn't really look at Sammie Jo. So little with a ridiculous wig on her head, a testament to her age and her fight with cancer.

She'd hugged her aunt, stood beside her with her hand clasped in that dry yet strong grasp that took her back to her childhood, and had found she couldn't meet those blue eyes so like Susie's. So like her own.

Thinking about the reception now, Allison knew instinctively that, unlike Daddy, Aunt Sammie Jo had never blamed her for having let Susie drive the car that horrible summer's night that ended in such tragedy. The one who most had cause to blame her never had.

But believing herself absolved during all those lost years was different from *knowing* it. And when Sammie Jo had hugged her tightly, then stepped back to look up at her, Allison had averted her gaze, more than half-afraid to see her instincts confirmed.

Because she hadn't forgiven herself? Because she hadn't "allowed" Susie to drive? Because she'd been crying so hard over Chas, over his announcement that he was going to marry Thelma Bean, that she'd nearly crashed the car herself before Susie insisted on taking the wheel?

Her father had known the truth. She could still see his drawn face, his dark Leary eyebrows pulled together in a black frown, his eyes tortured. His fingers pressing into her palms had felt cold and had trembled slightly. "My God, Allison, whatever possessed you to allow Susie to drive the car?"

Fifteen years later, his agonized words still sounded louder in her ears and heart than the real voices of the people inside Taylor's house. Allison closed her eyes. Unable to explain to him then why Susie had been driving, she was unable to explain now because he was gone, taken the same way Susie had been; by a sharp curve, a dip in the road and a truck where it shouldn't have been.

She hadn't even come home for the funeral.

The screen door squeaked a protest and alerted Allison to company. She relaxed slightly upon seeing her sister settle into the other rocker on the back porch. They sat in silence for a few moments, then Taylor said, "A bit overwhelming?"

Allison flashed a wistful smile in her sister's direction. "Like an avalanche." She ached to tell her about the past two months, the losses of memory, the terror of the panic attacks. She longed to be held in her sister's loving arms and called "honey" again.

Taylor chuckled. "Steve said the scariest thing about signing on with me is that he feels like he's marrying the whole town."

Allison's wistfulness shifted to a genuine humor. She liked Steve Kessler, who would soon become her brother-in-law. "He seems to take it in stride," she said. "He doesn't look like much fazes him."

"No. If he can put up with the boys, he can do anything."

Allison wondered if Taylor sensed an awkwardness between them, too. It was as if they were strangers pretending to be sisters, stage actors trying to feel their way through an impromptu role.

As if reading her mind and answering the question in a roundabout fashion, Taylor said, "And Carolyn? What do you think of her? You never met her when she was married to Craig, did you?"

Allison frowned over the questions, perhaps seeking censure in the reference to her long absence, an indictment of her studied withdrawal from her family's concerns. "I like her, too," she said simply. "And her husband."

"Pete's perfect for her," Taylor said, and fell silent for a few seconds before continuing. "Sometimes I forget she's not my—our—real sister."

Allison flinched a little at her sister's words but didn't want to make any comment, because she deserved whatever censure Taylor may or may not have intended. *Carolyn's been more my sister than you have been.*

"He reminds me a little of Craig," Allison said.

"That's what I said when I first met him. He doesn't anymore."

Allison glanced at her sister for elucidation.

"I loved Craig, you know that. But I wasn't blind to his faults. I don't think Pete has those flaws."

Allison thought about her easygoing brother, his willingness to let hard work and responsibility roll off his shoulders. She remembered his winning smile, his natural charm and his lazy assurance that he would always land on his feet.

She contrasted this with the quiet former FBI agent she'd met inside, a man whose every fiber bespoke commitment and protectiveness to his new family, his wife, his two adopted daughters, even the long absent Allison.

Another of those tension-filled silences threatened to swamp them before Taylor and Allison started to speak at the same time.

"You first," Allison said, laughing a little, more in nervousness than anything else.

She couldn't read her sister's expression. Too many years had passed since the days of slumber parties, wishful thinking and having to completely clean the bedroom before morning.

Taylor said softly, "I was only going to say I was surprised Chas—Doc—didn't stop by to welcome you home."

Chas. Someone had finally mentioned the dreaded name. Unconsciously Allison folded her hands across her empty womb, protecting that which she'd lost so very long ago. Trying ineffectually to protect herself.

"Oh?" Allison asked, unable to look at her sister, hoping

that she'd made the single syllable sound distantly curious. Doc who?

Her sister chuckled. "You had *such* a crush on him, remember?"

Allison forced a smile to her seemingly frozen lips. She couldn't speak and settled for an inarticulate sound. Until that moment, she'd always assumed that Taylor knew the truth, had known what had really happened the day Susie died. Now she knew otherwise. Because if Taylor had known the full details, she would never have teased Allison about having a crush on Dr. Charles Jamison.

In New York, during the past two months, she'd had to struggle every day, every *second,* to maintain some semblance of control on her errant memory. Here in Almost, no one cared about the immediate past; yesterday was just a touch away and tomorrow was at arm's length in that immutable present that existed for them. Here her strange mental aberration seemed almost inconsequential. Or it would until she experienced one of her attacks.

"Well, speak of the devil..." Taylor said, pushing herself out of the rocker and gliding down the back-porch steps, her hands outstretched to the man rounding the side of the house. "Doc! I knew you'd come by." She tilted her head toward the porch. "Look who's home...our Allison."

Allison tried to stand up but realized immediately that her trembling legs wouldn't have supported her. She clutched the arms of the rocker with such intensity that she felt the wood grain through her palms and fingertips.

It seemed to take forever for Chas to turn his head to look at her. Allison felt the shock of their gazes interlocking. Her heart pounded so rapidly and painfully that she couldn't hear what Taylor said next, though it made Chas smile a little and turn loose of her hands.

She relaxed slightly, realizing that the feelings that were sweeping through her, though paniclike, weren't anywhere close to the attacks that propelled her to run blindly, screaming, away from whatever prompted them. She was only suffering the normal, everyday terror of having to greet a former lover.

No big deal.

A piece of cake.

But she was still shaking like a proverbial leaf.

He had changed, of course. She tried telling herself that people's appearances did alter in fifteen years, that she couldn't expect him to be a kid anymore. He had to be forty-two now.

His sandy brown hair was streaked with strands of silver, and the lines on his broad, tanned face attested to his years of outdoor living and the many times he'd laughed. His lanky body had developed into what a man's body should be, lithe, supple and lean. His height once might have been called gangly or lanky; now he was tall and broad shouldered.

"Hello, Allison," he said.

The sound of his deep, rough voice sent a shock wave down her spine. She had once called it a burlap voice, warm and scratchy at the same time. He'd chuckled back then, a raspy, throaty sound that had lingered in her memory and now warred with the reality of hearing that raw-silk voice again.

"Chas..." she murmured, unable to do more.

The screen door creaked, and Allison jumped a little as Sammie Jo called for Taylor. "The boys want to try out their new video equipment Allison brought them, and I've told them they have to wait for you. Why...hello, Charles."

Taylor made swift excuses and disappeared with their

aunt into the kitchen, closing the back door firmly behind her. Shutting Allison outside in the twilight with Chas.

With the fear of a rabbit staring into the eyes of a fox, Allison cursed her own vulnerability that had been so recently and unwarrantedly thrust upon her. She watched Chas mount the few steps leading to the porch with a sense of impending doom.

He moved with a fluid, almost lazy grace. A man's walk. He leaned against one of the porch's four-by-four posts and shoved his hands into his jeans pockets. His broad shoulders blotted out the roseate sky.

God, she had loved him so. With every fiber of her being. Looking at him now, she didn't know what she felt. Different. Apart.

Was this part of that odd dissociation she'd experienced all too frequently in recent months, or was this merely the hard reality of a true time warp?

She hadn't seen him in fifteen years. And yet, seeing him again, she found that the same part of her that had ached for him all these years wanted him still. She felt tears burning her eyes at the strength of that want. And she wanted to curse him for making her experience that helpless longing.

She waited for him to speak, to tell her he'd seen her on television, to comment on the weather, to explain why he'd married someone else when he had claimed her body all those years ago. And rejected her for someone else when she had loved him so very desperately. So innocently.

Allison cursed herself for being such a fool. The past was long, long buried. She was only reacting this way because she'd been through so much confusion lately. Nothing more.

She held her face impassive as he frowned slightly, his eyes narrowing to study her. He'd always been able to read

her, back when she was a kid and he little more than that—
though the ten-year difference in their ages had mattered a
great deal to him then.

But he shouldn't be able to read her now. Not anymore.
He'd thrown away that right in their youth. When he'd told
her he was marrying Thelma, when he'd rejected everything they'd shared to spend his life with another woman.

"You know, it's funny," he said, looking as though it
were anything but. He fell silent.

"What is?" she asked, or tried to.

He hesitated, seeming to argue with himself, then
shrugged slightly, as if having lost the war. "I've thought
about seeing you here in Almost again. Too many times, I
guess. But I always thought I'd know just what to say."

She tried taking in the full meaning behind his words.
Too many times... She shook her head as if shaking off the
past. And what meaning would he take from that gesture?

"Did you find what you were looking for, Allison? I
know you're famous, but was it everything you wanted it
to be? Glitz and glamour...bright lights and sparkle?"

She felt her breath hitch in her lungs. Having him refer
to her own anguished words—disjointed phrases spoken
out of desperation the afternoon he'd dropped his decision
for their future together—thoroughly disconcerted her. And
that he would ask her that *now,* when everything she'd
strived for lay in chaos.

But most troublesome was the element of bitterness in
his tone. As though it had been *her* decision all those years
ago, as if what had happened afterward had been *her* fault.
It had been his casual attitude, then his announcement he
was marrying Thelma, that destroyed their love.

"No," she said, then amended her answer, "Yes."

He gave her a lopsided, seemingly rueful grin. "No ambivalence there."

"Ambivalence is all I feel," Allison said softly, and while it sounded like a quip or a lie, it was the raw, honest truth.

Chas didn't flinch or look embarrassed. He merely stilled, looking for all the world like a man who has heard the report of a gun and waits for the impact. After a few seconds, he sighed and withdrew his hands from his pockets.

"I think I'll get some lemonade. Can I get you anything?"

My heart, she thought. My memory. My naïveté...or maybe my suitcase so I can go back home to New York. Or run away somewhere far from anything I know, because I won't be knowing anything much longer.

"Nothing, thanks," she said, and this time she heard the tinge of sorrow in her own voice.

"I didn't think so," he said. It wasn't until he'd opened the back door that she realized he'd misunderstood her.

"Chas?" she called softly, not turning around, but aware with every perception in her body that he'd frozen in place. That she wanted—perhaps *needed*—to extend their moment of reunion, to put the past into place once and for all. Forever.

"Yes?"

"I...I take it back. I could use some lemonade."

Seconds later she felt his warm hands settle onto her shoulders.

She couldn't withhold the sudden tension that sprang up to meet his fingers. But she could fight the urge to relax into his grip, to let those broad, caring hands smooth away her anxiety.

"What's wrong, Allison?"

Dear God, she thought, too aware of him and much too aware of a desire to unburden herself, what *wasn't* wrong?

She shook her head and wished he'd lift his hands from her shoulders and, at the same time, wished he'd never stop caressing her stiff muscles and would draw her into his arms. Into an embrace that would be anything but safe, but would feel so heavenly, so perfect.

He leaned down and slowly, deliberately pressed a kiss to her temple. His warm breath played against her cheek, against her hair. His fingers tightened on her shoulders. His lips lingered. The moment seemed to stretch into infinity.

If she turned her head, their lips would meet. Such a small thing, she thought, just a simple movement, but it was far too difficult to accomplish. Far more dangerous than any strange memory lapses or panic attacks.

He stood erect and gave her shoulders a seemingly final squeeze but didn't remove his hands. She could hear him draw a ragged breath that matched her own. She felt tears gather in her eyes, ached for his touch, wished she had turned her head, wished she had met that kiss.

"Ah, Allison. After all this time…why did you come back?"

Chapter 3

Chas felt Allison's reaction to his question in her stiffening, already too tight shoulders. He wished he could take the words back while at the same time he stood, fighting an urge to shake an answer out of her.

She murmured something that sounded like *I had to,* but he couldn't be sure. He waited, half angry with her for being there at all, and at the same time, half crazed with a desire to hold her in his arms forever.

He thought that some things never changed. Years ago that young Allison he'd known so well, so intimately, had fallen silent then, too, shutting him out of her mind, her heart. Shutting him out of his life. Because she wanted more than a "one-horse anachronism of a town." Her very words in the face of his starry-eyed plans for the two of them.

"Have you been happy?" he asked finally, abandoning his earlier question.

"Have you?" she countered.

He thought of the past fifteen years with an odd dispassion, shrinking them to a mere few important moments. Moments without Allison.

And then he thought of the fourteen years spent with his son. Billy as an infant, his big blue eyes blinking with wonder. Billy as a toddler, racing into the clinic, a toilet-paper-wrapped cat draped across his baby arms. "Billy fixed the cat, Daddy!" Billy as a young boy, confidently lifting a horse's foot to treat a split pad. "Like this, right, Daddy?"

Had he been happy?

"Yes," he said simply, unconsciously tightening his fingers on her too thin shoulders.

He heard her sigh a little. From his angle behind her, he couldn't see her face, could only read the tension in her fragile frame, could only feel the anxiety pulsing up through his fingertips.

"And you, Allison?"

"Yes, of course I have," she said, and he knew with every fiber in his being that she lied.

She hadn't been happy. At times, maybe, but not all the time, and certainly not at this moment. He knew it with as much conviction as he knew that something was deeply troubling her now, saw it and felt it manifested in her tousled hair, her brittle hold on calm.

Once he might have asked what the problem was and received a prompt reply. Once he might have been able to figure out a way to solve whatever it was that was troubling her. But that time was long past, and Chas didn't have the tools to build the bridge she'd burned all those years ago and he'd razed soon after when he announced he was going to marry Thelma.

She tossed her head as she used to do, only now her hair was short and merely brushed his wrists instead of draping them with silk. As if she'd been reading a dim portion of his mind, she asked, "And...Thelma?"

His hands jerked convulsively on her shoulders, undoubtedly nearly crushing her. For a moment, he didn't know what to say. He fell back on the hard truth. "Thelma's dead, Allison."

He saw her hands grip and regrip the arms of the old oak rocker as if she were trying to mold it to a completely different shape. "I didn't know," she said. "How long...?"

"Nearly five years ago now," he said.

"I didn't know," she repeated.

Chas didn't know how he felt at that moment. Allison should have known. Someone should have told her. She should have come back to Almost then. She should have run back to him. A part of him had been hurt when she hadn't, though he'd never really expected it. Hadn't dared even dream she'd come back.

"I'm sorry," she said, sounding as if she were choking on the words.

He nodded his acknowledgment. It was so long ago now that he scarcely could conjure up the small details that comprised Thelma's personality. Not like he still could about Allison. Not in the way he'd always been able to remember Allison's every gesture, her every look. And, of course, he'd been able to watch her at least twice a month on *Timeline,* seeing her lovely face mature and gain character.

He opened his mouth to tell her any or all of his thoughts and was saved from such a damning disclosure by the back door bursting open when Taylor's triplets came spilling outside, trailed by their calmer cousins and his own son, Billy.

"Aunt Allison! Lookit over here!"

"How come you're crying, Aunt Allison?"

"She's not crying, doofus, she's only got the sun in her eyes!"

"She is too crying! Besides, the sun's already going down. You are crying, aren't you, Aunt Allison?"

Chas stepped away from behind her chair, amazed at how difficult it was to release his hold on her, but needing to shield her from the boys' curiosity more. She was crying? Why?

"Hey, kids, Aunt Allison's had a long afternoon. And she's on camera all the time. Let's give her a day off. Whaddya say?"

Billy, true to his thoughtful nature, suggested the boys film their dogs. "They're on the front porch," he added, brushing past them and leading the way to the other side of the house.

"Billy..." Chas called, and his son abruptly halted and turned back to face them, a half smile on his thin lips. His braces caught a late sunbeam and flashed for a moment.

"Thanks."

"Sure, Dad," he said, then he grinned, the crooked, slightly gamin smile that seemed to have such an effect on the girls. His mother's smile. "No problem."

Chas would have introduced them then and there, his son and the only woman he'd ever loved, but the moment slipped away as swiftly as the years had passed, and Billy rounded the corner of the house trailed by five Leary cousins.

"Your son," Allison said softly.

For some odd reason, he couldn't look at her, didn't really want to see the expression on her face. "Billy."

"I guess when I pictured you with your son, I had an image of a baby in my mind."

"He was that once," he said, forcing a smile to his lips, thinking about her in faraway New York, picturing him back home in Almost, holding Billy. A baby who completely captured his heart the moment he wrapped tiny, delicate fingers around one of his own.

She gave a ghost of a chuckle, and he couldn't resist looking at her. Then she finally, finally turned her head to meet his eyes. He could see the traces of tears and of some unexpressed, still deep sorrow gnawing at her, but her lips curved into a smile. "No wonder you've been happy, Chas. He's a fine young man."

Chas smiled, too, something shifting deep inside him. Dear God, help me, he thought. He'd known he'd loved Allison Leary all those years ago, had thought of her a million times since. But he'd never have guessed it could still hurt so very much.

"You must be proud of him," she murmured.

"I am," he said simply. "He's a good kid."

She nodded, as if agreeing with him. And perhaps she was. Her smile broadened, and he found himself returning it, a little sadly perhaps, but a smile nonetheless. The first shared smile they'd had in fifteen years. Maybe that bridge wasn't totally burned after all.

"And you, Allison...did you ever have any children?"

The smile slipped from her face, and her features seemed to draw in, as if she were consciously realigning her expression from guardedly open to profoundly neutral. But just before she looked away, he caught a glimpse of raw hurt and anger in her eyes.

"No. I never did," she said.

Allison could feel his assessment of her and kept her face as cool and impassive as was humanly possible. The flicker of surprise on his features before she'd turned her gaze away told her she'd imperfectly hidden her bitterness from him when he'd asked her about children. That was one subject she wouldn't discuss with him. Ever.

Luckily, perhaps sensing the extremely thin ice he was treading upon, he didn't pursue it. Instead, he fell back on a reliable reunion cliché. "It's hard to believe you've been gone so long."

"Fifteen years," she said softly.

"A long time, Allison."

"A long time," she agreed.

"Too long?" he asked, reaching a hand out to hang in the air between them.

Allison felt a surge of resentment toward him. "What are you asking me, Chas? Whatever was between us is in the past. And that past is fifteen years cold."

She leveled a look at him that would have reduced a lesser man to pure jelly. She'd had heads of state cower beneath such a hard look.

Not Chas. He didn't pull his hand back, and she realized with a faint flush that he wasn't ignoring her words; he was simply waiting to assist her up from the chair.

Somehow, in some indefinable way, he'd turned the tables on her and it was he who had control of this very strained situation. She didn't want to touch him again, yet wanted nothing more than to place her seemingly small hand in that broad, callused palm, to feel his fingers wrap around hers once again.

As if of its own volition, her hand rose and hovered above his. He reached up, as if in slow motion, and slid that tantalizing hand beneath her own, capturing it, holding her captive. As in her imagination, his fingers enfolded her to him, pressing her palm against his own.

"Allison?"

She couldn't seem to drag her gaze from the point where their hands met, skin to skin, cold to warm touch. His warmth seemed to flow through her, igniting something she'd prayed was long, long buried, had tried believing for years.

"It's never too late," he said, mocking her futile prayers.

She wasn't sure what she read in those deep brown eyes, but knew he was wrong. Some things were late the very instant harsh words were spoken. And some things were better left permanently late, forever unvoiced.

"It can be," she said honestly.

He pulled her up from the chair, not allowing her to hesitate any longer. He held her firmly, not letting her rock on her unsteady leg. And when she gained her balance, he didn't release her hand but instead folded it to his chest so that she could feel the strong, hard beating of his heart.

Her own pulse felt thready and unsure.

They stood so close together she could smell the clean, fresh scent of his newly washed hair, the faint whiff of whatever soap he'd used, something that reminded her of open fields and golden grain. And she could smell that familiar, oh-so-familiar odor particularly his, a rich, slightly tangy scent that reached straight to her taste buds and made her eyes feel heavy with want.

He raised his free hand, gliding it across her face, cupping her cheek in his palm in a gesture both tender and possessive.

"That's up to you, Allison. I'm just glad to see you again."

Mesmerized by the feel of his warmth against her face, ensnared by his gaze that held too many desires, too many demands he had no right to expect of her, Allison told herself to step back, to pull away from him.

Where was that panic and fear now, when she could have used a measure of it? Why, standing so close to Chas Jamison, the man who had irrevocably changed the entire course of her life, wasn't she running away?

"This is crazy," she murmured.

"Not seeing you in fifteen years is crazy," Chas said, and drew her closer, tilting his head slightly before lowering his full, warm lips to hers. "This," he murmured, "this is the first sane thing I've done in years."

Somewhere in the distance, she heard children giggling, heard the soft voices of an impromptu welcome-home party in Taylor's loving home. She wanted to pull away from Chas, to run back to New York and whatever fragments of a well-ordered life she might have left behind.

But instead, she leaned into this country vet with lips like velvet, hands as strong as steel and as gentle and knowing as an artist's, forgetting the past, forgetting the past fifteen years of solitary dinners and midnight heartache. And blessedly, miraculously, forgetting the past two months of torment.

With his scent filling her nostrils and his touch holding her to the present, she could forget all but the feel of his hands and lips, his hard, lean body pressing against hers, the taste of his mouth, the insistent pressure of his arms.

"Ah, Allison," he murmured, folding her against his chest, pressing his face into her hair, his lips against her temple.

She gave in to the sheer pleasure of being nestled against his broad chest, letting her face absorb the deep, now slightly faster pace of his heartbeat. She reached around him and held on to his back, feeling the warmth of his body emanating out from beneath the thick cotton sweater he wore and molding her palms to the contours of his shifting muscles. She ached to lift it and slip her hands underneath to meet his skin directly. He would never know how she struggled not to give in to that desire.

She mouthed his name without giving voice to it. But he shuddered as if she'd pressed a kiss to his chest and held her even more tightly. Warmly. Safely. And with something more, something filled with his own longing and wants.

Now that Thelma was gone, now that her own life was in chaos and disarray...*now* he wanted her.

She pushed away from him, not swiftly, but with finality. Without quite meeting his eyes, she spoke to his laugh lines, the evidence of both his age and his time in the sun, his warmth, his compassion.

She forced a false smile to her lips. "Well, Chas, that was certainly a welcome."

He didn't say anything, though she could feel a new tension radiating out from his still body.

"We could use more of that kind of thing in New York," she added, and stepped away from him, hoping her legs would support her. She moved carefully, refusing to allow him to feel the slightest tinge of pity for her limp.

"In New York," he echoed.

She flicked him a quick glance and couldn't read his expression. "I do have to go back, you know," she said.

"Back."

She felt a stirring of resentment. Had he really thought a single kiss and a too warm hug after fifteen years would make her forget her responsibilities, her career, however turbulent that might be at the moment?

"Of course. I do have a life, you know," she all but snapped, and was sorry the second the words slipped from her tongue.

But was sorrier still when she saw the way he seemed to harden as though being slowly turned to stone.

His eyes darted to hers, then away again. But the darts found their way to her damnably unwary heart.

"Of course you do," he said. "I just wanted to welcome you home—back to Almost."

Now he stepped back, away from her, edging toward the

door. "I guess I'd better say hello to everybody. Town politics. You know how that is."

She said she did and she felt nearly ill with the way she had distanced him and demeaned that kiss.

He wrenched the back door open with a controlled violence.

When she would have said something more, though she had no idea what that might have been, he raised a hand to forestall her and spoke himself. "It's been a long time, Allison. Maybe too long for some things. But I don't think it's just seeing us again after all this time that's making you jump every time you hear a noise. You're acting like someone on the run."

She didn't know what to say. She felt stripped of all defenses except that news mask she'd so carefully honed over the years. And even that seemed to be melting beneath his discerning study.

He sighed and looked nearly resigned. "I'll be around if you want to talk, Allison."

She couldn't speak, though everything in her wanted to.

"We could always do that, couldn't we?"

She shook her head slowly. That was the one thing they had never been able to do...*talk.*

He knew what was wrong with an animal just by touching, by looking at it, by gazing into its tortured eyes. Just as he'd always been able to do with her. And she could talk to anyone on earth, drawing secrets out that would be revealed to the world. But talk? The two of them? Never.

"It's not such a hard thing, Allison," he said. "You just have to want to let someone in."

With that he left the porch, letting the door drop shut behind him.

Soft as the sound was, it felt like a slap.

"I want to," she whispered, staring at the closed door. "Oh, Chas...I've always wanted to let you in."

Allison lay in the darkened guest room listening to the night sounds of her sister's home. All the townspeople had gone home a couple of hours earlier, leaving her to face Taylor, Steve and the boys without the protective mass of well-wishers. After two hours of nearly excruciating awkwardness, she'd pleaded exhaustion and a headache and fled to the sanctuary of her room.

She longed for the quiet and comfort she'd once known in her apartment in New York City. There she could have curled up in the big padded chair on her narrow balcony and listened to the hum of the city, the pulsing beat of so many million people's hearts, aches and needs.

In the safety of that lonely chair, she wouldn't have been forced to lie in the dark, aching and needing to understand the dynamics of a family she didn't even know anymore, or ponder another panic attack and yet another loss of two or three hours.

There in that empty expanse of an apartment, she could have pretended her life was complete. Often did so, in fact. And though she would have known it for a lie, she would have felt comfortable with the falsehood because there would have been nothing to contradict it, nothing to flay her with the truth.

Now, after two months of unmitigated confusion, with the soft laughter of a sister she hadn't seen in fifteen years, the teasing rumble of a soon-to-be brother-in-law she hadn't even met before today and the cracking voices of three identical boys, she felt more alone than she'd ever felt in her life. She felt forced to confront the emptiness of her life, the superficial elements that composed her everyday world.

Where was the warmth, the laughter? The jokes among colleagues, the teasing, the frenetic pace of her world in the city and in the news department was certainly exciting and rich, but once home, where was the simple human warmth?

What had she called it earlier, while afraid to get out of the car and greet her sister? Empty-life syndrome. The latest in pop-psychology disorders. There would undoubtedly be groups forming in every neighborhood soon. ELS Meeting, 8:00 p.m., In The Library. Refreshments Served.

Throughout the long evening, she'd been forced to brave the past at every turn. After his kiss on the back porch, Chas had gone inside and had stayed, for the remainder of his short visit, on the other side of any room she'd entered. But somehow some chemistry between them had seemed to alert everyone in the room that the two of them should be talking together. Eyes would swivel from one to the other, faces poised and eager.

Aunt Sammie Jo had approached her many times, touching her, talking of Susie as if Susie might have appeared at the door at any moment. And she'd stood before Allison, looking so frail and tired with her leathered hands and her face drawn and pinched.

Just glancing at her had torn Allison's heart into ragged pieces. *It was my fault,* she'd nearly blurted out a hundred times. *If it hadn't been for me, Susie would still be alive.* But she'd kept silent, guilt choking her.

Uncle Cactus, Sammie Jo's husband, hadn't said much at all, only hugged her a little longer than she ever remembered him doing so in her youth. And his craggy snow white brows had twitched as he'd looked away from her, his eyes suspiciously shiny with tears.

And the boys, Taylor's amazing triplets, so much like Craig, their uncle, but so different, too, had pummeled her with questions, statements, stories and demands for her attention. Reminders all three of a life she could never have, of children that would never be.

And Chas, with his callused hands, silver in his hair, and soft, pliable lips, calling back every emotion she wanted buried long ago.

And his son, Billy.

Too much memory was far, far worse than too little, she thought in disgust. And she, of all people, would surely know.

She sat up abruptly and swung her legs from the bed. She limped across the dark room to her suitcase, digging inside until she found the pack of cigarettes she'd carried with her since quitting three months before. She also unearthed a slender pack of matches from a restaurant she loved in New York.

She shook a crunchy-dry cigarette free from the rumpled pack and struck the match. Her fingers were shaking, both around the cigarette and the match. The flame flickered and danced, orange light playing across the walls of the room.

She took a deep breath, then shook the match out and, with a hitched sob, dropped the unlit cigarette into the trash can beside the dresser. She opened a window to blow away the sulphur odor and knelt before narrow aperture, drinking in the clean, cold desert night air.

She could feel winter in the night where she couldn't during the day, could smell it in the dry, cold scent of the unfurrowed, frost-covered fields.

She closed her eyes and felt a desperate longing for that girl she used to be. The one who trusted easily, who believed in all the promise of the universe. The one who wasn't scared or frightened or couldn't remember some things. And she wanted the hard, tough reporter she used to be at *Timeline,* the cool customer in the face of adversity and deadlines.

She didn't want this soul-sick confusion of past and present colliding. She didn't want to confront the demons from the past when she could scarcely recall with any degree of clarity a single day in the past two months.

She opened her eyes to stare out the window at the white vista of flat lawn, flat, empty field beyond the highway and felt that sob she'd stifled earlier fighting for escape.

She wouldn't cry. She'd had tears well in her eyes, even had a few spill free in this strange afternoon, but she hadn't given way to crying in the strict definition of *crying.* And she wouldn't now.

She clamped her jaw tight, holding back the sob. Forcing that flood of undirected emotion back to the depths from which it had sprung.

"No," she said aloud, forcing herself to comply, exerting the self-discipline she'd learned years before to come into play, the same discipline that had so eluded her of late.

Both facets of herself, the young, trusting girl and the hard and polished woman, seemed so far away, so buried beneath the confusion that swamped her now. They were elements lost in the fragments of memories that seemed scrambled and unconnected, in the panic that would steal in and make her tremble only to disappear with equally inexplicable swiftness.

She pressed a finger to her lips, holding in the sharp, hot keening she felt rising. Strangely the touch reminded her all too well of the feel of Chas's lips on hers. Warm, strong, demanding and somehow offering a safe haven.

A tear streaked down her cheek as she stared out the window.

Some shadow shifted out front, looking for a moment

like a man lurking in the dark. Her heart jumped, and she felt a jolt of terror streak through her.

Just beyond the window, she saw a man's arm, stretching out, ready to…to what?

She didn't know. She didn't care. Her heart raced, her breath caught and held, snared in her throat. Panic. She clamped her hands over her mouth to hold back her scream of terror.

Not here. Not in Almost. Not when she was with her family.

She felt herself gag slightly against the urge to shriek out her fear.

But the wind strengthened and gusted across a rose of Sharon bush, causing its leafless, spindly limbs to wave with more vigor and the man-shadow became a bush once again, the evil arm a mere branch.

After a few seconds of utter disbelief, Allison was able to draw a deep breath and swipe the tears from her cheek. She dragged her hands through her hair, lifting her fluff of blond hair from her forehead, and waited for the rhythm of her heartbeat to steady and slow.

What on earth was wrong with her? The doctors in New York had said it might take a while for her attacks to pass and that she would soon be fine. She could only wait for the moments to pass, for her heart to steady. And somehow, now that she was back home in Almost, welcomed back into the fold of the neverending community, she thought that she might just be able to beat whatever tortured her. She might just be able to survive the mysterious malady. Like the flu, she might just get over it.

As she had gotten over Chas Jamison?

But she had done that.

Until she saw him again.

The man with the greasy black hair and stained clothes stood outside the house with the yellow trim, watching the darkened house, one window in particular. He'd seen her clearly outlined in the brief flicker of a match.

He'd held his breath, wondering if she would actually light the cigarette he knew she wouldn't want, would never want again. But he saw no telltale glow from a lighted tip. She'd dropped it. Abandoned the attempt.

Good girl. She'd given them up three months ago. For him. Because he'd asked it of her. He'd demanded it of her. Not that she'd ever thanked him for it.

When she opened the window to her bedroom and had knelt in front of it, he'd felt her longing from where he stood in the shadows. He'd felt her aching and had reached out for her only to realize it wasn't him she cried for so sadly. It never had been for him.

How he loved her and how he hated her. Polarities. He drew back into the shadows, but lingered there, buffeted by a bitter, cold desert wind that seemed echoed in his heart. And he vowed to keep watch over his lady until such time came as she would be his forever.

Which wouldn't be very long at all now.

''Dad?''

Chas turned from his blank concentration on a test tube to see his son framed in the open doorway of the clinic. ''Hey, there, kiddo. Dishes all squared away?''

''Naw. I decided we waste too much time on dishes, so I just threw them all away.''

Chas tossed a pencil at his smiling son and grinned himself as the boy caught it without even glancing at it.

Instead of just saying a quick good-night and heading for his room and whatever homework awaited, Billy stood just inside the door, tossing the pencil up into the air and catching it. Idle, dexterous, even agile, but his face too carefully neutral.

"What's on your mind?" Chas asked, sitting back in his chair.

He'd seen that particular studied indifference before. It usually preceded the more intense discussions he and Billy had. Sex. Girls. Thelma's illness.

Billy cut him a swift, assessing glance, then flicked his eyes to the pencil flipping end over end in the air. He caught it again before he answered. "Taylor's sister...you know, Allison."

Chas's stomach knotted swiftly. He forced himself to relax. If the mere mention of her name could affect him so, he'd better get a grip on himself. She'd made it clear the past was the past and that was the way it should stay.

But even knowing that, he couldn't stop himself from thinking about the way her silken skin had felt beneath his hand earlier that evening. About the way her lips had parted for him.

"What about her?" he asked hoarsely.

"Did you know her? Back when, I mean?"

If anything, he found himself tensing even more. "Yes, I knew her."

Somehow putting it the past tense seemed a betrayal of sorts.

Or a lie.

He couldn't quite look at Billy, but had to ask, "Why do you ask?"

"I dunno," his son said. The pencil pinwheeled again, and deft fingers plucked it from midair.

"Sure, you do. What's up?"

Billy shrugged. "I just wondered, that's all."

"Wondered what?"

Billy's eyes cut from the pencil to Chas in a swift, nearly

apologetic glance. "Oh, nothing. Just something Mom said once."

Chas felt like that whirling pencil, tossed into the air without any awareness of how he'd gotten there.

"What was that?" he managed to ask calmly enough.

Again the eyes. Again the pencil. "Oh, it was a long time ago, you know."

Chas waited.

The pencil became a miniature baton. Up and over. Up and over, caught between middle finger and forefinger, endlessly spinning, but so controlled.

"Mom said that you and Allison were…well, you know, like…"

"Like what?" Chas asked through utterly dry lips.

The pencil clattered to the floor, and Billy swiftly snatched it up, rolling it in his fingers. "Like…lovers or something."

Billy wasn't looking at him, but Chas knew he would soon. He instinctively felt that if he didn't manage to school his features to some semblance of calm, his son would see every truth on his face. Every raw and painful truth. And some truths a child should never see. Ever.

Chas felt a moment's anger at Thelma for having told the boy anything at all. Immediately following this anger was a supreme pity for Thelma, for a woman who had been a good and loving mother, though a sad one, for a woman who had tried the best she could to make a family, a home. And he felt the sorrow he'd known from the first moment with her, the sadness of knowing she would always dream of another man while never truly loved by the husband she had.

"That was before your mother and I married," Chas said, letting the stark honesty in his voice cross the few feet to where his son stood uncomfortably rolling that slender pencil in his fingers.

The pencil froze, and Billy's eyes lifted to meet Chas's. Clear blue eyes, questioning but not doubting, locked with his own brown eyes. "Did you love her? Allison, I mean?"

"Yes."

How simple it was to tell the truth to Billy, the simple truth he'd never once really told Allison. The entire universe seemed open to him at that moment. Like an epiphany, it seemed to slam into his soul, into his heart; he'd never said the words to Allison. *The* words.

"And now?" Billy asked.

"Now?"

"Yeah. Like she's back. And like Mom's, well, you know, like that's not a problem." Billy stopped fingering the pencil and frowned heavily. "That sounded bad, but you know what I mean, right?"

Chas smiled, even though a grin had never felt more strained on his face. The simplicity of youthful thinking: the world was a huge, colorful place but conveniently pigeonholed with tidy boxes.

"That was a long time ago, Billy."

He heard the echo of Allison's words and restrained a grimace. *Ambivalence is* all *I feel.* He knew exactly how she must have felt. He felt it now and understood her. Ambivalence didn't have anything to do with indifference; it was being ripped into two parts, equally drawn to the torn halves.

"Yeah, but feelings don't just go away or anything, right?"

Out of the mouths of babes, Chas thought. And was still thinking about Billy's innocent question six hours later and miles from sleep. And he still had no answer to give him and less than none to give himself.

Chapter 4

Allison thought Taylor's wedding day dawned as if her sister had ordered it straight from her dreams, bright and clear, and unseasonably warm.

"You look stunning," she said honestly.

Beautiful as her sister was in any garb, she'd never looked lovelier nor more radiant than she did in her simple, full-length, cream linen gown flecked with shots of teal and gold. She had the grace and poise of a woman of years and the joy and sparkle of a girl.

Taylor laughed. "I feel more comfortable in jeans, but what the heck, I thought Steve should see me in a dress just once. Besides, with you looking like that, I doubt anyone will notice me."

Allison shook her head, smiling, not believing her sister's words for a second, though she loved the simple teal gown her sister had selected for her maid of honor.

Someone knocked on Taylor's bedroom door. The knock was followed by the door opening a crack.

Allison was struck by the fact that both she and Taylor turned in unison and called, "Yes?" Maybe it was simple genetics, or maybe some things from the past were so ingrained that they would always surface.

Carolyn, the sister-in-law she'd never known before she'd come back home, mother of her two nieces, slipped through the doorway, shutting it behind her.

"It's just me. Are you ready?" Carolyn stopped and broke into a slow, soft smile of real appreciation. "You look lovely. Both of you."

Watching her, Allison thought that Carolyn, wearing the same style of dress in the same shade of teal, seemed far more at home with the sister role than she herself did. This woman should have been the "matron" of honor. Carolyn was far more a sister to Taylor than she had been.

She tensed a little as Carolyn moved forward to stand between Taylor and Allison before the beveled, three-tiered mirror that had always stood in Momma's bedroom. It now reflected all three Leary women—two by blood, one by marriage.

There was no mistaking the fact that Taylor and Allison were sisters; both had the same blond haired, delicate features from their mother and the dark, mobile eyebrows of the Leary clan. But Carolyn could have been a taller one of them, as well, with her honeyed gold hair, her clear blue eyes and her narrow chin.

"I wish Daddy could have been here today, to give me away," Taylor said, fluffing one of her flounces.

Allison couldn't help it. She looked away, but not soon enough to miss the look of concern on Taylor's face, the puzzlement on Carolyn's.

It was Carolyn who broke the slight pall. "I'll go tell Martha Jo she can start the music…okay?"

"Good idea," Taylor said absently.

Allison turned away from their dual reflections, wishing her sister had less news sense and would let the subject of family drop. But she knew it was a forlorn hope...wedding days were dates to be etched in memory, times to remember the past, say farewell and move on to a beautiful future.

Carolyn slipped out of the room, and the silence seemed to chastise Allison for having made Taylor uncomfortable about anything on her wedding day, however unintentionally.

"Allison..."

"Yes?" she asked, trying to sound bright, as if she were wholly unaware of anything amiss.

Her sister wasn't fooled, of course. She never had been.

"What did Daddy do or say to you that makes you uncomfortable to even talk about him?"

Allison waved her hand as if brushing away her sister's words. "Nothing. Don't worry about it."

Instead of heeding that advice, Taylor crossed to lean against her dresser. "Are you ever going to tell me about it?"

"About what?" Allison stalled, not meeting Taylor's eyes. She picked up their mother's gold-and-teal evening purse, Taylor's "something old" and handed it to her sister.

Taylor took the bag, which had determined the color scheme of her wedding, as it had been their father's rather unusual wedding gift to their mother all those years before. She caught Allison's hand before she could snatch it away.

"Whatever it is, is it the reason you stayed away all these years? The reason you didn't even come back for Momma and Daddy's funeral?"

"Taylor," Allison began, agonized. "Your wedding...Steve..."

"I'd like to know," Taylor said. "Make it a wedding gift, if you like."

Allison felt trapped. Of all terrible things to want for a wedding present. But a far worse one to give. Luckily her years in the news business had given her plenty of practice at slipping out of awkward situations.

She forced a bright smile to her stiff lips and shook her hand still caught in her sister's. "What is this, last-minute jitters? Steve's going to think you're backing out."

"Allison..."

"Taylor..." Allison met her sister's eyes with an unflinching stare. Then she forced a small chuckle and posed dramatically. "Come on! It's time. The past is the past. Your future awaits."

Allison waited with her arms outstretched, as if embracing the universe, until Taylor relaxed, apparently accepting her sister's words at face value.

"The future does await," Taylor said softly. "Doesn't it? There were times I never thought it would be possible."

It was possible for people like Taylor, good people, nice people, Allison thought. People who weren't going crazy.

"But I still wish you would tell me whatever it was that kept you away so long."

"Let it go, Taylor. Don't spoil anything," Allison urged, drawing her hand free and crossing to the door to open it with a flourish.

In a way she was sorry she hadn't just told Taylor about the hurts from the past, just lanced that old and festering wound and spilled it into the clean, bright and healing concern her sister felt for her.

It seemed so minor now, so *old* a hurt when compared with the turmoil of the past two months. Especially since in the past few days, nothing untoward had happened. A few struggles with panic, but nothing terribly worrisome.

Maybe she should switch from reporting to psychology, she thought. Give a person a huge, horrible problem to make them see that the problems that troubled them before weren't quite so huge.

"Won't you please tell me about the past?" Taylor asked again.

Allison had never talked about any of the past with any human being. She frowned, thinking about that. She had told someone, sometime, hadn't she? No. She shook her head as if shaking the errant thought away.

Taylor, misunderstanding her frown and the shake of her head, reached out to touch her face.

Allison withheld the shudder of horror that swept through her. But she sighed in relief when the panic attack didn't burst into full bloom. All she felt was the love and tenderness of Taylor's touch on her cheek.

"Go out there and get yourself hitched to that Texas Ranger," she told her sister.

And as a radiant Taylor swept past her, Allison knew a moment's desire to catch her sister's arm, to just blurt out her guilt and the reasons she'd stayed away so very long. To ask Taylor to just stay a moment longer, to talk to her, to listen for a moment as she tried to smooth over the past fifteen years of absence with a few long-overdue words. And maybe, if they were spoken, she'd be able to confide her recent fears, the memory lapses, even her concerns for her sanity.

But she didn't know her sister anymore and perhaps had never known how to talk about such things. Most of all, however, she didn't want to spoil Taylor's wedding day, and any explanation of the past or present would do just that.

Taylor paused at the end of the hallway, seemingly waiting before stepping into her living room, the guests and Steve.

She turned suddenly to clasp Allison's hand. "It's so good to have you back home," she said, unknowingly echoing Chas's words of a couple of days before.

"It's good to see you again, too," Allison responded, changing the meaning slightly.

Taylor looked at her for a moment, as if tasting her sister's shift in words. Then she nodded and raised Allison's hands to her lips. Her eyes filled with tears. "I love you, little sister. Never doubt that. Ever."

Allison felt her own eyes prick with tears.

"I love you, too," she said, meaning it with all her heart, but aware how strangely the words sat on her tongue. It was as if she'd never said them before.

Taylor nodded again. "That's all that matters, then, isn't it?"

Martha Jo, who ran Almost's only boardinghouse, started playing a remarkably adept version of the traditional wedding march, and Taylor gave Allison a slight nudge.

Carolyn stepped up beside them. "You two ready?" she asked.

"I'm ready," Taylor declared. "I don't think I've ever been more ready for anything."

Allison drew a deep breath as Martha Jo started the second play-through. It was her cue. Her entrance. She drew a deep breath and, after a backward glance at her smiling sister, stepped into the living room and proceeded slowly to the front where the minister from the Almost Methodist Church waited by the softly glowing fireplace.

She was quite used to people looking at her; she was essentially on stage every day for a living, just behind a few brighter lights and cameras. But this felt different, far more in view than any coast-to-coast broadcast. These were all faces she knew, people who had grown up with her, cried with her, scolded her.

She nodded at Aunt Sammie Jo as she passed and at Uncle Cactus, who grinned broadly. She gave a smile to Pete and her nieces. She winked at the triplets flanking a very handsome Steve and his best man, and avoided meeting Chas's brown eyes and only half nodded in the general direction of the left side of the living room where he stood in a Western-cut suit beside his son in the crowd of familiar faces.

She took her place to the left of the minister and was joined almost immediately by Carolyn. On the right side stood the triplets, a beaming Steve Kessler, and his best man, Tom Adams, a short, stocky man with ruddy face and bright, laughing eyes.

Once Carolyn was in place beside Allison, Tom lifted his hand and gave Martha Jo a signal and she began the wedding march with vigor as Taylor walked into the room.

A collective sigh of pleasure emanated from the assembled crowd of friends and family. And as one, all eyes followed Taylor's slow progression down the center of the room. Even Allison's.

But unlike the rest of the crowd, Allison was trying desperately not to break and run. Not because of Taylor, never that. In fact, it was only the sight of Taylor's lovely face, flushed slightly with joy and anticipation, that kept Allison rooted to her place as attendant.

Her heart scudded in painful, too rapid beating. Her fingers felt numb and shaky. If Taylor handed her the bouquet at this point, she would simply drop it from her lifeless fingers. Her head spun in waves of dizzying fear. She wanted to run; dear God, she *needed* to run. To escape. Because if she didn't, she didn't know what would happen but it would be the worst possible thing imaginable.

Not now, she begged of her chaotic mind. Not *now*. But knowing her fear was irrational, knowing there wasn't a single danger in the world for her to be frightened of in this warm, cozy living room filled with loving family and friends, didn't matter one iota in the face of her abject terror.

Why now? What had triggered this? Not even trying to concentrate on that all important question could quell her fear.

Dimly she heard the wedding march continuing. Through a haze of wild dread, she saw Taylor approaching Steve. If only she could remain where she was. Inside she was screaming. Outside she was shaking. She begged all the gods combined to just be able to remain where she was, not to have the black fog of blind panic descend upon her. She wanted nothing more on earth than not to break away and run screaming from the room. But her legs were moving before she could stop them. And a scream was building in her throat.

Suddenly strong, warm hands wrapped around her shoulders. She started violently and would have uttered a yelp of protest had Chas not leaned close to her ear. "Shh. It's okay. I'm here."

He pulled her back against his chest, keeping his hands on her shoulders, pressing them slightly, impressing himself on her. Letting her feel his warmth, his strength, his awareness that something was terribly wrong with her, holding her there by sheer force of will.

His lips at her temple moved, brushing her hair with his warm breath. "It's okay, honey. Just draw a deep breath and relax. Everything's fine now."

Everything *wasn't* fine, she wanted to cry, but Martha Jo had stopped playing and the minister had taken both Taylor's and Steve's hands in his own, folding them over each other, turning his gentle, nonthreatening gaze from one to the other in smiling approval.

"There's nothing to be scared of," Chas murmured. "I'm right here."

Allison leaned against him slightly, feeling the waves of panic subsiding, trusting him for that moment to ward off whatever it was that haunted her so. She blinked back tears of relief and let her eyes wander to the crowd facing her to see how much of a spectacle she'd made of herself.

She needn't have worried. Tears filled many a pair of eyes in the crowd, but they weren't for her; they were, as they should have been, for Taylor, for the beauty of the ceremony before them. No eyes held any curiosity for the anxiety that had nearly propelled her from her sister's wedding. Not one pair rested on her.

Only Chas had apparently witnessed her near flight. Even Carolyn, right next to her, appeared unaware of her hysteria, though she glanced a bit curiously at Chas's unexpected presence behind her sister-in-law.

And still he held her against him, subtle pressure from his hands thrumming a soothing rhythm through her shoulders. And he didn't turn her loose until it was her turn to hug and kiss the new bride and groom, though he stayed very close beside her.

Throughout the short reception following the ceremony, Allison felt Chas's questions burning into her mind. It was as if he were yelling the queries at her, his very silence pounding at her like an incessant hammer. As always after one of the inexplicable panic attacks, a rough headache swamped her and thundered in her head. Chas's careful surveillance of her didn't help to abate the pain, for all that he'd saved her by preventing her flight.

And she was equally careful not to find herself alone with him. Of all people, she didn't want to try to explain to him that she was suffering from some strange and bizarre ailment, a mysterious haunting that left her nearly mindless with fear and sick afterward with a blinding pain and a general sense of malaise. For him in particular she had to remain the cool, tough television reporter, the woman of glitz and glamour.

No matter how much she might want to confide in him, to lean against that broad chest and just pour out the fear, the despairing sense of doom she felt, she had to remain aloof, strong. Because whenever she was around him, all she wanted to do was to simply be held and reassured, as he'd done during the wedding ceremony.

But no amount of reassurances would really matter, because the terror was irrational and without pattern. It would come back, and he wouldn't be there to stop it the next time. She'd needed him once before in her life, desperately and futilely. She'd never allowed herself to need anyone again since, and she wasn't about to turn to the one person who had let her down so monumentally once before.

She wasn't looking forward to the moment when Taylor and Steve would be leaving for their honeymoon and she would be left alone with the boys. And Chas would surely linger in the expectation of talking with her, of discovering what had happened that afternoon.

Chas kept his eyes on Allison as he joined the crowd in waving farewell to Taylor and Steve. Allison looked about as ready to collapse.

He'd stuck to her like glue throughout the seemingly endless afternoon, dying to ask her what happened, what had frightened her so, but had thought better of it when she studiously avoided his eyes and turned a shoulder against him more than once.

He was no physician, no psychiatrist, only a country vet

in a little dot of a town in the Panhandle, but he knew stark terror when he saw it. And Allison had been ready to bolt.

He'd caught hold of her just before she sprang into action. He'd felt the impact of her shoulders against his palms as she was already leaping forward. If he'd been a weaker man, a man unused to exercising a firm hand on such animals as cattle or horses, he wouldn't have been able to ground her.

He'd felt the waves of fear rippling through her and, as closely as he'd stood behind her, he'd been able to feel every nuance of her ragged breathing, her trembling body, and had known she still ached for flight.

He was sure some people wondered why he'd suddenly walked up behind Allison and half hugged her right in the middle of her sister's wedding ceremony, but he was pretty certain he was the only one who had caught sight of her fear. But then, unlike the rest of them, he hadn't been watching Taylor; he'd been staring at Allison.

He'd seen her poise, her grace and, despite her limp, her lovely walk to the front of the room. He'd seen her soft smile for Sammie Jo and Cactus Jack. He'd witnessed her wink at the triplets. She hadn't been frightened then. And she'd smiled when she'd nodded at Steve and Tom. It had only been after Tom Adams gave Martha Jo the signal to begin to play the wedding march for the second time through that her eyes had widened, that her breath had become hitched.

Like a horse caught in a thunderstorm, she'd been ready to bolt, to run blindly out of the room, desperate to escape and neither knowing nor caring what greater danger she might be running toward.

She wouldn't talk to him about it; he knew that much. And he would be leaving soon himself, unable to think of an excuse to stay beyond the short round of cleanup. So how to stick close enough to be able to be there should that panic rise again?

As if in answer to his silent plea, less than a half hour after Taylor and Steve left, Sammie Jo bustled into the kitchen, her wig askew, dragging two of the triplets by an ear into the kitchen with her. The third one trailed behind them, one hand on his own ear and dangling a piece of broken video equipment with the other.

Chas saw the first smile he'd seen on Allison's face in hours. She masked it swiftly by the simple expedient of covering her mouth with a single finger, holding her lips compressed.

He nearly chuckled aloud at seeing her amused.

"Oh, dear," she said, her voice muffled. "What happened?"

"What happened was this trio of hooligans decided they'd get themselves a little peep show is what they did. So they rigged up the camera on a remote and let 'er run while all the ladies was walking up and down the porch steps."

"That isn't what we— Ow!" Jason tried protesting, but was halted midstream by a twist of his earlobe.

The triplet behind Sammie Jo—Chas thought it was Josh, though it was difficult to tell when they were all dressed up—swallowed convulsively, then burst out, "We didn't mean to do what you're saying, Aunt Sammie Jo!"

One of the others took up the chorus. "Honest. We didn't know—"

"How were we supposed to know it would just catch feet and stuff. Honest!"

Josh, or whichever one he was, danced out of range of Sammie Jo's feisty eyes and well out of reach of her hand. "Let 'em go! We didn't mean anything."

She turned loose of the other two boys and placed her

hands on her thin hips while they rubbed their ears and looked pained beyond imagination, though having felt her grip, Chas wasn't terribly surprised.

Sammie Jo made a slow circle, eyeing each of the miscreants. "And who's going to pay for this broken equipment, I'd like to know?"

"We didn't know it would get stepped on," Jason said, rubbing his ear.

"We'd already filmed the farm guys like you said. For a documentary," Jonah added.

"So we thought a documentary of Mom's wedding would be cooler."

"Yeah, like, we didn't think—"

"Darned right you didn't think!" Sammie Jo snapped. "But that doesn't fix the equipment, or make up for Martha Jo twisting her ankle falling over the danged stuff. Lucky for her that Tom Adams can't keep his eyes off her, or she'd have fallen for sure. But he caught her just in the nick of time."

"You gotta believe us. We didn't know it would hurt anybody."

Martha Jo entered the kitchen about that time, limping just a little, less noticeably than Allison did, in fact. "I'm fine, Sammie Jo, really. No damage done."

Chas thought he'd never seen Martha Jo looking prettier, with her face slightly flushed and a stray strand of hair tickling the nape of her neck. He thought of the many times people in Almost had tried pairing the two of them. Just as they'd tried with Taylor and then Carolyn.

He flicked a glance at Allison, who no longer looked amused. She looked ready to bolt again. He turned to see what she was looking at with such fear.

All he could see was Martha Jo, pointing her finger at the boys. "You guys! You're gonna owe me."

The boys burst into their litany of innocence. If they had once had the courage to look up, they would have seen every adult but Allison smiling.

Again Chas looked from where Allison stood, obviously fighting an urge to run, to Martha Jo, a woman who couldn't hurt a fly if her very life depended on it. But just behind her he could see Tom Adams, nearly half a head shorter than Martha Jo, grinning from ear to ear.

Sammie Jo, never one to back down from a fight, wasn't finished with her temper yet, though after a long and pointed double take seemed somewhat mollified by Martha's glowing looks. "I'm glad to hear you aren't hurt too badly. But that doesn't take away from what these boys have done. Haven't had the fancy stuff three days, and already going and breaking it."

Josh cried out, "But this isn't the new stuff."

"And we didn't *mean* to break anything, Aunt Sammie Jo!"

"Double honest, we didn't."

"Shush, now. Meaning to do something and doing it are two different things."

Chas saw Allison cover her mouth. To anyone else, it would appear she was trying hide a smile. As she had earlier. But to him, it looked as if she was trying to withhold a scream. Her eyes, wide and frightened, lifted from the shadows of the hallway and turned to his.

He felt the force of her appeal for help as if she physically thrust it at him. He felt rocked by the sheer agony in her gaze.

Suddenly, inexplicably he was frightened for her. What troubled her so much that she would turn to him?

Jason groaned. "Community service," he said.

"Darned straight," Sammie Jo barked, though her voice

broke on what Chas knew was a repressed chuckle. "Two weeks."

Allison dragged her hand from her face.

Chas felt her effort and inched toward her.

"I can always get the equipment replaced," she said. She cleared her throat. "It's still under warranty."

Without looking at her niece, Sammie Jo said, "That's good to know, honey. And that'll be just about the right amount of time for the boys to work, thinking about how they'll be more respectful of people in the future and will be more careful with their things. Won't it, boys?"

"But—"

"No 'buts,'" she snapped.

"Yes'm," came three downcast replies.

Chas edged still closer to Allison, aware of her shallow breathing, the side glances she took at the back door. Was she afraid someone would enter suddenly, unexpectedly…or was she mapping out an escape route?

Sammie Jo paced the kitchen in short, staccato steps. "Now, let's see, you've already fresh painted Martha Jo's place just a month back."

"Her son had to help us," Jason said hotly. "He made the bomb!"

Sammie Jo leveled a sharp look at him before lifting her eyes to Allison. Not meeting an amused kindred glance, she turned her attention back to the boys. "*And* you've already done the beds at Alva Lu's and painted the trim at Charlie Hampton's…"

"They can work with me for a while," Chas said.

Sammie Jo turned to give him an appraising stare. Her eyes softened, and a slight smile tilted her lips. "Why, thank you, Charles. That'll do just fine."

Her face remained as soft when she turned back to the

errant preteens. "And you'll do everything he says and not bother any of the animals, is that clear?"

The boys had brightened considerably. They'd often told Chas that working off the community-service hours Taylor had long ago established as the only means of discipline was best at his clinic. They had Billy to follow around and the animals to pet and feed. And often Chas would let them exercise the horses that might be in for whatever doctoring was needed.

And now he would have an excuse to see Allison at least two or three times a day. Maybe she'd open up to him, tell him what was troubling her.

He looked over at her again. Her eyes were on the back door.

If he'd thought of it, he might have broken the camera equipment himself.

Chapter 5

The man whose last name was Quentin watched the departure of the wedding couple from a safe distance some one hundred yards away.

He'd learned about the wedding from the ancient man who hired him to work his fields. And for a split second of raw fear, the first he'd felt in months, he'd been afraid he'd seriously misjudged Allison and that she'd returned home to marry the country stud, a mare in heat, running home for a repeat performance.

But it had been her sister, the graceful woman with all those boys, who had married some Texas Ranger. Now that was a particularly ironic twist in Quentin's plans. Who would have guessed Allison would have a Texas Ranger in the house to protect her?

But the Ranger was leaving town, his only thoughts on his new bride.

However, he decided, even if the Texas Ranger weren't leaving town, he'd never have looked twice at the battered old pickup or its present owner. And no matter how cautious the Ranger might be, he'd never equate the theft of a car in Lubbock—and the murder of its owner or the murder of a hitchhiker—with an itinerant farmworker helping break ground and do soil preparation in Almost.

And now that the Ranger was leaving town for his honeymoon, his little FBI buddy would be heading out also. And Almost would be virtually lawless. The man renamed Quentin chuckled. What a town. And what a concept, Almost lawless.

He smiled, not the patented Hollywood smile he'd given the café people in Anton, but a tight grin of mastery. A smile he knew better than to let others see; for some reason, it frightened them.

But he had cause to smile. Everything had been working according to schedule.

Not everything, perhaps, but who could have guessed that Allison would have forgotten him? Who would have guessed that a steel-trap mind would have soft, malleable mesh in it somewhere, a mesh that allowed all traces of her memory of him to disappear? Was that his fault? How could he have taken that peculiar possibility into consideration?

Once he would have been fascinated by this seemingly aberrant behavior. He might have studied it in depth. But those days were gone. All that mattered now was reaching Allison. Making her pay for all the pain, all the misery she'd put him through.

He drew a deep breath, held it and expelled it slowly, forcing himself to relax. The time was right. And the plan was working. Hadn't he discovered her exact travel arrangements? And hadn't he flown into Lubbock a day before her, stolen the car and pulled the title with only the registration papers? And hadn't he met her at the airport just as he should have, just as he had promised her he would?

And hadn't she walked right past him as if she'd never seen him before in her life?

And weren't they both here now, in the ridiculous little town she'd said she hated but, down deep, loved so much that she'd cried when telling him about it, begging them to welcome her back home, to be enveloped into their small-town fold?

She'd rejected everything he offered her. She'd forgotten those Almost tears, those pathetic little pleas, but he hadn't. He hadn't forgotten a single detail she'd told him.

As he watched the wedding guests milling around the front yard of Taylor's house, he toyed with the fishing line in his pocket. In his mind, he could hear Allison's sleepy voice. *There isn't a trace of standing water for nearly a hundred miles, but every man in Almost has fishing gear.*

He tried to pick Allison out of the crowd leaving the reception now. But she remained inside, hidden from him again. But she wouldn't be for long. And then she'd be his forever. The way she was meant to be. He pulled the fishing line from his pocket and let one end of the coil spiral to the ground.

She'd be hooked. And by a bait she'd given him just three months before. A gruesome bait to be sure, but one that would reach the deepest part of Allison, would touch her at the most fundamental of terror levels.

He chuckled aloud. Oh, yes. I'll hook you then. Line and sinker, Allison. Hook, line and deadly sinker.

The cleanup finished and fine dishes once again lifted to their niches in the china hutch that had once belonged in her mother's dining room out on the ranch, Allison fought a headache as she bade farewell to Aunt Sammie Jo and the few others who had lingered to assist with all the mess.

She sank into the living-room sofa and dropped her head on the back with an audible moan. The silence surrounded her like a soft, warm blanket. She congratulated herself on the fact that she'd passed every minute of the time since she'd been in Almost without a memory lapse.

In fact, except for a few seconds of lost time at the airport luggage carousel and her swift—but marginally controllable—panic attacks, she'd really suffered no more than just the natural tensions surrounding coming home after a fifteen-year absence and her own doubts about her mental condition.

She tried not thinking about the peculiar holes in her memory, but as always, her mind, that reporter's mind that sought out mysteries, shot straight to the problem. Car accident, memory loss. It had to be physiological, then. Cause and effect.

She couldn't remember anything from the moment of the accident until waking in the hospital room. And from that point on, everything became sketchy. But her first real sense of time displacement or lost time had been during her stay in the hospital.

She remembered seeing the door open in her hospital room and then a nurse suddenly standing beside her bed. But three hours had lapsed in between.

Could she be suffering a multiple personality disorder? She'd done an interview with a woman who claimed to have ten personalities, and nine of them were documented by her psychiatrist. The woman frequently encountered moments of "lost time," suddenly "waking up" in different clothing than she remembered wearing, in different places than she'd expected, one time even in a foreign country.

"Er...Miss Leary? Allison?"

She froze for a moment, not opening her eyes. She thought Chas had left quite a while before. Her heart jolted once, painfully before she realized that he would never have called her Miss Leary. She opened her eyes to see his son, the boy who looked nothing like Chas but conveyed every nuance of his presence nonetheless.

The boy ran his hand across his face in a gesture she'd seen Chas do a million times in those days so long ago. He hitched a shoulder up a little on the left side, as if apologizing for something before acknowledging the deed had been done. And this was something she'd also seen Chas do.

"Hi, Billy," she said, and the smile that came to her lips was uncomfortable. This was *Thelma*'s son. The woman Chas had married instead of her. Unconsciously, her hand stole across her flat stomach.

Would he have married her if he had known the truth? It was an unanswerable, fifteen-year-old question. And one that belonged to the dark and murky past. Except it wouldn't stay there.

Billy grinned at her. It wasn't Chas's grin, but every bit as warm and generous. "Dad and I talked about it and we think I oughta hang out here tonight. With the guys."

The worst of Allison's headache melted away by the magnitude of his offer. She'd been half dreading a night with the triplets, not that she hadn't already fallen for each of them and not that they weren't good boys; it was just a lot to cope with.

But she felt obliged to offer a weak protest.

As his father would have, he brushed her feeble objections aside with a wave of his slender, boyish hand. "I want to, really. We're going to mess around with the video stuff."

She raised her eyebrows. "I thought it was broken."

Billy shook his head. His dark, nearly black hair curled tightly against his head and shone faintly blue in the light from the lamp. "That was my old setup," he said.

Allison cocked her head. "But the boys got in trouble because they broke the equipment."

"Oh, Dad already knows it wasn't theirs. But he said they're better off having something to do for a few days. Besides, with them around, I get out of some of my chores."

Allison chuckled at the conspiratorial grin on the boy's open face. "But surely I should tell them they're not in trouble."

"Well, yeah, but Dad says that since they *did* break equipment, whether it was new or not, they still owe the community service. And even if it didn't work very well anymore, Dad says you'd probably appreciate us not telling them that until *next* week."

Allison chuckled again. She'd half expected to feel a measure of resentment toward this boy, this young man, if for no other reason than that Chas had fathered him and married his mother *and abandoned her in the process.*

Instead, gazing into his clear blue eyes, she found herself inexplicably drawn to him, as if whatever she'd once felt for his father was reborn in him somehow. A basic goodness, a fresh, open outlook on life, the child who would become a good man.

"And he's usually right. My dad, I mean."

For fifteen years of her life, she had thought the opposite, that Charles Jamison had treated her as badly as a man could. That Chas had been wrong to abandon her, to leave her for Thelma. That he'd lied and hurt her in the process. As wrong as wrong could be.

But this young man had been raised by Chas. And the love between them was evident in the boy's assessment of his dad, of the pride he held for him, the depth of emotion in the timbre of his still changing but already deep voice.

Whatever wrongs Chas might have done in the past, and in her mind they were still huge and varied, he'd done right by this boy. Oh, *so* right.

In the shadows of the front porch, waiting to leave until he knew Allison's decision about Billy staying, Chas closed his eyes and listened as the two of them talked. Just hearing those voices mingling together, rich contralto and shifting baritone, was music, a symphony he'd never thought to really hear.

He'd read articles of people who'd had surgery to gain hearing for the first time, and cried upon hearing certain sounds others took for granted...the ticking of a clock, the scratch of a dog's paw on a back-door screen, a mother's voice. But not even a Chopin sonata could sound as haunting and as alluring as hearing his son's voice playing a countermelody to Allison's.

And when they laughed together, not heartily but softly, exploringly, as if testing the waters between them, something painful and sharp turned inside him. He would do everything he had done for the past fifteen years to have known Billy, to have lived with him, to have loved him. Oh, but how much he wished Billy had been Allison's son.

He opened his eyes at the damnable thought. It was as if he were wishing Billy to be someone else. Billy was who he was, what he was, because he was Thelma's son. And all the wishes in the universe couldn't change that, nor should they.

"Well, Billy, if you don't mind it too much, I'd really love to have you stay and help me out," Allison said inside.

Chas strode from the front porch and walked into the

night as swiftly as if all the demons from the past were biting at his heels.

Allison heard the tapping in her sleep. In her dream, it came from an enormous grandfather clock, one she knew, in that strange way of dreams, was really her father. Only instead of the hours of the day on his face, he had the months of the year neatly marked out. The hands were pointing to November.

Tock…tock…tick-tock.

"It's time, Allison," the father-grandfather clock said, speaking in her father's voice. "It's time to bury the past." The clock that had once been her father handed her a large shovel and pointed a long, spindly arm at a flat expanse of bared earth. Farm workers dug in the ground far beyond this place, their dark heads bent down as if praying.

She couldn't disobey her father-clock and the insistence of his tock-tocking. She took the heavy shovel into her hands and wrapped her hands around the wooden handle. She could feel the coarse grain digging into her palms. She rammed the shovel against the earth, hearing it making a sound much like her father-clock, though somewhat muted. It went in easily, and she began digging the hole, a grave for the past.

Tock…tock…tick-tock. "Keep digging, Allison," her father's voice said. When the hole seemed enormous, a maw yawning up at her, she reached beyond the huge mound of displaced earth and picked up a small strongbox with two handles on either side. The top was marked Yesterday, and in the dream, she knew what lay inside, however impossible. She began to cry.

Tock…tock…tick-tock. "Do it, Allison."

She couldn't. She couldn't lay that precious little dream into that dark, dark grave. She turned to run away from the hole, from the father-clock and his November demands, and tripped over the shovel. The box flew from her hands, and she was flung from the dream, her hands stretched out to catch the precious box, tears running down her face.

Awake now, in the darkened bedroom of Taylor's home, she sat in her bed, upright, chest heaving from the strange nightmarish dream, pulling her hands back to her chest, to clench them against her breasts.

Tock…tock…tick-tock.

She whirled toward the bedroom window, swiping at her wet face, her eyes clear of tears now, wide with sharp fear.

Something hung outside her window, something that dangled into the gap revealed by the partially opened curtains. For a moment of pure shock, she saw what it was and denied it with equal swiftness.

In that one second of awareness and rejection, she slipped back in time. She lay on the cooling asphalt, her vision blurred. She could smell the burned rubber from the tires. And she could smell the sharp, coppery tang of blood. Could taste it as well. She could see Susie sprawled not five feet away, still, not moving. And she could see Susie's hand, stretched out and curled, as if beckoning her, pleading for her cousin's help. It was only after she reached for her cousin that she understood that Susie still lay in the car.

And in the window of the bedroom now, fifteen years later, she could easily make out the details of a hand. Disembodied, tapping at the window. A hand. A human hand.

She gasped and frantically scooted back on the bed without any conscious thought. Her back pressed sharply against the headboard, though she scarcely felt the bite of the wood against her skin. A gargling precursor to a scream caught in her throat and fought for freedom.

A thousand possible explanations flitted through her mind—she was still asleep and dreaming, the triplets were playing some joke on her, she was having one of her "spells" and was really seeing something far different than a severed hand—but none of the possibilities could stem the scream that built in her throat, the shriek of terror demanding immediate release.

The boys, her mind reminded her. Don't wake the boys. Don't scare them.

But the scream didn't care about children or quiet, sleeping townsfolk nearby. The scream had a life of its own and fought free, ripping the peace of the night, drowning out the horrific tock...tock...tick-tock of the lifeless fingers against the window.

She lost all sense of time, thought or anything else but the scream and the hand.

Her bedroom door flew open, and four sets of wide, frightened eyes met hers as her nephews and Chas's son flipped on the overhead light.

Her scream still echoed, and her mouth was still open, trying to sustain the terrible sound.

Four voices, three high-pitched, one low, demanded to know what was wrong. But she couldn't answer, only point to the window and follow their gazes as they all looked at the window. The overhead light had blackened the window so that only the curtains and a narrow swath of black were visible.

"What was it?" Billy asked, his voice cracking with fear and adrenaline.

"Was somebody out there?" one of the triplets asked.

"Creepy," another affirmed, but more as if he were excited than scared.

"I'm going to turn off the light," Billy announced, and did so.

One of the boys swore.

But not because he was seeing what his aunt had

screamed about, for there was nothing at all in the window now. No hand, no dead fingers. Nothing at all.

Just like all the other times in the past few months. Terror, visions, strange memory losses...and nothing.

"I don't see anything," one of the boys said.

"Me, either," another affirmed.

Billy turned the light back on. "You guys stay here, I'm going to go check outside."

"No!" Allison all but yelled.

The four sets of eyes turned in her direction for a second time.

"What did you see?" Billy asked.

"Yeah, what was out there?"

"Like, was it a man or something?"

"She can't talk with everybody talking."

"So what'd you see, Aunt Allison?"

She was struck by being called "aunt" so naturally and so easily when she'd woken them from deep sleeps by her screaming.

"A h-hand," she managed to say. Her throat was dry and scratchy, painful from her scream.

"Whoa! Like just a *hand?*"

"Awesome!"

The triplets dashed to the window before she could utter a protest. They crowded into the windowpane, jostling each other, cupping hands around their faces to block out the light.

"I don't see anything, do you?"

"Was it, like, just floating there or what?"

"I'll bet it was a tree branch or something."

"Doofus, we don't have any trees by the window."

"Well, she musta seen something normal, right, Billy?"

Billy was looking at her with a closed expression, something rather like a cross between concern and doubt.

"Yeah, Josh, something." Then to her, he said, "I think I should call Dad."

"No," Allison stated again, too forcefully and too swiftly. Billy looked startled and the triplets turned from their contemplation of the window to stare at her. "No. I don't want...I was probably just having a nightmare...I'm fine now."

She ran a wildly shaking hand through her hair and drew a deep breath, looking from the triplets to Billy. The mere thought of waking Chas up in the middle of the night, of having him rush over to rescue her from another hallucination, was just the medicine she needed. It was the cold glass of water thrown squarely into her flushed face.

"What time is it, anyway?" she asked.

She received four differing answers, but all attesting to the earliness of the hour.

"I'm fine now. Sorry I woke you guys up. Must have been a n-nightmare."

Four murmurs of acceptance rippled through the room, but their eyes were still wide with residual startlement. Two of them began telling her about nightmares they had endured.

"Will you be able to get back to sleep?" she asked finally, when the nightmare stories wound down.

Four heads nodded. Three carried identical expressions of total doubt on their faces. Billy looked worried.

Allison, as reluctant to turn out the light and be alone again as the boys apparently were, asked for her robe, slipped it on and rose from her bed to stand on shaky legs. "Since I woke you all up in the middle of the night, what do you say I make us all some hot chocolate or something?"

She thought it was Josh who came up to put his arms around her. And Jason who led the march from the bedroom to the kitchen. But it was definitely Billy who turned on the porch lights and peered out the windows at the still night.

"The dogs are all still asleep," he said.

"Yeah, they didn't even wake up when Aunt Allison screamed."

"I thought someone was getting killed. Like, really!"

"Boy, you can scream *really* loud, Aunt Allison. I about wet my pants!"

"How come the dogs didn't bark, Billy? Don't ya think that's weird?"

Chapter 6

Chas snatched up the receiver and barked his name on the second ring. His eyes couldn't seem to focus on the clock on his bedside table.

"Something weird's going on, Dad," Billy said on the other end of the phone.

The sound of his son's voice in the middle of the night and the hushed words slapped Chas instantly awake, and he was on his feet before he even thought.

At his father's demand and in a swift, breathless recitation, Billy described Allison's supposed nightmare and the scream that had woken the boys.

"But the thing is, Dad, something *is* wrong with the dogs. Like they won't wake up. They're still breathing and everything. I mean I can see their chests moving and all, but it's like they're drugged or something."

"Stay put, Billy. Don't go outside!"

"I won't. I was too scared. I mean, like scared of messing up evidence or something."

Chas closed his eyes in sharp relief. Thank God there was still a boy left in the young man. He'd still been young enough to be scared to go outside, and old enough to know the wisdom of not doing so. And his son had been practically raised in the clinic, so he could be relied on to know enough to recognize a drugged animal and to understand the simple fact that anyone aside from a vet who would want to drug one had some ulterior motive in mind.

Chas asked after Allison and the boys, and Billy told him they had all gone back to bed. Frowning heavily, he asked why Billy hadn't called him sooner.

"Allison didn't want me to. She was pretty adamant about that, Dad. Like she almost yelled for me not to call you. But she was upset, you know?"

Chas felt himself wince at this last statement, but managed to summon praise to Billy for calling him and told him a second time to stay inside. "Make sure the doors are all locked. And check the windows. I'll be there in a minute."

And he was, not even having taken the time for socks or his boots, just shoving his feet in a pair of garden tennis shoes. Billy met him at the door and, for a second time, recounted the night's events in a hushed whisper.

One professional look at the dogs and he knew his son had been right; they'd been drugged. He was relieved to discover that their heartbeats were neither too rapid nor too slow. He did take three blood samples, one from each of them, to analyze once back at the clinic. In the meantime, he'd have to hope that the boys' dogs would revive quickly enough with the small doses of epinephrine he administered to each of them. After that, they would simply have to sleep off the effects of whatever drug they'd been given, because he wasn't going to leave the house.

Chas wanted to take his flashlight and check for footprints outside Allison's bedroom, but didn't want to frighten her any more than she already had been that night.

Billy had told she claimed to have seen a disembodied hand tapping at her window. Sounded like something right out of a nightmare, and he would have believed exactly that had occurred but for the evidence of the sleeping dogs.

He wondered if someone from Steve's past might not be pulling a little grotesque harassment of the Texas Ranger, but discounted the thought nearly as soon as it crossed his mind. And he was relatively certain the targets weren't Billy or the triplets. Teenage pranks didn't usually extend to drugging pets. It was almost an unwritten rule that pets remained untouched. In that respect, the Golden Rule always seemed to apply.

And if someone wasn't out to harm the boys, that only left Allison. A woman who had nearly run from her own sister's wedding, who started at each little sound. Who looked caught between confusion and fear, exhaustion and despair every time he saw her.

He paused in the act of examining the window locks. There had been one time since her return that the look of fear had been absent from her lovely face…when he'd held her in his arms. For that blissful moment, when her body relaxed and she'd melted against him, she hadn't been frightened. He would have bet his life on it.

But what was scaring her so? Why would she assume she'd had a nightmare instead of believing her own eyes? Contrary to popular belief, he knew that people more often *did* believe their senses, no matter how bizarre or outlandish.

"You go on to bed now, Bill," he said, unaware he'd shortened his son's name to its more adult status until his son gave him a startled, then pleased grin.

He smiled back. "You did just the right thing tonight, son."

Billy's grin broadened. "Thanks, Dad. I…I'm glad you're here now, though."

"Me, too," Chas said. He gave Billy a rough hug and propelled him toward the hallway.

Once Billy was gone, he went out onto the porch to check the dogs again. Still sleeping, still drugged, but now, after the epinephrine injection, moving a bit and thankfully very much alive. He peered out into the darkness beyond the yard, hoping to catch a glimpse of the creep who would drug children's dogs and do something as hideous as frighten a sleeping woman and children.

But just as he couldn't fathom the kind of mind that would allow someone to terrorize women and children, he couldn't see anything out of the ordinary, either.

He went back inside, locked the door carefully and was turning to go check the back door when he heard a gasp behind him and whirled to face Allison.

Her hand on was on her chest, and her eyes were wide with startlement and fear.

"It's okay," he said quickly. "It's only me."

"W-what are you doing here?" she demanded in a thready voice.

"Billy called me," he said. He held up a hand to forestall what he assumed would be her protest. "He had to, Allison. He was pretty sure the dogs had been drugged."

Impossibly her eyes widened even more and cut from his to the window flanking him. "Drugged?"

"Yeah. He was right. I don't know what drug was administered, but they're still out even after the epinephrine I gave them. They should be coming around any time now."

"There *was* someone out there?"

Chas thought she was unaware she'd backed up a pace until her back was against the corner of the hallway. Confounding him, what he read on her face wasn't anything like fear or puzzlement, but a staggering look of pure and simple relief.

"Allison?" he asked.

"Oh, thank God," she said.

Chas caught her before she slid down the wall to the floor.

He told himself that he held her in his arms for comfort, nothing more. He assured himself that pressing her face to his chest, stroking her flushed face and smoothing her tousled hair were strictly in the name of solace. He was a noble friend, a guardian for the night.

He was a damned liar.

He was holding her tightly to his body because it felt right to keep her there. He stroked her hair because it was a magnet to his hand. His lips pressed against her forehead because he wanted to kiss her, to tell her everything in his heart, however confused and uncertain.

She, on the other hand, merely rested against him, neither hugging nor clinging, responsive at the lowest of levels, the way a sister would respond to an older brother.

"Allison?" he murmured after a few moments, when her breathing was steadier, her muscles relaxed somewhat.

"Mmm?"

"What's going on?"

She shook her head against his chest. Her hand fluttered at his waist.

"Tell me."

"I don't know," she said. "Honestly. I don't know what's happening to me."

"But something is."

"Something...yes."

"Tell me," he urged.

She stirred in his arms, and he was sorry he'd asked any questions when she pushed away from him slightly and ran her hands through the hair he'd imperfectly straightened. She flicked him a somewhat embarrassed look.

"Do you suppose Taylor would keep any alcohol in this house?" she asked.

He smiled. "If she doesn't, I'm sure Steve does. I've never met a policeman yet who didn't have a bottle of bourbon around somewhere."

Allison wrinkled her nose but turned toward the kitchen. Following her, Chas noticed that she knotted her robe tightly around her waist after pulling it sedately closed. She might be treating him like a brother at the moment, but she wasn't unaware of him. Not at all. And that thought made him feel a universe better.

He divided his time between a careful watch of the opened curtains and Allison as she rummaged through the cabinets for the cache surely hidden somewhere. The night was dark and still, and Allison found the liquor in the fourth cabinet she opened.

He drew the curtains, fighting the sense of being watched and knowing it wasn't true. Together they selected a Napoleon brandy, and she searched a few more cabinets seeking snifters. Finding none, she poured them each a small amount in juice glasses.

Without waiting for a toast, she tossed hers back with what seemed a practiced flick of her wrist, but actually revealed her ignorance of the alcohol. She choked violently, and Chas held back a chuckle as he supported her while spasms racked her unprepared body.

He led her to the table and pushed her into a chair. He sat down opposite her and waited until she regained her breath to ask her again what was going on.

She gave him a rather watery glance, then wiped her eyes. "I wasn't kidding when I said I didn't know. I really don't."

"What do you *think* is going on?"

"Until tonight, until you said the dogs had been drugged, I thought I was going crazy."

Chas assimilated this without visibly reacting. Allison crazy? Never. Hot tempered maybe. Risk-taker certainly. But crazy? Nope. Not possible. But it was the flat acceptance in her voice that made him understand that whatever *was* happening had been going on for some time. Long enough that she said the words as if bored by them.

"Why would you think you were going nuts?"

She didn't look at him now but at her crossed and folded hands resting on the table. "I've been experiencing what the doctors call 'fugue states,' where my memory seems to be erratic at best. Usually short-term, seemingly inconsequential things. But there's lost time, unaccountable minutes or even hours."

"You haven't been abducted by aliens, right?"

She chuckled weakly, then cleared her throat, a throat probably still raw from her screams and from coughing after downing the brandy. "Don't think I haven't considered that," she said. "In a lot of ways, I fit the profile. Missing time. Scared of my own shadow. Forgetful."

She shot him a look he could only have called teasing. He was glad to see it and grinned when she said, "Somehow I wouldn't have pictured you in the UFO-believer category."

"Oh, you know me, Allison, I'm curious about damned near anything."

She smiled, but the gesture was perfunctory at best. And he knew why. She *didn't* know him. She'd known him in the past. She didn't know his interests—beyond Billy and his own practice. She didn't know his opinions, his tastes, his preferences, even what his house looked like. And he didn't know her anymore, either. He felt the chasm between them threatening to yawn wide again.

"Why don't you tell me when this...fugue thing started?"

She nodded and closed her beautiful eyes. "About two months ago." Her eyes slowly opened, and she gazed down at her hands, making a diamond of her forefingers and thumbs. "I was involved in a car accident."

Chas knew about the accident. He frowned. "A head injury could account for the fugues, something neurological could explain the missing time, the spot-occurrence memory loss."

"I know. So the doctors claim, but they say there's nothing like that in my case. It's a complete mystery."

"Especially because a head injury doesn't account for drugged dogs," Chas said. He didn't add that it wouldn't account for the drugged dogs unless it was Allison doing the drugging.

But unless she really was crazy, her relief at knowing that a human agent had been responsible for whatever terrified her put paid to any notion of mental distortion.

He said, "Taylor told me it was a pretty bad accident. You were in the hospital for quite a while, weren't you?"

Allison nodded again, flexing the diamond shape into a butterfly, then back to a diamond. A crooked smile shifted her lips. "Taylor was mad at me for not letting her know until afterward."

"Can't blame her," Chas said.

Allison lifted startled eyes to meet his gaze. "Why?"

"You're her sister, Allison. She loves you. She cares about you," he said, genuinely surprised at her question.

"She hasn't seen me in fifteen years," she said defensively.

"As Billy told me a couple of nights ago, feelings don't just die, Allison."

"Is he so sure about that?" she asked.

Chas knew they had strayed from whatever was troubling her to far more global issues and far-more interpersonal ones. He had the distinct feeling that how he answered her bitter question might determine the course of whatever relationship they might have in the future.

A tremendous weight to place on one little "Yes, Allison, and so am I." But he said it anyway.

Then, when she remained silent, he added, "Feelings can change, shift even, but they never just *die*."

She nodded as if he'd confirmed something she'd dreaded hearing but knew all along. "I'm not sure about anything these days."

"Just since the accident?"

She nodded again. Her hair glimmered in the light from the overhead lamp and glistened pure gold. Chas had to lay his hands flat on the table to keep from reaching out to touch it.

"Is there any pattern to these fugues?" he asked, forcing himself to stick with the topic at hand and to keep from touching the subject so close to hand.

She shook her head. "I don't think so. And don't think I haven't gone over everything."

"When did they start?"

"In the hospital. The first one I can remember is hearing someone coming in the room and turning to see who it was, then the next thing I remember it's three or four hours later and the nurse is in my room."

Chas frowned. "That's not uncommon, Allison. You were probably on some kind of painkiller."

"That's true. That's what I told myself at the time. But see, Chas, every time one of them happens, I have an absolutely unreasonable fear build up inside."

"Like today at the wedding?"

"Exactly. And speaking of which, how did you—? No, it doesn't matter."

"I was watching you, not Taylor."

She blushed and flexed her fingers again. She cleared her throat. "I was just looking at Steve and…and Tom Adams?…and then it hit. I had to run. If you hadn't been there…"

"You'd have carved a path right through the center of the guests and gone straight through the wall, cartoon style."

She gave a wan chuckle and looked up at him. "Seriously, though, I would have bolted."

"I know. But you didn't."

"Thanks to you."

Chas felt like his own fourteen-year-old, ready to scuff his feet in the dust and hang his head. "Part of the job," he said.

"You country vets must have quite a job description."

"We do. It's in the country-vet handbook—never take your eyes off beautiful women who return home after a lifetime and never let them run from a room when the organ music starts to play."

Her brow furrowed. "It wasn't the music, you know. That had already been playing and didn't bother me then. It was…oh, I don't know."

"Sure, you do. You're the only one who can."

"But it's not like it was a certain light or the sound of a chain rattling or anything obvious. At least, I don't think it is. Because it happens all the time. I was riding in a cab going uptown last week, at least I think it was last week—

I'm not really sure. See, I don't drive much anymore, and not at all in the city.''

Her eyes unfocussed a little, and Chas knew she was remembering the car accident.

"You were riding in the cab…" he prompted.

She started a little and gave him a weak smile. "Anyway, I was staring out at the people, not even paying attention. Suddenly I was terrified. I had to get out of the cab. I had to run. That's all I could think about. Running. Getting away…escaping.''

"From what?"

"From…from I don't know. But you want to hear something really funny about all this?''

"I'm all ears," he said dryly, knowing whatever she said wouldn't be very funny at all.

"Somewhere in the back of my head, I seem to equate all the panic with quitting smoking. At least, I always want a cigarette whenever I'm coming down from a panic attack. Isn't that crazy?''

"How long ago did you quit?" he asked, never having known she'd smoked at all.

"About three months ago now.''

"And any problems back then?''

"Not really. I just quit. One day I was smoking, then I took a week off, and sometime during that week I just gave them up.''

Though she was looking directly at him when she said the words, Chas had the chilling feeling she wasn't seeing him. And her voice sounded strange as she spoke, as if she were reciting something not particularly interesting.

"You must have really wanted to quit," he commented, pursuing the thought process for no discernible reason other than the fact she'd brought it up.

She frowned. "No. I mean I don't know. I smoked almost two packs a day. Then I just quit. One day I was smoking, then I took a week off, and sometime during that week I just gave them up.''

Chas felt a cold tingle work down his spine. Allison had just repeated verbatim her earlier comments. She didn't appear even remotely aware of having done so. Part of him wanted to ask about the cigarettes again, but a bigger part didn't want to hear that crazy, flatly inflected little speech for a third time. Tomorrow perhaps, or another day. But not tonight.

However, he did have to ask one very important question. ''Are you still on any painkillers, Allison?''

''What? No. I gave those up when I quit the physical therapy.'' She gave him a quick and sad little smile. ''Drugs were a good theory for a while for me, too. But no dice.''

Chas wanted to ask if the painkillers had been for her leg, if her limp stemmed from this accident or the one long ago, but he didn't know how thin the ice was that now lay between them. For the moment, they had found a safe place to stand; while talking about whatever was plaguing her, they had a common ground. Any reference to the past, however oblique, might prove the one bit of extra weight that would shatter their fragile support.

''Does Tom Adams look like anyone you know? Does Steve? You said you were looking at them when you felt the urge to run come over you.''

''*Urge* isn't quite the word, Chas.'' She really chuckled this time, though her face was still deathly pale. ''It's more a flat-out, dead panic. What do you do with a horse that spooks too easily, that breaks into a lather at the slightest thing?''

Chas smiled and settled back in his chair before replying. ''You're not a horse, Allison.''

"Some people I've interviewed would argue that point," she countered. "Though not recently. I don't remember *them*."

He chuckled this time. He was struck by her ability to laugh at herself. He didn't know if he would have been able to joke about something so frightening as fearing he was losing his mind.

"So what would *you* do with a spooked horse?"

Chas studied her for a long moment, feeling the tension in the room shift, knowing—without thinking about how—that she'd asked him something entirely different. Her eyes met his, a hint of the old Allison present, the sassy gal with the wind-tossed mane of hair.

He was aware that she was dramatically changing the subject, that she was ducking whatever was bothering her, a neat side step from a very uncomfortable topic. With all that she'd been through, he wasn't about to force her.

Besides, he would have to have been a robot, devoid of any feelings, to ignore the flicker of fire in her blue eyes, the shyly teasing smile she wore.

He pushed to his feet, slowly and carefully, keeping his eyes locked with hers, letting her see every movement, every gesture, even his thoughts. He stayed by the end of the table, but held out his hand to her, palm upward. "With a horse, I would work on making her feel so cozy she doesn't have to panic anymore."

"And how do you do that?" she asked, looking from his hand to his eyes.

He shook his hand a little, coaxing her to place hers in his. "I would let her see she can still have all the fears she wants, but she doesn't have to be scared of *me*. I'm not going to grab her or slap her. I'm not going to hurt her in any way. I'm just going to stand here and let her come to me."

She lifted her hand and slid it into his. "You let her think she can trust you," she said.

He folded his fingers around her slender hand and just held it, slowly stroking his thumb along the fine planes of her delicate knuckles. "I let her know she can."

He lifted his hand slightly and pulled just the merest fraction toward his midsection.

"And that makes her feel cozy?" Allison asked, rising to her feet and allowing his grip to steady her.

"Oh, no," he said, drawing her still closer. "I'm old-fashioned. I happen to believe that every scared thing needs to be held."

"Is that right?" she asked, but to his delight she stepped closer.

"That's right. So I give her space, then I wrap my arms around that space."

He released her hand and for a moment didn't move at all. Then slowly, achingly slowly, he lifted his arms and wrapped them around her. He didn't try to pull her closer, simply stood there, nearly at arm's length, but encircling her nonetheless.

"And then?"

"And then I wait for her."

"How long?"

"As long as it takes."

Her eyes widened slightly. "And what does she do then?"

"If I'm very, very lucky, she'll step forward."

With a faint smile, Allison moved another step closer. "Like this?"

His heart was pounding so fiercely now, he was surprised she couldn't hear it. "Exactly like this," he rasped.

"And then...?"

"And then I hold her close. Let her know she's safe. Let her know that I'm there to take care of any other worries."

She slid her own arms around his waist and pressed her palms flat against the contours of his back, making him shiver with a sharp, hot want of her.

Her hands, trembling only minutes before, were steady now on his back, and knowledgeable. They roamed across his back with a sure and sculpting touch, strafing the lines from his belt to his neck, cupping his shoulders and molding her fingers to the valleys of his muscles there.

"Ah," she said. "And then...?"

Chas couldn't answer her. He couldn't think what she meant. He could only gaze at her heavy lids, her slightly parted lips, the rapid rise and fall of her chest, the robe slipping open to reveal a satin tease of a chemise. "Allison..."

"Yes?"

The single affirmative, issued more as a question than a statement, undid any remaining resolve. He pulled her even closer and lowered his lips to hers, any tenderness forgotten, all gentle thought lost to a raging desire for Allison.

His hands roamed her back, her hair, the contours of her silken face. And at the slightest sound from her, he would have come back to the surface of his plunge into lunacy, but she pressed harder against him, her breasts flattening against his ribs, her hands pulling him firmly to her.

She tasted of brandy and something of mint, and he pressed his tongue against hers, warring with it, drinking her, arching against her, needing, aching to be a part of her. And she met him equally, straining against him, moaning a little as her sweet tongue played with his.

Ah, it had been so very long. This untrammeled, unfettered freedom to touch, to taste and drown in her sweet scent left him weak in the knees, but feeling stronger than he ever had in his entire life.

Then, baffling him, she chuckled. He continued his kiss, lowered his lips to nuzzle the sharp points of her collarbone and the hollows at the base of her lovely throat. And she chuckled again. He couldn't help but smile in response, no matter how puzzled.

She arched a little, and he lightly drew his teeth across a jutting nipple, then drew it into his mouth through the satin.

"Chas…"

"Mmm?"

"If you tame a spooked horse this way…somebody's gonna lock you up."

Chas caught her to his chest and laughed aloud.

Allison laughed with him, not because she thought what she'd said was so particularly hilarious, but because it felt so very right to be in his arms again.

She'd been through a full range of emotions that night, every night for the past two months, but none of them more certain or more readable than the one she felt now: accord.

This was a man she had once loved desperately and lost. She'd thought of him off and on, with a little more emphasis on the "on," for some fifteen years. And now, like the little girl she'd been then, she was turning to him for safety. Like a knight of old, he'd rescued her that morning, then come to protect her in the night.

But she wasn't a girl anymore. She was a woman, confused and tormented with fears for her sanity, yes, but a woman. And with a woman's desires and knowledge, she'd allowed him to tease her, coax her into his embrace, and with a woman's surety she'd made him laugh aloud, a laugh she'd been unaware of craving for nearly fifteen years.

She savored the emotions he brought forth in her. Peace,

charm, even a bit of the playful. *Accord.* Nations negotiated for years to achieve it. Neighbors went to court and counseling to find it. Couples strove for it. A union devoted to compromise, a treaty disallowing war, a camaraderie, two former lovers finally becoming friends after all this time. A gift.

Strangely, in the middle of feeling nuts, in the midst of uncertainty and now every possibility of danger, she felt better than she had for days...years. She felt strong, free, effervescent with sheer life force.

She'd done an interview about three months ago with a psychologist who had claimed that a Jane didn't fall in love with a John so much as she fell in love with how John made Jane feel about herself. She'd done her usual hard-hitting interview, happily punching a hundred different holes through the guy's theory, but now she wondered. She might have to look the guy up and apologize. If she could remember his name.

"What did you say?" Chas asked her.

"What?"

"I thought you said, 'I can't remember your name.'"

She chuckled again. "No. *You* I remember."

He let her loose a little to cup her face in his hands. "Do you, Allison?"

"Yes." She could say it without awkwardness now. Guarded, perhaps...careful, certainly. But no longer feeling awkward.

He brushed her lips with his. The touch of a feather, the breath of a breeze. His cheeks were rough with unshaved beard, and his eyes were shadowed from lack of sleep.

"What time is it?" she asked.

"About five."

"Good heavens. And you have work tomorrow...today."

He smiled and leaned his forehead against hers. "I usually get up about now, anyway."

"I'm sorry Billy called you."

"I'm not."

"Neither am I, to be honest," she said with a chuckle. Her smile faded as she remembered the exact reasons he had come to Taylor's house that night. "Thanks, Chas."

"Any time. It's what I'm here for."

He'd said that once before, in those long ago days. *Any time. That's what I'm here for.* But he hadn't been there. He'd married Thelma instead. And raised Billy. And she'd been without him and without children.

She resolutely shoved those thoughts from her mind. She didn't want to spoil the moment, the feeling of peace. Even on a quest to put some closure on the past, some things were better left unsaid.

His smile faded as he stared at her and the warmth in his eyes shifted to flame. He drew his hand down her shoulders, across the bare expanse of her upper chest, then lower, slowly, enticingly, rising to cup a breast, lifting it slightly as if testing the weight of it, then molding her to him, his forefinger and thumb caressing her already hard nipple. She moaned a little and pressed against him, feeling his want for her.

"Allison..." he whispered, then softly kissed the sensitive skin beneath her ear.

All she could think about was the fire he was creating in her, the warmth of his body against hers, the slow, seductive stroking of his hands, one on her breast, one exploring the contours of her waist, the slope of her thighs, her flaring hips.

Her robe fell open the rest of the way, and she could feel the chill air as he pulled back slightly to trail his tongue along her collarbone. His breath, hot and rapid, thrummed against her skin, making her shiver and arch to him.

His hands felt molten through her satin chemise. The silky material might as well not have been there, for she could feel every nuance of his hands against her.

She knew she should stop him, knew also that he would halt immediately should she ask. Instead, she pressed still harder against his firm length, aching for more. Wanting nothing more than to not think for a moment, to not wonder what was happening to her mind. She wanted just to feel and to pretend for this one moment that she was fine, that no dangers mental or otherwise could exist. And just for this one moment of rare intimacy, she wanted to pretend that she belonged to Chas and always had.

As if reading her thoughts, he began to stroke her more firmly, molding her to him, neither roughly nor abruptly, but surely, knowledgeably, hungrily.

When she'd last felt the power in those strong hands, she'd been little more than a girl, a starry-eyed dreamer on the threshold of life. Relishing the feel of his hands upon her now, she was fully aware that she was a woman with a woman's heartaches and wants. And every pore of her body desired this man. Had always done so.

No matter how badly he'd hurt her in the past, no matter how many tears she'd shed in his name, she still wanted him. She literally ached for his touch, craved the feel of his hands on her body, and leaned into sensations she hadn't felt for fifteen years and yet recognized with every fiber of her being.

"Ah, Chas..." she sighed as her head lolled forward onto his shoulder.

He pressed a kiss to her bared throat. "Allison...it was always you, Allison," he murmured, his lips trailing down her shoulder, freeing the thin strap of her chemise with his teeth.

But he was wrong, she thought, even as she shivered while he trailed kisses down her arm, nuzzling her, circling the globe of her bared breast. It hadn't *always* been her. Somewhere, at some time, he'd found Thelma, rejected the "always" and had married, raised a son.

His hands on her body, strong hands, confident and assured, seemed to be trying to erase the truths of the past, the hurts of long ago. And though she would never have admitted it in all those lost fifteen years, most of the pain did ebb at his touch.

But not all.

Some hurts remained, permanently vulnerable, forever endangered. But with his lips against her bare skin, his hands roving her every curve, it was so very hard to think about the past. The very long ago, dark and distant past. And the sound of his ragged breathing as he suckled her breast stole the last vestige of her resolve to stand away from him.

Chas knew he should stop, should call a halt to the mindless, utterly perfect satisfaction of holding Allison in his arms once again, of tasting her, of feeling her perfect breasts in his hands.

Her body melded to his, pliant and soft, and her hitched breathing spoke volumes. He knew she wanted him every single bit as much as he wanted her, and the knowledge infused him with strength, with even greater passion.

Some dim and sane voice in him demanded that he let her go, that he *talk* to her about the past, about the odd occurrences of the present. But damn it, he told himself fiercely, he'd made sacrifices all of his life, and nothing on the face of the earth could force him to make this one, the one of letting her go now.

Luckily, for the both of them perhaps, one of the boys' dogs started barking.

Chapter 7

"Turn off the lights," Chas said calmly, sliding the strap of her chemise back up and tugging her robe closed. He gently pushed her toward the hallway and the light switch. "I'll open the curtains."

If he'd snapped the command or even looked the slightest bit perturbed, she might have felt fear or worry, but as it was, she only obeyed him, stepping to the doorway leading out of the kitchen and drawing her hand down the switch.

In that strange way of light refraction, the room they stood in was instantly plunged into total darkness while outside the room, the night world took clear shape and definition. She could see the posts and ceiling joists of the porch and beyond it the broad backyard, the low chain-link fence and still farther the flat, flat plains that surrounded Almost, a stretch of land that sparkled silver in the moonlight then melded into darkness somewhere far away.

One of the dogs—Allison didn't know which one—was

running along the back fence in an unsteady, ungainly lope and barking furiously at something in the great universe beyond. It was a high-pitched, frantic yapping, perhaps a reprimand directed at whoever had drugged him, or perhaps just a loud statement of life. It was impossible to tell which.

Allison could just make out Chas's large form silhouetted against the window. He didn't look as though he was worried about any intruder. He appeared to be looking for the first rays of dawn, relaxed and comfortable with what he might see.

And yet she could feel his tension from where she stood. He wasn't looking for the sunrise; he was searching the darkness for any signs of the person who had terrified her earlier, a man who had drugged the boys' dogs. A *real* person, but one who was obviously something straight out of one of her nightmares.

"I don't see anything, do you?" she asked finally.

"Yes," Chas said softly without turning around. "You gotta come see this, Allison."

She made a cautious way around the table and chairs and joined him at the window. She felt the warmth emanating from him before she actually stood beside him. She paused to take in his scent, a combination of outdoors and a spice she couldn't identify but that she knew was uniquely his. And then he reached out his hand for hers, clasping it unerringly in the dark. She sighed a little as his warm fingers enveloped hers.

The old clichés were wrong, she thought, stepping into that warm spice, tingling to the feel of his arms wrapping around her and molding her back to his front. Familiarity did *not* breed contempt. No, on the extreme contrary, it bred intimacy.

What on earth was she thinking? To be embraced by this man, the man who had most hurt her in her life, was tantamount to losing what little sanity she had remaining. But she leaned back nonetheless, allowing his size, his strength and his very aura of peace to capture her emotions and wholly override what was left of her mind.

"Look toward the windmill at the Speckler Ranch. You remember where it is?"

She did, but she didn't see what he wanted her to see.

"Just beyond the outline of the windmill."

He lifted a hand and pointed. Her heart started pounding in a furious rhythm.

"You see it?"

"W-what?" She had to force the single word from her lips and felt as if she were trapped in his embrace.

She couldn't see what he wanted her to see. Beyond his pointing finger lay madness or worse, and she had to run. Just run. As hard and as fast as she could.

Now!

She stiffened in his embrace, shifted to her good leg, prepared for flight. But he held her tightly, his arm a band of steel around her midriff.

"A deer. Do you see it?" He raised his other hand to press it firmly against her chest, holding her in place, not allowing her to run, though he couldn't possibly have known the extent of her need to bolt. "Isn't it beautiful?"

Her heart thudded against her rib cage, undoubtedly thundering against his hand, irregular and painful. She couldn't seem to gain her breath. And yet the panic that had flooded her ebbed slightly. His words? The deer? His broad, warm hands, which were intimately splayed above and below her breasts, holding her fast against his still body, bracing her, blocking her escape?

"Do you see it now?" he asked, hugging her slightly, shifting her direction, redirecting her focus.

And, the panic fading, the shards of night coalesced and

allowed her to see what he'd been looking at. A mule deer. A doe. Head raised, poised, listening to the barking of the dog, cautious, ready for flight. Like herself.

Chas whispered against her temple as if the deer could hear them, "She's a beauty, isn't she?"

Her heart rate was slowing, and her breathing seemed to be trying to match his slow, steady respirations. "She is," she whispered back. She could still taste the raw, grainy spittle of fear.

"She's part of a herd that drives Alva Lu Harrigan crazy by getting into her garden once spring comes."

Allison drew a tight, sharp breath and strove to appear normal. How often had she had to do just that in the past few months—lying to co-workers and colleagues, faking a nonchalance she was far from feeling? She forced herself to focus on the deer and on Chas's words and touch.

"Alva Lu would be upset if a butterfly landed on her fence post," Allison muttered tightly, coercing herself to remember the too many times of being in trouble with the prissy-faced woman.

Chas chuckled. She was amazed to feel his laughter ripple against her back, and more amazed to discover the sensation was mildly erotic and further served to dull the razor edge of her fear.

"But then Alva Lu would bring you her prize-winning pie just because she thought you might need a taste of pecan."

Normality. Simple and sweet. Her fear dropped another dramatic few degrees. "You really do like it here," Allison said, half-amazed at the strength of her voice, awed by her own ability to stay put. And warmed by his love of this tiny little desert town in the heart of nowhere.

She knew she could move away from him now without

the need to run, but was reluctant to lose the warmth of his arms, the depth of the solace she found there.

"Yes, it's home," he said simply.

"I used to love it," she said. Even to herself, her voice sounded wistful. And perhaps a bit accusatory.

"Maybe some part of you still does," he stated. She couldn't tell if he sounded meditative or was simply making a statement of fact.

"Maybe," she hedged, knowing she lied. She loved this strange and unique part of the world so much it hurt. But it had been far easier to leave it behind than to see it and not be a part of it anymore. From the moment Chas had told her he was going to marry Thelma Bean, she'd become a visitor only. A transient.

And now she was just a woman who had come home for her sister's wedding, hoping to find her sanity again, only to discover it was more elusive than ever.

On some level, Almost was inextricably linked with her feelings for and about Chas. It had been easier to leave him forever than to watch him raising his son with another woman. Easier to leave them all, Taylor, her parents, Aunt Sammie Jo—all of them. Everything that had comprised her life.

But it felt so good to stay still in his arms, to feel his entire body enfolding hers as his hand had enwrapped hers earlier. So warm, so strong. So peaceful. So *sane*.

The land beyond their view began to lighten as the sun sent the first rays of morning over the horizon. The silvered fields glistened, adorned with precious frost. And pale blue fingers of light stretched across the lightening sky. The deer turned and walked on stiff legs behind the stock tank and windmill. Four deer, all does, wandered out from the other side and began moving into the west, following the night.

"There they go," she said, wholly unnecessarily.

"They'll be back."

"Tomorrow?"

"When they want to," he said, pulling her a bit closer to his chest, a fraction deeper into his warmth. "When they're ready."

"Where do they go?"

"Just away."

"Aren't they in danger?"

"Of course," answered the man who was a country vet. "But they'll be fine."

"How can you be so certain?" she asked a little dreamily, lulled by his heat, his strength, the breadth of his compassion.

"Because they're magic deer."

A surprised chuckle escaped her. "Magic deer, huh? Not too many of those left around these parts."

"Nope," he agreed, and pressed a kiss to the nape of her neck. "But good things always happen when you see one."

"Do they? And we saw four."

"Mmm, so the good things are quadrupled," he murmured, then lightly grazed his teeth across the narrow expanse of her back that the robe exposed.

"Yes," she sighed, tilting her head to allow him even greater purchase. Her fear had completely faded now, and in its place, engendered by his mouth, his full lips, his tongue, was a delicious and heavy languor.

"Allison?"

"Mmm?"

"What scared you a minute ago?"

She tensed, but at the gentle, soothing pressure of his hands, his body spooned to hers, she allowed herself to relax again. "I don't know, Chas. I honestly don't."

Chas withheld a groan as she pressed back against him,

unwittingly applying pressure where he least needed any persuasion.

He thought wryly of the sacrifices he'd briefly cataloged for himself a while back, when he'd told himself he *deserved* the moment, the bliss of Allison in his arms again. Now he thought that not one sacrifice he'd ever made in all the years held a candle to the one he was making now in not giving in to his desire for her, hers for him.

But she needed to talk about what was frightening her. She needed his help to understand what was happening to her. So with the greatest reluctance on the face of the earth, he was bringing them both back to the present, to the realities inherent in dogs being drugged, to children possibly wandering in, to the potential dangers surrounding his Allison at the moment.

"When we were looking at the deer..."

"Yes?" She slid a hand to his jean-clad thighs and stroked deeply, enticingly.

He had to grit his teeth for a moment, warring with the raging fire she was knowingly reigniting in him. Finally he was able to ask, "You were ready to run again. Why?"

She stilled so thoroughly that he felt the tension springing from her body. He realized that she hadn't been aware she was stroking him as a device to steer him away from discussing whatever had scared her.

She felt ready to spring from him, to fly again. He continued to hold her tightly to him, hating himself for making her face the unknown, inexplicable fear, willing her to understand that he was only doing it for her. And perhaps, on some deeper, more selfish level, for *them*.

"What do you mean?" she asked. "I'm fine."

"Allison, I've spent nearly every night of the past fifteen years recalling every aspect of your personality, the way you laugh, the way you wrinkle your nose when you don't like something someone's saying. I *know* you. Whatever's going on with you, around you, it isn't all just coming from inside your head.''

She said nothing, but Chas thought her stillness held a different quality, an arrested, questioning immobility.

''I know that you think we're strangers, Allison. That we knew each other a long time ago, that we were lovers and then we weren't anymore. End of a sad story. But it doesn't work that way.''

''W-what way?''

''Ambivalence doesn't mean indifference, Allison. It only means feeling two distinct ways about something. Opposites, good-bad, happy-sad, love-hate. I can't ignore you, Allison. I can't pretend that you're okay and do nothing about it. And I'm not ambivalent at all. Not one little bit. I'm telling you right now, I'm going to help you figure this out. Whatever happens with you and me, I'm going to be right here for you, do you understand me?''

As he waited for her answer, he felt the stiffness leaving her rigid form. Slowly, an inch at a time, she relaxed against him until finally she was pliant and resting easily in his arms again.

''I...I'm not ambivalent now,'' she said finally. ''And I'm not running, either,'' she said finally.

''And why is that, Allison?''

''Because this feels so good, so right. Here in your arms, I mean.''

Chas looked up at the ceiling of Taylor's kitchen and closed his eyes against the empty expanse of soft yellow. He was dying from the desire to do the right thing, but he'd be wholly unable to do that if she continued leaning against him, her soft body pressed to his, and with words such as she'd just spoken hovering between them.

He wanted to abandon the quest to help her untangle

whatever nightmare chased her. All he wanted to do at that moment was to turn her around and kiss her until tomorrow was forgotten and yesterday was forever buried.

And if he did, he would be turning his back on Allison. She needed to be free of the fears, the panic attacks. And he needed to help her. It was that simple. And oh, so very difficult to do.

"Did you see something out there that I didn't? Before the deer?"

"No...I don't think so."

"Allison, maybe someone could help you pinpoint when all this began."

"It began with the car accident."

"Are you sure?"

Again he felt that speculative stillness, that poised alertness coursing through her.

"No," she said slowly. "No, I'm not sure, Chas. I think the memory lapses may actually have started before the car accident. I just didn't remember that until now. I wonder why?"

"Have you talked with your doctor about the lapses?"

"Of course. But we were only talking in relation to the accident. We know from the X rays that I didn't suffer a fracture or anything. No brain scrambling."

"What about hypnosis?"

She went utterly rigid in his arms. "What about it?"

"Couldn't a good hypnotist take you back to the precise moment all this started? I mean, wouldn't he be able to figure out wh—"

"No!" she burst out.

He knew that his nearly offhand suggestion sparked a conflagration of some kind in her. She broke away from him, all magic shattered, the deer forgotten, the warmth of her soft body stripped away. Her eyes were wide with anger and a fear he couldn't begin to fathom but understood had something to do with whatever tormented her.

He didn't try to stop her or restrain her this time. "What is it, Allison?"

"What? Just because I don't happen to believe in that mumbo jumbo—"

"Fine," he said. He lifted his hands and dropped them again. "It was only a suggestion."

"Not for me. Never again."

"Again?"

"What is this, the inquisition? I simply said I didn't want hypnosis. Why should that create such a furor?"

She didn't know why she was so angry with him. And strangely she wasn't any longer. This anger was similar to the panic attacks that assailed her—there one second and completely gone the next. Only this one seemed triggered by something Chas said. Or rather by his suggestion that she seek psychiatric help.

"Allison, I'm sorry."

With the draining of the swift anger came remorse. "No, Chas. It's me who's sorry. I...I don't know why I reacted that way. Just testy, I guess."

"You've been through a lot lately," he said slowly, as if tasting the atmosphere while formulating his words.

She wanted to explain, even opened her mouth to do, but what would she say? How could she tell him that her anger at him was as mysterious to her as her memory lapses, her lost moments of time, her irrational panic attacks? She resorted to the half truths and half assurances she'd become accustomed to using in the past couple of months.

"I'm sorry, Chas. You're right. I probably should seek some kind of psychiatric help. I'm just tired," she said, and could see by the look on his face that she'd done nothing to allay his concern. If anything, she'd heightened it.

Chas was frowning heavily, and eyeing her as if she were about to suddenly fly apart and start shrieking. She didn't want him looking at her that way. Not Chas. Not ever.

She should never have come back home. She should have known she couldn't run from her troubles, that they would follow her home. She'd felt a moment of hope when she learned the dogs were drugged, a sick hope, certainly, but hope nonetheless. If someone had drugged the dogs, then perhaps she wasn't insane, didn't have some dread brain dysfunction. Maybe someone was using psychotropic drugs on her, the new designer drugs that distorted all perceptions of reality, that could even bend the subconscious mind.

But she'd panicked *after* the dogs were drugged, and for no discernible reason. She'd felt panic even while in Chas's embrace. She'd wanted to run away, escape, race blindly through the house and outside into the fearsome cold night.

"I think I know why you wanted to run, Allison."

"What?"

"Actually I don't know the 'why,' but I think I know the trigger for it."

"What is it? There's nothing," she said. But she watched him, hoping against hope that he'd discovered something she hadn't. She glanced at the window and back to him. "What did you see?"

"You were looking at Tom Adams this morning…yesterday morning…right? Exactly at the moment he signaled Martha Jo to start playing the wedding march?"

"And…?"

"And you wanted to run tonight, but only after I pointed at the window to show you the deer."

Allison thought about Tom Adams giving Martha Jo a

single-fingered go-ahead. Reviewed her panic at the window only moments before. She shook her head. "It can't be that. I think about it and it doesn't scare me."

Chas looked at her for a long moment, then slowly raised his hand toward the dawn-lighted window and deliberately pointed outside.

She followed his eyes to his steady hand. Her heart had started beating a bit faster at the moment he lifted his arm. And jolted into hyperspeed when he balled his fist, all but one finger.

"Allison..." she heard him say, but it was from so very far away. He couldn't reach her. Couldn't hold her now, wouldn't be able to stop her terrified running.

He turned his hand until that finger was pointing directly at her. "And now?" he asked.

But she scarcely heard him. Everything in her told her to run, to run as far and as fast as she could. *Now*.

Chas caught her before she so much as turned. He held her tightly against his chest, cradling her, smoothing her hair, murmuring words of assurance.

"It's okay, Allison. It's all right now. You know what's causing it now."

Tears of confusion and fear sprang to her eyes. And relief let them spill free. "But why, Chas? Why would something so simple scare me so? I must really be going crazy."

He thought he might know what haunted her, but didn't know enough to speak his half-baked theory aloud. As Alva Lu Harrigan would have advised, "Ideas are like pies—they need to sit for a while before cutting into them."

So, in the dawn light, he held Allison in his arms, the way he'd longed to do for years, unwilling to lose her to whatever demons tortured her and vowing to never let her be frightened again.

But even as he rocked her, promising all would be well,

swearing to be with her, he felt a dark certainty that he was lying to her, that his promises were empty. How could he protect her against an unknown assailant, an unknown quantity? It—the unknown he—could strike at her anytime, anywhere and when she was most likely to be vulnerable.

He wasn't a Pete Jackson of the FBI and he wasn't any Steve Kessler, Texas Ranger. He was only a country vet with a fifteen-year-old son and an ache where his heart used to be.

But just maybe, if he never let her out of his sight, out of his arms, perhaps then he'd be able to protect her.

As if negating his thoughts, she sighed and pulled herself free. She ran a hand through her hair. She looked at the floor, his hands still held out to her sides though no longer touching her, and finally lifted her eyes to his face.

"Someone's brainwashed me, haven't they?" she asked.

Chas let his arms drop to his sides. He hadn't forgotten she was a reporter for one of the toughest news programs on television, and he'd never lost sight of her brilliance; he'd only swept those simple facts under the rug of his concern for her, his need to protect her.

He fought a minor skirmish with the desire to tell her to let him handle it, let him figure it out. So he could…what, present it to her as a pretty package? *Look what I figured out for you, Allison. Now you'll have to love me, right?*

He realized he'd been as foolish as any of the triplets, and as childish in thinking she would appreciate his wrapping her in cotton wool. She was vulnerable now, yes, and scared with good reason. But she was no one's property, not a porcelain figurine to be kept on a shelf and admired. She had brains and heart. And she had courage.

And what she needed from him was his *help*, not strong-arm tactics and heroics. And she needed his complete honesty.

"Hypnotized," he said. "That's what I think. Same thing."

He saw the flinch that caught at her and watched her ponder his single word. Her nose wrinkled. "But I thought no one could be hypnotized against their will."

"You don't remember being hypnotized?"

"No. Never."

"That's what you said earlier. But you said 'Never *again.*'"

He wanted to draw her into his arms again when she frowned heavily and ran a hand across her brow as if easing a headache.

"I did say that, didn't I? When I was so angry at you a while ago. And I was angry for no reason."

"Not for no reason, Allison," he said wryly. "I was pushing you."

She waved her hand as she turned from him a little. "Oh, that was probably a good thing." She began to pace, the same way she used to do when agitated over something when she was younger. "No, the anger was like the panic, it just slammed into me, then backed off just as quickly."

"Has that happened a lot?"

"The anger? No. I don't think so." She ran her hands down her robe, ducked them into her pockets, then out again. She moved to the kitchen drawers and opened the top one and closed it again.

"What are you looking for?" he asked.

She turned to stare at him blankly. "What?"

Chas felt a chill work down his arms. "You were looking for something."

She looked down at her hand still resting on the drawer's knob. She gave a shaky laugh. "Damn. After three months, you'd think the habit would have faded. I was looking for a cigarette."

Chas drew a deep breath, then told her what she'd said earlier when she repeated herself about quitting smoking, the flat way she'd spoken, the dull expression on her face.

"And it was verbatim, Allison."

She shoved her hands into her pockets then, unaware she was pulling the robe open in the front. "Three months ago. I quit three months ago. But I didn't go to any hypnotist to do so. I just quit."

"During that week you took off."

Allison frowned. "You know, it's funny, I really don't remember anything about that vacation."

"Nothing at all?"

"The first couple of days...I can remember those. But nothing else. Just quitting smoking."

Chas experienced a strangely murderous longing to wrap his hands around the throat of whoever had done this to Allison, whoever had erased her memory, whoever had left her with terror and gaps and was even now apparently haunting her. A stalker? Was that what this was, a case of a stalker?

As he took in the implications of this thought, he derived a grim pleasure in the realization that the psychotic responsible for whatever was happening to Allison hadn't reckoned on Almost. In a town as small as Almost, a stranger would stand out like a punk rocker in Bible school. It would only be a matter of time.

"Chas..."

"Yes?"

"What if I never figure it all out?"

"You will, Allison," he said, wishing he were as confident inside as his voice sounded. "We will."

"But what if I don't know all the triggers and I have a panic attack right in the middle of an interview, while I'm on the air, or in public somewhere, like has happened before.''

She paced toward the sink and whirled suddenly, unaware that he was standing stock still, a coldness seeping through him.

She suddenly slapped her forehead. ''The pointing. That explains it. I've been absolutely unable to watch the cameraman. He signals us and points when we're about to go on. Oh, Jimmy must have thought I was crazy! Chas? What's wrong?''

He was still standing perfectly still, feeling the effect of her words reached deep into his heart and tearing some vital piece loose.

He'd just consoled himself with the notion that it was only a matter of time before they nabbed whoever was doing this to Allison. But at her words, he realized with the force of a thunderbolt that they didn't have all the time in the world.

In just a few days, Allison would be returning to New York. The psychotic hypnotist or stalker or whatever he was could simply wait for her there, another nutcase in a big, big city.

But it wasn't only the thought of her being unprotected so far from him that made him feel physically ill; it was the awareness that she would be leaving Almost.

Leaving him.

Again.

Chapter 8

The man calling himself Quentin kicked a low-slung nubby chair across the threadbare living area, then threw a metal wash pail against the dirty mirror in his equally dirty trailer. The mirror shattered but didn't nearly satisfy the rage boiling inside him.

He knew he was out of control, felt the fringe of madness lapping at him, but continued nonetheless, kicking at furniture, throwing whatever wasn't already destroyed or nailed down.

Allison still loved her country stud. After all the stud had done to her, after he'd impregnated someone else and married her, after he'd abandoned Allison...she still wanted him.

God, to watch them kissing in the lighted window of the kitchen. To watch her willingly wrap her arms around the stud's neck and let him kiss her, let that man touch her body when she belonged, body and soul, to *him*.

He slammed his fist against the slivers of glass littering

the battered dresser. A thousand tiny fragments of his rage splintered and danced in the air for a moment, capturing his attention, diffusing his pain.

He brushed the larger bits of glass from his hand, ignoring the rivulets of blood, not even wincing at the sharp reminders of the remaining shards. He ran his hands down his body, unknowingly smearing his own blood on the already bloodstained work shirt. He smoothed back his hair and schooled his features to calm composure.

He wished he still had the false glasses; he would push them up his nose, and that would further settle him.

But he knew only one thing would really ease the torment inside him…ridding the world of the woman who caused it. And ridding her of the man who had stolen her from her rightful caretaker.

He left the trailer, closing the door carefully behind him, and stood on the front stoop, breathing deeply of the fresh, cold air. It would be even colder by midday as a winter storm was predicted to sweep through the area. Ice, sleet. Blizzards in the desert.

But by midday, he would be hot. As hot and fiery as he would need to be.

He flexed his hands. The one with bits of broken glass in it began to throb a little. But pain had a way of making him think clearly.

He wondered if it would make Allison think clearly.

He hoped so.

When Chas left to go feed the animals at the clinic after a quick check on the boys' dogs, Allison swiftly locked all the doors and windows.

While he'd been there with her, she'd felt distanced from the trouble, even calm about it. She'd felt safe with Chas.

But with him gone, the enormity of what might have

happened to her came crashing in. And as the boys stirred from their rooms, grumbling about breakfast and not wanting to do any community service right now, "'Cause, gosh, it's a Saturday and we shouldn't have to give up *all* our time, 'specially since it wasn't our fault and wasn't even our video equipment," the real magnitude of the problem flooded her with renewed terror.

Only this terror wasn't the mindless, running, screaming fear, it was rooted in solid, painful possibility. If someone had drugged the dogs in order to more easily terrorize her, then that someone was right there in Almost. And so were the boys. Her nephews and Chas's son. If they stayed close to her, by proximity alone they could become targets for whoever, whatever was after her.

And if that happened, she would never ever forgive herself. She'd already caused the death of one cousin; she couldn't bring danger down on Taylor's sons. Oh, please God, no.

While the boys ate their cereal, listening to winter-storm warnings on the radio, Allison stood at the kitchen counter making a list. A list of every moment of time loss, spot amnesia and the senseless, terrifying panic attacks.

Somewhere in that list was a pattern. Some discernible pattern.

She was a reporter. She was—or had been until recently—one tough cookie. She made her living looking for patterns, digging through seemingly endless mountains of material to discover that often elusive connection.

Why hadn't she fought this the way she would have tackled a recalcitrant story? She'd been so accepting of the victim role that she'd lost sight of her own strengths. In her case, she thought with some disdain, it hadn't been a matter of fearing fear itself, but rather fearing the fear of it.

The boys were finished with their breakfasts and off to get dressed before she was halfway through her list.

She began with the car accident, then thought perhaps Chas was right in that the car accident hadn't been the source of any of her trouble, but just another incident in the middle somewhere. And for the first time, she actually considered the notion that the crash may not have been an accident at all.

She shivered as she understood the implications in the fact that she had no memories whatsoever of the moments following the crash. Before, yes. But after? Not one. She told herself this was a common complaint in accident victims. But how common was it really? Specifically what had triggered her memory lapse? What if it was something to do with whoever was after her? Because it now seemed very, very likely that someone was.

A stalker. She shivered at the thought.

She pondered the questions Chas had posed just a couple of hours earlier and his supposition that her quitting smoking had something to do with everything.

She grinned a little wryly at that notion. The hazards of quitting smoking. She'd like to let the surgeon general know just a few of the possible dangers surrounding her now that she had quit. Maybe he would put a little boxed warning on the side of the packet.

She consulted her list:

November 15—Start vacation.
November?—Quit smoking.
November 28—Some difficulty on the set. Memory loss? First known occurrence of spot amnesia?
November 28-30—Nightmares.
December 20—My birthday. Went out somewhere. Can't remember where.

December 21—Car accident. What really caused it?
Who was driving the car behind me?
December 26—Lost time. Spot amnesia.
December 27—Lost time.
December 30—Run/panic. Spot amnesia.

The list continued through her release from the hospital
on January 10 up, more than two dozen other incidents of
lost time or spot amnesia, until the final entry:

February 23—Panic during Taylor's wedding. Later:
nightmare/harassment? Dogs drugged. Hand in window. Discovered pointing hand to be a trigger for
panic. Note: hand in window wasn't pointing.

She made a second list, this one comprised of questions
only.

When and how did I really quit smoking?

Why does the sight of someone pointing make me
panic? Posthypnotic suggestion?

What's the name of the psychologist I interviewed
on the love story? Why can't I remember? When was
that story aired?

Have I been given a drug of some kind?

What was the significance of the hand in the window last night? Who would know about Susie's hand?

Why was my father a clock in my dream? Why was
he telling me to bury the past? Why were the hands
on November—because that's when my troubles really
began? Or is my unconscious mind trying to let me
know when things really started to get wacky?

Was I hypnotized against my will? If so, by whom
and why?

Are the children in danger if they stay with me?

Allison only knew the answer to the last of her long list of questions: *Yes.*

If something happened to the boys, it would be her fault and hers alone.

Just as it had been with Susie.

Chas realized he'd been listening for them with an acute tension only during the moment he exhaled a pent-up breath of abject relief when he heard the boys' voices approaching the clinic.

He stripped the long plastic gloves from his arms, dropped them into the dispenser and washed his hands before going out to greet them. He needed the time to get his hands to stop their high-school trembling.

He'd been analyzing the blood samples he'd taken from the dogs. He was relieved to discover it was only a mild sleeping narcotic he would administer to any animal prior to an anesthetic for surgery.

But it wasn't a drug anyone could buy over the counter, and one very unlikely to be found anywhere but in a veterinary clinic. With sudden suspicion, he checked his own supply of the drug. And found at least six vials missing.

The bastard had been in his clinic. Had stolen from him. When, how?

Taylor's wedding. Everyone in town had been there. Everyone but one stranger who had been rifling through the clinic, stealing drugs to knock out children's dogs. So he could frighten Allison.

Where would he draw the line between frightening and physically harming?

"Hey, Doc!"

"We're here!"

"Come on, Aunt Allison!"

Chas stepped outside to greet them.

Having seen her only a scant two hours before, he thought he should have been inured to her powerful allure. Instead, all the old enchantment he'd felt not two hours earlier—and all those fifteen years ago—came flooding back and in its wake seemed to grow and magnify in the renewed exposure.

As a veterinarian, he'd never studied plants all that intensely, except those that affected domesticated animals. But in a quick flash of understanding, he now understood the fascination so many biologists felt for the greenery. Allison was like the sun that made his blood flow, the magic that made him feel alive.

And every time he saw her, he was thrown back to a decision made so long ago, a decision he could never allow himself to regret, and he ached for what she'd said to him that long-ago afternoon, and hurt for the bitterness in her tone and the hurt in her eyes.

But it wasn't the past anymore. This was a gorgeous morning, and Allison was walking toward him just as she had in a thousand unfulfilled dreams. Troubled, in possible danger, but still Allison. His Allison.

And despite the deep emotion he felt in her pliant body against his, in her kisses, he'd stepped back from her, not because he didn't want her, but because she needed him to simply be there for her, not need anything from her.

All this and more was clear on her face now. He detected a new resolve in her, something different from the frightened, tearful woman he'd held in his arms that morning. Her limp was scarcely detectable now, her stride more certain, her shoulders squared as if prepared to go into battle.

Even from his distance from her this morning, he could see the strain that had settled on her like a pall was slightly mitigated by some newfound strength. She gave him a short, businesslike wave and was careful not to meet his gaze. He glanced at Billy, trailing just a few steps behind her.

Billy nodded a little, his face solemn and manlike. The official escort. The boy who was transforming into a man turned his watchful gaze back toward Allison, as if prepared to catch her if she so much as appeared to stumble.

The triplets, unaware of anything at all unusual, bounded forward with their normal enthusiasm. "If we do all your cleaning and stuff, can we ride one of the horses?"

"Is Charlie Hampton's horse here this week?"

"Did you fix his leg?"

"Doofus, of course Doc fixed it. He's a *vet*."

"Has everyone had breakfast?" Chas asked the group at large, but looked at Allison.

She nodded, but the boys all exchanged rueful glances.

"We had *cereal*," Josh said. His expression said that Allison had fed them rhinoceros liver.

Chas couldn't hide his grin and he tried sharing it with Allison, but she wasn't looking at him. She was staring out at a group of farm workers breaking the soil in the nearest Hampton field. A heavy frown scored her forehead.

"Allison?"

She started slightly and turned to face him, squinting a little in the bright February sun. Her eyes seemed slightly unfocused, as if her mind were a thousand miles away.

"You okay?" he asked.

She nodded. "It was like in my dream last night," she said cryptically.

One of the triplets looked up. "What was? Did you see another hand in the window?"

"Like, *way* cool."

"Ah, it was only a dream," Jonah said.

Chas was proud of Billy for keeping the boys in the dark about their pets. Knowing them as well as he did, he was fairly certain if they thought there was any danger, they'd find a surefire way of getting right in the center of it.

At the boys' questions and as her surroundings once again centered in her thoughts, a cautious, guarded look replaced that lost-in-time expression. She nodded a second time, with more definition, a slight smile curving her lips. But there was none of the terror-induced intensity he'd glimpsed on her face the night before—this morning.

He'd been so right. She needed the big brother now. Some part of him knew it was all she was willing to accept from him. He told himself he could do that. He could serve that role…as long as he didn't look at her, stand anywhere near her or think about the way her skin felt beneath his roughened hands.

"You're sure?" he asked, wondering if he was pushing her because he wanted her to lean on him, to let a spark of that passion for him peek through again.

She shot him a quick frown and gave the boys a swift glance that let him know she didn't want them to know about her curious malady—or torment.

He thought the shadows beneath her eyes were accentuated by the extreme pallor of her fair skin. Had something else happened since he'd left her at the house?

He dug in his pocket and withdrew his wallet. He fished a twenty-dollar bill out and handed it to Billy. "Why don't you take the boys down to the café and get them something a bit more substantial than cereal. I plan to work 'em hard today."

He gave the boys a wink before they dashed away, and within seconds they were a good thirty yards ahead of Billy, whooping loudly over the biscuits-and-gravy treat in store for them.

"What is it?" he asked Allison the moment they were all out of earshot. "Has something else happened?"

She gave him a wry look that told him clearly that what had already happened was certainly enough. "No. It just occurred to me after you left that whatever is wrong with me, hypnotized, going nuts...I brought it home. I brought it right back here to Almost. To my sister's children."

He drew a deep breath. "Allison, that's where you're supposed to go when you have trouble...*home*. To your loved ones. That's what family is for."

He wanted to add that was what *he* was for, but didn't. Couldn't. Not yet. Not until the haunted expression was totally erased from Allison's face. And even then there were no guarantees she would want to hear him out.

"But not the children," Allison said. "I want them safe."

"Let's call Carolyn," he suggested. "They can stay out there with her. Maybe you should, too."

"No!" Allison said. "Just them. I don't want anyone near me until whatever is going on is over."

"You're going to play hell with that game, Allison."

She looked at him questioningly, frowningly.

"You're not leaving my sight from now on."

She gave a tremulous smile, her frown fading. But she shook her head. "Not even you."

"I'm not going to argue with you, Allison," he said, and grinned at her.

She smiled back, a little wistfully, he thought. He wondered if she had the mistaken idea he wasn't arguing with her because he'd been even remotely persuaded by her refusal to have him stand by her every minute of the day. As Sammie Jo would say, she'd catch cold with that thought.

He reached out and took her arm, linking it through his. "Come on and see the critters."

She moved with him easily, not looking behind her as she'd done just two days before. He kept his hand covering hers and tried not to feel gratified that she maintained a steady pressure on his forearm.

She very nearly seemed the old Allison as she made the rounds of his small clinic with him. She still remembered most of the simpler ailments and cures. As was common in the harsh days of winter, he had several animals housed at the moment.

Most were regular patients—a pig who ingested something that didn't agree with her, a rarity among pigs; a collie in for spaying; a pup he had isolated, suspecting parvo virus.

Some were strays he'd picked up while making his rounds to the outlying areas or the large-animal visits—a cat missing one front paw and soon to deliver a litter of kittens. He'd surmised her injury resulted from a skirmish with a coyote or an owl and was amazed at the cat's survival. And there was a male pup not two months old, as well as a five-year-old spayed shepherd cross with big, sad eyes.

The strays had probably been abandoned by some city dweller who mistakenly believed that turning an animal loose in the country would give it a fighting chance at survival. Instead of which, it was a slow and painful death of starvation that usually claimed the unwary pet, that or their wilder cousins, hungry and predatory.

"What'll you do with her?" Allison asked, cocking her head at the shepherd cross.

"I don't know yet," Chas said honestly. "She's too scared to be of much use to any rancher. She's okay with Billy, but he's been around her for about a week now. All she did the first three days was huddle in the corner of the cage and shiver and snap. Her pads were bloody—"

"From running or from hunger?"

"A little of both, I think. She had cuts in addition to the tenderness that comes of dehydration. Billy and I started leaving the cage door open whenever we were inside here, thinking she might be less fearful if she knew she could move around."

"And that didn't help?"

"No. She's had too rough a time of it."

Allison knelt down before the cage. Chas could see it was a difficult task, one that caused her hurt leg some additional stress. He wanted to warn Allison to be careful of the dog, but sensed that a part of her needed to reach out to the stray.

The dog flattened her ears as Allison held out her hand to let the dog take in her scent. The stray bared her teeth for a brief second, then whimpered as if in apology or expressing that deep sense of empathy she felt emanating from Allison.

"Poor, poor girl," Allison said in a low, soothing voice. "You've been through such a bad time of it, haven't you, girl?"

The dog whimpered again and lowered her head submissively.

"You've been so scared, didn't know what was happening to you, didn't know who to trust...isn't that right, pretty girl?"

Chas felt his heart constrict when he saw that tears had filmed Allison's eyes. He thought she might have been talking of herself. And perhaps, in a way, she was. Perhaps, on some level, she needed the absolution from herself, the permission to feel shaken and hurt, fearful and mistrusting.

He wasn't surprised when, at Allison's gentle touch behind the dog's ears, the tail that had never wavered once softly beat against the concrete floor and a pink-and-black tongue darted out to swiftly taste Allison's skin.

"But you're going to be fine, aren't you, girl?" Allison continued. A tear spilled onto her cheek. "We just need to get you better, then everything's going to be all right. You're not going to just sit back and take this anymore, are you? You're going to be just fine."

The hesitant beating of the shepherd's tail on the floor steadied and intensified. She gave a soft whine as if acknowledging Allison's promise. Or maybe giving one in return.

Chas thought he had never loved Allison quite as much as he did at that precise moment. Whatever had gone on between them in the past, whatever obstacles remained in the future, he would always remember this moment, the exact second Allison acknowledged her vulnerability and chose to fight back at the demons haunting her.

If she had any idea how wistful she looked, how fragile and yet how valiant, she would never have turned to gaze up at him. He knew her well enough to know she would hate being thought of as vulnerable. And yet every fiber of his being responded to that evidence of vulnerability...and inner strength.

"You told me some of those things this morning," she said. "The things I just said. I knew how they made me feel."

"I love you, Allison," he said, and was never so sorry over having opened his mouth and speaking in his entire life.

Shutters dropped immediately, locking him out, closing him off. She looked away, her face a perfect example of a mask, hiding whatever she was feeling inside.

If he could have taken the words back, he would have. If he could have thought of anything that would smooth them over, blur them somehow, pass them off as something an old friend might say, he would have done that, too. As it was, he could only stand there over her, unable to lie to her or take the words back, frozen by the truth he'd incautiously spoken, afraid that in speaking them he'd destroyed whatever small bridge they'd created in the couple of days since her return to Almost.

But the look on her face, the softness, the luminous sparkle of tears in her eyes, the extreme vulnerability combined with that tensile strength, had all combined and out the words had come. A tiny package of pure, undiluted dynamite. And in speaking them, he'd blown his big-brother role to smithereens.

"Chas, I don't want you to misunderstand this morning."

Yes, he thought, he'd set fire to that tiny bridge, blasted it with four little words that should have created the finest span in the universe, but instead had destroyed it. He remained silent, waiting for her to speak, dreading the words she might say.

Because he couldn't take his back.

"You can't love me, Chas. You don't know me. Not the real me, the me I am now. You're in love with a girl in the past."

Was he? He didn't think so. "I held the woman of the present this morning. Held you in my arms. Kissed you."

"Yes, you did. And I kissed you back. And you, of all people, should know that a kiss—or more—certainly doesn't constitute a commitment."

Her bitter words sliced through him with the sure cut of a well-honed knife. He felt a flicker of anger work through him. Anger at her unfairness. "You were the one that didn't want a commitment, Allison."

She pushed her way up from her crouch beside the stray

shepherd. The dog whimpered and edged toward the opened door of the cage.

Though slightly ungainly because of her injured leg, she managed to convey a stateliness, a regality he'd seen surrounding her on television but never in real life, and she turned to him with the coldest eyes he'd ever seen.

"But then I wasn't the one sleeping with two women at the same time, was I?"

Chas frowned, thoroughly rocked by her statement. "What—?"

"What kind of a commitment did you have in mind? I'll marry the cake and have the icing on the side?"

"What in the hell—?"

"I may not be able to remember things that happened a month ago, but I remember every detail of the past, Chas."

"So do I."

She didn't say anything to that. She was busy patting her pockets, nervously looking into her handbag.

"You don't smoke anymore," he said through clenched teeth.

He'd never once imagined that she'd think he'd been with Thelma Bean while loving *her*. While *loving* her. He'd naturally assumed she'd heard the talk he had, that she'd known Thelma had been seeing one of the Wannamacher brothers, both wild in those days, both in prison now.

Yet all these years, Allison had thought him capable of…culpable for the most dastardly of behaviors.

Whatever shutters had dropped in Allison earlier at his foolishly uttered words were nothing compared to the slamming of a steel door in his heart at that moment.

She looked over at him, then sighed as she let her purse fall back to her side. "I don't want to argue with you, Chas."

It was his turn to remain silent. A part of him was still

reeling from her unjust and false accusation. But the bigger part was just plain angry. As angry and hurt as the day she'd mocked him all those years before when he'd enthusiastically outlined their future together and she'd thrown it in his face.

He'd be double damned if he'd tell her the truth now. Loving her or not. Maybe she was right. Maybe he did love a pretty picture from the past. But she'd just shown him that what the past cast in concrete could be repeated in the future.

In the past, she'd flung his intentions to the wind and slapped him for having them. In the present, she'd ripped his admission of love into small, irreparable shreds.

"Can't we simply let the past stay there and be just friends now?" she asked.

Big brother Chas, he thought bitterly. "Sure," he said. "Friends."

In his own defense, his misspoken admission, ill timed and hastily blurted out, had carried no expectation with it. It was simply and honestly the truth.

But he saw now that truth had many strange byways, and facts were far from representing absolutes. It was a fact that he'd loved Allison all those years before. It was a fact that he loved her now, however angry he might be with her, however unjustly she'd just accused him, no matter how long she'd misunderstood his motives, his nature. But those facts didn't mean a thing when the truth was that fifteen years of pain lay between them. Fifteen long years.

"I...I'd better call Carolyn," Allison said. "Unless the boys are going to stay here with you today, for community service?"

Chas thought it was one of the tougher things he'd ever done to push his feelings down—way down—and assume that loveless mantle of "just" a friend.

''We'd better call Carolyn,'' he said finally, deliberately linking them by using the plural. ''Because, like I told you, you're not getting out of my sight. Not while someone out there wants to mess with your head. So that means Billy'll have to go to Carolyn's, too. And we'd better do it soon— a storm's coming up. It's supposed to be a doozy.''

A half hour later, Carolyn drove away with not just the triplets, but Billy, as well. And Chas stood beside Allison, waving goodbye and thinking that spending every waking minute with this woman he claimed to love would be nothing but pure, unmitigated hell.

And from the expression on her lovely face, he was fairly certain she felt the very same way.

He would work hard to vanquish whatever chased her, but he knew that in striving to free her, he was killing any dream of ''them'' as a unit, ''them'' as a couple.

Because if and when they discovered who was tormenting her, they would finally have to face the past. And that was something that would probably destroy them both. Due to the simple fact that he would never be able to apologize for the past. Because of Billy, he'd go back and relive every single second of the past fifteen years to spend them with Billy.

He was thankful when Allison pulled a few folded sheets of paper from her purse. She handed them to him silently and hunched her shoulders against the rapidly chilling wind.

He quickly scanned the list of dates and times she'd experienced her so-called mental aberrations. And read her list of questions. Then he read the whole thing again.

By the time he looked at her again, the anger he'd felt had faded, and the last tinge of it he relegated to a place behind that closed steel door in his heart.

"You spent Christmas in the hospital?" he asked. "Alone?"

"Y-yes," she stammered, as if she were admitting to doing something wrong.

He thought of the friendly Christmases he spent with Sammie Jo, Taylor, even Alva Lu Harrigan. An Almost Christmas was about togetherness and family. Love.

The lock on that steel door felt molten hot in his chest. The thought of her being alone in New York, spending every Christmas without her family, without the warmth, the tenderness and the joy nearly caused him to swear aloud at the pain it brought him. The mental image of her in a hospital, lonely and scared, battered and hurt, gnawed at his very core.

"We're going to fix that," he managed to growl finally.

"What are you saying?" she asked, frowning up at him.

He took her arm and guided her toward his house, a square, one-story, ranch-style house adjacent to the clinic. At least he could channel some of the anger in a positive direction now. He had purpose. A mission.

"Today isn't mobile-vet day. Any emergencies can reach me on the cell phone or in the house."

"Chas...what's going—?"

He swung her around and pulled her to his chest. Her eyes were wide. He didn't think the startled expression had anything to do with fear, but he couldn't read exactly what she was thinking. He still could see the strain on her face, but he could see something else now, as well, hope maybe, or perhaps it was only desire.

He lowered his lips to hers swiftly, surely, capturing hers with total command.

He thought she held still for a second in surprise, and possibly even in momentary resistance. *You can't love me,* she'd told him in the clinic.

But he did. And even though the past was a time bomb waiting to explode any second, they had this moment, this present, and he was going to seize every blessed minute of it.

He turned her loose as abruptly as he'd grabbed her to him. Her eyes were slightly dazed, her lips parted and moist. He ached, physically *ached* to lift her up into his arms and carry her into his house like some knight of old.

Instead, he propelled her toward his house, keeping hold of her arm, half supporting her injured leg, a wild need to secure a corner of the present infusing him with energy and strength. And, whether she liked it or not, love.

"We're going to haul out that holly and you're going to have an old-fashioned Christmas," he said, throwing open the front door of his home and guiding her inside.

She chuckled and let him push her through the doorway. "But it's—"

"No 'buts,' Allison," he ordered, letting the door fall closed behind him. He took her into his arms and kissed her soundly, deeply, thoroughly impressing the present on her, and in his mind and heart.

She sighed in response and then laughed a little. "You're crazy," she said.

He caught her to his chest, running his hands down her slender back, the curves at her waist, the fullness of her breasts. His kiss deepened still further, and he groaned as her tongue warred with his, her kiss mobile and strong, giving back as fully as she accepted.

He dragged himself to the surface and wrenched himself free of drowning in her enchantment. Today was her day. A Christmas present. The "present."

She stared up at him with luminous eyes, a soft curve lifting her slightly swollen, thoroughly kissed lips. Everything in him demanded he sweep her back into his arms again, kissing her, making love to her, on the floor, on the sofa, he didn't care where. But he only lifted his hand to her face instead and cupped it tenderly.

"This is your day, Allison. A day I'm not going to let you forget."

Chapter 9

Allison thought the moment could not have been more perfect nor more memorable if she'd orchestrated every nuance of every second to impress it in her mind forever.

From a closet in the hallway, Chas hauled out box after box of Christmas decorations. When she tried stopping him, he only handed her another box and steered her toward the living room.

As she stacked the seemingly endless array of boxes, she caught glimpses of Chas's life in his furniture, the paintings on the walls, Billy's school photographs in little bronze frames and the general clutter.

The furniture, styled in large solid pine with neutrally colored cushions, was sturdy and manly. The coffee table was also pine and of a simple, mission style. It held newspapers and a couple of veterinary magazines in addition to a pile of Billy's corrected homework.

The curtains were nubby and thick, another neutral tone shot with flecks of brown. The pillows on the sofa picked up the brown and wove it through the room. It was a man's room but with tasteful, thoughtful touches. It was a *home*.

She contrasted it with her apartment in New York, sparsely decorated, clean, light, *empty*.

"This is the last of it," Chas said, hauling out a huge box and plunking it on the floor. "The tree itself."

"Chas, this is silly," she stated, knowing it was but still longing for it in some part of her soul.

"Yep," he agreed cheerfully, opening the large box and pulling out and undertaking the assembly of an eight-foot blue spruce look-alike.

He'd obviously put the tree together many times, for he deftly manipulated limbs and staves so that it became a tree in a matter of minutes. Standing in the corner of the room, it looked so real and so fresh that she could almost smell the rich scent.

Chas sorted through the boxes and opened one with a grunt of satisfaction. He pulled out a stack of old albums and handed them to her. "Here, you take charge of these."

He pointed over at a recess in the wall where the stereo presumably rested. For a moment, staring at his pointing hand, she felt the ragged edges of panic threatening to seize her. But she forced herself to follow his finger's direction and turned to look for the record player.

Who even *had* albums anymore, let alone a stereo to play them on? she wondered. Obviously, Chas Jamison. Fighting the fear his pointing finger had engendered, telling herself it was only some strange impulse triggered by her subconscious, she resolutely thumbed through the albums in her arms.

Perry Como, Bing Crosby, Anne Murray, Tina Turner, Dolly Parton, Lena Horne and so many other artists singing Christmas carols old and dear. An eclectic collection united by a single theme. She turned to look at Chas, busily engaged in winding a long strand of small lights around the tree.

This was a side of him she'd never have dreamed existed. A wholly sentimental, childlike quality infusing his concentration on the tree. He was doing this for *her,* she thought in some awe, even as some dim portion of her mind knew he was also doing it for himself.

Half the gift isn't in the receiving end, she knew. It was in the act of giving itself. Of sharing. And he was sharing something private and special to him. His music, his tree, the small treasures he'd accumulated over the years. He was presenting them to her out of season, out of rhyme, but with joyful, enthusiastic determination.

A day for her to remember. What a remarkable gift to proffer a woman suffering from spot amnesia.

She pulled out an Andy Williams album and settled it on the spotlessly clean record player. On top of it, she slid Bing Crosby and then Kenny Rogers, and followed his renditions with a Glenn Miller Big Band Christmas. She smiled a little as they poised in seeming midair, ready and waiting.

She depressed the switch, and the first record fell to the already spinning dais. She watched as the arm lifted and moved to delicately rest the needle on the grooves. Christmas bells tinkled in the background, and pianos and clarinets heralded the rich, mellifluous voice of Andy Williams calling out his "Joy to the World."

Behind her, his hands spanning her waist, Chas started singing along, a rich, slightly off-key and raspy baritone. A sudden and wholly unexpected stab of happiness pierced her and made her feel hopeful for the first time in months. True hope, rare and precious. She turned to embrace the moment and the man who was giving it to her.

She told herself that whatever he'd said in the clinic and

whatever she'd answered back didn't matter at the moment. Because this moment wasn't in the regular flow of time.

Unlike his nearly forceful passion in the doorway to his house, the fierce demand of it outside, he slowly, gently ran his hands down her hair, her shoulders and arms and back again.

His rich brown eyes met hers with utter warmth, complete tenderness. A light smile played on his full lips.

She thought again of his words, of her own, while in the clinic, then ruthlessly shoved them from her mind. He was giving her Christmas, a day out of time. She would accept it for what it was and not let it be clouded by the past, by bitter feelings of hurt or pain. She would accept it in the spirit it was being given, wholly and openly, not coloring it with outside interference and doubts.

As if he read all this on her face, he leaned forward to press a kiss to her forehead, slowly, gently, and lingered there a moment, making a silent vow or a promise, the kiss its seal.

He lowered his lips, and his tongue teased her lips apart, tickling her a little, tasting of coffee and his own unique flavor. He teased her lips with his own, then trailed feather-soft kisses along her jawline, making her sigh as he followed the kisses with his fingers, as if blurring them into her skin.

She snared his slowly moving forefinger with her lips and sucked lightly, drawing him into her mouth, flicking him with her tongue. She reveled in his sharp intake of breath and gasped herself as he caught her earlobe between his lips and tugged gently.

Strangely she felt no divorce of rationality in her mind. She was giving in to the day, the moment. There were no conflicts between ''should'' or ''shouldn't.'' One didn't question a present of this magnitude; one could only accept it or decline it.

And she was accepting it. Every bit of it. This day was hers now, the first that was truly hers in months. Maybe years. She would savor every taste, touch and smell of it. She would luxuriate in the oddity of the music, the strangeness, the singular elements of Christmas in February, and mostly she would, on this rare and memorable day, prize the man giving it to her.

When he cupped her breast with a strong, warm hand, she pressed into him, letting him know the extent of her acceptance, her desire for him. And when he slipped his hand beneath her sweater to have closer contact, she arched back to encourage his quest. And when he released the clasp of her brassiere, she moaned a little as he caught her full and aching breast in his hand.

This time Chas knew no barriers would be raised between them. He hadn't planned for this, had harbored no such hopes for it, but he wasn't a fool, either, and all twelve of the lords a-leaping combined with the eleven pipers piping couldn't make him stop now. Only Allison had that power and she was leaning into him, her body pressed tightly to his, her breast heavy and full in his hand.

He'd wanted to sweep her up and into his arms earlier, had wanted to whisk her across the threshold into his home, but had held back. There was nothing to stop him now, and he knelt swiftly and lifted her up and cradled her against his chest.

Her arms slipped around his neck, helping him distribute her weight, but not stiffening for escape or struggling to be set down. Instead, she raised her face to him, eyes nearly closed, lips slightly curved into a somewhat dreamy smile. He lowered his mouth to hers, tasting again her moist desire.

Without saying anything, not wanting anything to shatter the moment, he turned and stepped around boxes until he'd crossed the room and carried her to his bedroom.

As Andy Williams began singing "Silent Night," Chas lay Allison upon his bed and stretched out beside her. She looked up at him, her lids heavy, her breathing slightly rapid, her lips parted in invitation, a request he confirmed immediately.

Perhaps because the song in the other room was sweet and soft, slow and lilting, so were their embraces, their kissing. Chas felt their bodies already assimilating a rhythm, long and deep, passionate yet tender, as each reached out to the other in mutual recognition of the yearning thrumming between them.

And as that song ended and Andy Williams began singing of chestnuts roasting on an open fire, the flames sparked between them and a deeper blaze ignited. And by the time Williams worked to "We Three Kings," Chas couldn't hear the music anymore; his ears were ringing with the sound of Allison's soft sighs and his own heartbeat.

He helped her free of her sweater and pushed her silky bra from her dewy skin. He took one pert and hard nipple between his lips and tugged at it, making her sigh and cup his head in her hands. As he laved her puckered aureole and teased her nipple with his tongue, she moaned aloud and gripped her hands in his hair, pulling it somewhat. He grazed the rock-hard pebble with his teeth, and she squirmed beneath him, holding him to her with her trembling hands.

His own fingers released the catch of her jeans and tugged the zipper open. He could feel the heat rising off her and suckled with greater alacrity as he slipped his hand between her jeans and silken panties, shucking the jeans from her lithe hips.

He abruptly released that nipple and swiftly caught the other with his mouth, drawing it between his lips to meet his flickering tongue. Her hands ran through his hair, alternately pulling him to her and caressing him in deep, hunger-driven strokes.

The feel of her soft, satin skin, knowing she wanted him fully, maddened by the desire to rip the remaining obstacles free so that he could plunge into her served to steady him, to make him linger over each small pleasure. He loved the contrast in texture between her silken undergarment and the slightly scratchy feel of the denim jeans. He savored the rocklike hardness of her nipple and the velvety softness of her full breasts. He lingered over the stiff curls pushing up at the loose undergarments, teasing her by running his fingers ever so lightly across the wisp of a barrier.

Had he ever wanted a woman this much, this hungrily? Once. It was perhaps no irony that it was the same woman. He shoved the fifteen-year-old memory from his mind. That was one contrast and comparison he didn't want to consider at the moment. This was the here and now, the glorious and perfect present, and he wanted no shadow of the past to interfere with it.

He rose to pull her jeans free, and his breath caught at the sight of her nearly naked form sprawled upon his bed. One of her arms was lightly draped across her forehead, hiding her eyes from him. Her breasts were lustrous with his own moisture and splendid in their shape and form, large and round, spilling to the sides as if demanding his hands be there to cup them upward.

Her body tapered sharply to a narrow waist and flared again almost immediately, winging out to full, curved hips. Her smooth stomach dipped to a gentle valley at her navel and rose again to curve to her mound.

She was glorious. "You are beauty personified," he

murmured, running his hands from her collarbone, over her breasts and the soft soft skin at her navel and down to her jeans.

He pulled her pants free, uncertain for the first time since they'd come into the house, afraid of hurting her injured leg. As he removed her shoes and pulled the jeans off, he studied her legs, searching for signs of her injury.

There was no need for intense scrutiny; the scars were readily visible, barely healed scars neatly crisscrossing her right upper thigh, dominantly displayed and vivid as a fearful reminder of her recent accident. And behind them, faint and less perfectly straight, were other scars, reminders of that accident long ago that claimed her cousin's life and nearly stole hers.

For a moment, he wanted to say something, to ask about them, then he slowly leaned forward and pressed a light, very gentle kiss to them. Old and new.

She shivered beneath his nearly intangible touch, then sighed and raised a hand to his face to stroke it equally delicately, as if memorizing the planes of his features.

"I have a new pin in the leg. It really doesn't hurt anymore. It just takes some time to get the hang of it," she murmured. She hadn't said *a* pin. She'd said a *new* pin. Had he known she'd received one back when Susie was killed? If he had, he'd driven it from his memory.

He shifted his lips to the velvet-soft skin just above her panties and traced the outline of her last remaining article of clothing with his tongue. She squirmed and parted her legs a little when he reached her thighs.

"Chas..." she murmured, perhaps in warning, maybe in supplication.

Her hands plucked at his sweater trying to free him of it, and he yanked the cotton cable knit from him, tossing it somewhere far beyond the bed. He heard his own swift hiss of intaken air as she laid her cool hands flat against his shoulders and kneaded softly, learning him, exploring his muscles, his bare skin.

Within seconds, her hands seemed supple fire, hot and light, delicate and sure, igniting every inch of his exposed chest and back with flames of molten need.

He could hear her slightly hitched breathing, as if her breath were catching in a throat too constricted to allow easy intake. He knew exactly how she felt; his own breath was ragged and harsh with the severe controls he was placing on himself to take his time, to wile away hers.

When her fingers tugged at the belt of his jeans, he rolled from her to yank them free. She helped him then by slowly pushing his briefs down over his buttocks, sliding her hands along the planes of his back, his cheeks and around to encircle him with her hands, cupping him, drawing him back to her.

He closed his eyes in sudden, sharp pain—not that she was hurting him in the slightest, but with the strongest need he'd ever felt before in his life. As her hand slowly rose and achingly slowly lowered along his shaft, every fiber in his being warred with the need to just turn and sink into her.

But the time for words had arrived. "Allison..." he all but croaked, stilling her wickedly sweet hands. "Let me get something," he said brokenly.

Though her hands were already immobile beneath his, he felt her still even further, the way an animal might stiffen in fear or wariness.

"I can't have any more children," she said softly.

Chas didn't move, either, shocked into utter paralysis at her words, his hands resting upon hers which were yet holding him. She hadn't said she couldn't have children. She'd said any *more* children.

A thousand questions trembled on his lips, hovered there, ready to spill free, but he checked them, having more restraint now than he had in the clinic earlier. There would be time for questions later, when the day wound to a close, when Christmas was over and the presents long opened.

"And you?" asked his matter-of-fact reporter love. He could hear the smile in her voice.

He grinned a little in response, felt some of the tension slipping from his body and felt her hands shifting beneath his, gripping him with greater strength and renewed purpose.

He could tell her now, let her know the truth about Billy, about himself. But that, too, would be to talk of the past, to bring up old hurts and pains, to try to explain away fifteen years of longing. And of bitter desire.

"No one since Thelma."

Her hands wriggled beneath his, and she hitched them slightly to unfetter her movements. He was somewhat surprised to discover that not a whit of his desire had ebbed in the slightest. In fact, in some strange way the total freedom of their conversation, short and tense and utterly confusing as it had been, made him all the harder, all the stronger beneath her sure touch.

"Chas..."

"Mmm?"

"Won't you ever turn around?"

If she'd asked him to leap from a tall building at that moment, he would have. And clear the one beside it.

He swung around and pinned her arms above her, holding her firmly to the bed. He chuckled a little as she rose to meet his kiss with full alacrity. Holding her with one hand, he used his other to edge her panties from her, careful of her scars, anxious to be rid of the silk once it cleared the marks on her leg.

"Around enough?" he asked, smiling down at her.

"Oh, yes," she said simply, smiling back.

Keeping her hands beneath one of his, he reveled in the feel of her strong grip around his hands, more holding him there than he was her. He nuzzled her uplifted breasts and slipped his free hand between her thighs to tickle her legs apart.

"You don't have to hold me," she said. "I'm not going anywhere."

"No dice," he said. "I'm not taking any chances."

She chuckled, and her breasts jounced against his face making his smile broaden and his fingers at her apex dip to stroke her.

She arched upward and drew in her breath sharply. And he lowered his mouth to her flattened stomach and flicked his tongue across her sensitive navel. She writhed beneath him, whispering his name.

As his fingers found her liquid opening and slipped inside her, she bucked up to meet him, her breath drawing raggedly, her body luminescent with passion, dewy with want.

Reluctantly he released her hands, but he was far more avid in his quest to taste her, to bury himself in her. To his delight, she didn't try stopping him and parted her legs still farther to allow him access. An invitation he accepted with all his heart.

Can't have any more children. The words reverberated in his head like a refrain, like a discordant melody line to the harmony he felt with her. But as he brushed her crisp curls to the side and flicked his tongue across her, making her leap to his lips, he found he could think of nothing else in the world but tasting her, making her writhe, making her beg for him to join her, to join with her, to sink himself and drown in her.

* * *

Allison didn't know when he had released her hands. Minutes ago? Seconds ago? Or had they been free all along? She knew nothing but pure sensation, his hot breath against her apex, his delicate, sure tongue tasting her so intimately, his fingers gliding in to tease, only to withdraw again, tantalizing her still further.

"Please..." she murmured, or was it a whimper, so strong was her desire to have him fill her. "Chas...oh, please."

But he remained deaf to her entreaties, moving faster against her, in her until the universe began to quiver and flatten. She felt everything in her still in utter concentration and total abandonment. The eye of a hurricane, the core of a tornado. Then the universe imploded as spasm after spasm racked her body, seemingly sending it into a thousand pieces.

Chas had stilled also, waiting for her, ready to catch her and bring her back down, holding on to her firmly as if wholly aware of her momentary disappearance. He slowly withdrew his fingers from her, and she cried out a little as he did so, aching for the feel of him even still.

But when he raised his head and she saw his eyes, heavy lidded with want, his face nearly rigid with fierce petition, she opened her arms and called him to her, hungrier now for the feel of his full length inside her than she had been even seconds before.

He poised above her for a moment, as if gauging the extent of her acceptance.

"Please, Chas," she said again, hoarsely, her voice raw with all new and even more heightened desire.

"Allison," he said. Naming her, perhaps claiming her, as he slowly, deliberately slid into her until buried deep inside her. "Oh, my lovely...lovely Allison."

His eyes were tightly closed and his jawline rigid, as if

in great pain. She knew how he felt, for nothing in her life had ever prepared her for the exquisiteness of feeling him so deeply held within her.

She closed her legs around his back, holding him securely to her, and wrapped her arms beneath his to bring his weight down upon her, needing to feel the solidity of his body pressed to hers, flesh to bared flesh.

Tucking his arms beneath her shoulder blades, he grasped her shoulders with his broad hands, holding her tightly, rocking her downward to meet him as he slowly began thrusting into her.

"Ah-h-h," she cried at the same time as he groaned aloud and buried his face in the hollow of her neck as his body slowly, surely melded into hers, the most primal of meetings, the most glorious of unions.

One now, they parted slightly only to meet again, over and over, faster and faster. Harder still, he drove against her, and she rose to draw him even deeper, clinging to him, reveling in every thrust, each driving push of his rock-hard body, his rippling muscles and his single-minded want.

She felt herself clenching around him, her own focus growing narrower, tighter as she spiraled closer to a second fragmenting of the universe.

She had loved him so, once upon a time. Feeling him inside her again, loving his body, loving the way he made her feel, she tried shutting her mind to all but the sensations he roused in her. But tears of joy, of memory, of extreme desire, sprang to her eyes nonetheless.

His breathing changed, became erratic and labored. His heart thundered against her breasts. His fingers dug into her shoulders, and he growled her name over and over as he plunged into her.

She gripped him as tightly as she possibly could, feeling she were riding a storm, being swept away by one. The room faded; the world faded. Sharp spikes of light shattered her vision, and she felt herself tightening, another implosion ready to rip through her.

And suddenly he went perfectly still. He cried out her name, arching against her as he held her fiercely to his chest, thrusting his head back, loosing a groan of such intensity that she felt it ripple through his back.

And then she felt him inside her, hot and sharp, not spilling so much as erupting into her, and the intensity of her own triggered spasms caught her unaware, flinging her senseless. She would have been wholly lost if he had not held her to him so tightly, so lovingly.

It seemed to her that hours, perhaps days, passed before his rigid form began to relax. He shuddered and pressed hard, utterly possessive kisses to her jawline, her shoulders, her lips.

He shifted as if to pull free from her, but she tightened her legs, locking him in, refusing to let the moment end. He sighed and released his strong grip on one shoulder to lightly brush her dampened hair from her forehead. He trailed his fingers down her face and gently, tenderly kissed her.

She heard the record player change another record. She hadn't been able to hear the music for who knew how long. As the first song began to play, Kenny Rogers singing in his distinct voice, she began to chuckle.

Above her, Chas grinned down at her. "What's funny?" he asked, relaxed and oh, so very warm over her.

"The song," she said, and chuckled anew as he cocked his head to listen to the chorus of "Come, All Ye Faithful."

He began to laugh, too, his body rippling against hers. He rolled them over in a swift motion, cradling her above him, holding her close, still within her, but all intensity spent.

Still chuckling a little, he gazed up at her. "Merry Christmas, Allison."

She laid her head down against his broad chest, nestled into his arms, cherishing the slow, rhythmic caresses of his hands on her back, the steady rise and fall of his chest, the lulling beat of his heart, listening to the music, knowing that this perfect day would have to end, that the troubles that waited for her hadn't disappeared, that danger still lurked in the shadows, that the past remained unresolved, unfinished, unburied.

But as the record paused and Kenny Rogers began singing his version of "Oh, Holy Night," she prayed that the morrow would wait, that this day would last forever.

A futile dream, an impossible one. But she wished it nonetheless.

"Shh," Chas whispered, as if he'd been reading her mind. "We're here now. That's all that counts."

Oh, if only that were true, she thought.

Chapter 10

Chas busied himself in the kitchen, assembling a Christmas platter of taste treats, leftovers he'd carefully kept in the freezer. He'd had no inkling then to what use he would put the roast turkey, the various cookies and candies, the unusual pastry hors d'oeuvres.

As a widower in a town the size of Almost, he seldom had to actually carve out a meal on his own. Invariably Sammie Jo, Martha, Mickey Peterson or Alva Lu Harrigan would happen to prepare just enough extra to feed he and Billy. And in an area devoted to the growing of food and the raising of cattle, sheep and pigs, he had a freezer literally brimming full of the choicest meats, which had contributed to his turning into a pretty handy guy to have around a barbecue grill.

Sammie Jo had once told him to stop feeling guilty about the largesse offered him. "You're the only doctor we have for better than fifty miles, Charles, and if we want to repay you some way or another, it's not for you to argue or go around feeling guilty about it.''

"I'm a vet," he'd said.

"Really? And who got up at three in the morning last week to fix up Homer Chalmers when he pitched down those ridiculous steps of his?"

"I only put a bandage on his head," he'd said.

"That and twenty-one stitches all sewed neater than Alva Lu coulda set them. 'Sides, you don't have anybody to fend for you."

He'd shrugged then, accepting all the favors and gifts, knowing it made his life easier in a thousand different ways. And now, sliding the large platter into the microwave and setting the timer, he was glad he'd given in.

Now assembling a dessert plate with bits of fudge, divinity, toffee bars and other delectables contributed by half the town, he wondered who "fended" for Allison in New York. And suspected she had no one.

The microwave dinged, and he pulled the platter of turkey slices, mashed potatoes and giblet gravy, candied yams and the traditional green-bean-and-mushroom soup with onion-ring casserole from the large oven, while tossing the reheated homemade buns like a juggler to keep from burning his fingers.

In not having to fend for himself, he'd learned the secret of masterful preparation; he added a couple of fluffy sprigs of fresh parsley and a light sprinkle of freshly ground pepper to the whole plate.

He kissed his fingers and tossed the kiss to the air. "And voilà! Ze vet becomes ze amazing master chef." He turned to find Allison grinning at him from the doorway to his kitchen.

The effect of seeing her in the doorway, dressed in nothing more than one of his shirts, sleeves rolled to the elbows, shirttail hanging nearly to her knees, her hair tousled, her face flushed with the heat from his fireplace and her smile nearly blinding in intensity, was a purely visceral one.

He felt as if someone had seized hold of his heart and squeezed tightly.

She had. *Allison.*

"I didn't know you were there," he said, purely from reflex. He wanted to toss the carefully arranged platter to the floor and drag her back into his arms.

"So, master chef, what have you whipped up for us? I'm starving." She walked seductively toward him, perhaps not intending the seduction, but managing all too effectively nonetheless.

Her eyes widened when she took in the array of food-stuffs. Then they softened as she looked back up at him. "A real Christmas dinner?"

"With all the trimmings," he said through a tight throat.

"I think I'd better take that," she said, and removed the platter from his outstretched hand.

She set the plate on the island bar and popped a finger in her mouth to erase a dab of gravy that had spilled to the side. She gave him a swift glance that cut right through him.

"If you want to eat—" he began, only to have the words wither and die in his throat as she deliberately dipped a finger into the gravy pooled in the center of the potatoes and came sassily, saucily toward him, single finger out-stretched.

"You're playing with fire," he said hoarsely, capturing that finger with his lips and her pliant body with his hands, pulling her to him.

She laughed and arched back in his hands, trusting him not to let her fall. Her entire being radiated enchantment. He remembered how she'd laughed so long ago, just in this carefree, unfettered way, secure in herself, her attractiveness, her beauty, in those days when she had been secure in her love for him, his for her.

He was aware that she'd deliberately set aside the past and her troubled present, that she'd shoved them to some dark corner of her mind.

Gone were the shadows beneath her eyes, erased as magically as the gravy had disappeared from her fingertip. God knew there was so much to talk about, so much to figure out, but standing there, holding her from falling, loving her so much it ached, he could only continue with the pretense that one day out of time could matter, that their one day together would heal all wounds, large or small.

But he was all too aware that it was only a pretense, that the shadows would darken her eyes again and make her face seem pale and frightened.

"Come see the tree," she urged, straightening up, a child again, all bright eyes and sparkling personality.

He half flipped her in his hands, catching her as he spun her around.

She chuckled, and his heart swelled at the natural sound.

"Lead the way," he said, grinning as he propelled her toward the living room.

She stopped just inside the room so abruptly that he ran into her, nearly pitching her forward. He caught her and held him back against him, much as he had in Taylor's kitchen what seemed like months ago, but was actually only some six or seven hours earlier. But he wasn't keeping her from flight this time, no arms serving as steel bands to still her too rapidly racing heart, her flight. This time his hands easily, naturally sought her curves and held her loosely to him. Molding her, loving her.

She waved her hand at the miraculously transformed living room.

All boxes were gone, the tree was fully trimmed and she'd even streamed some garland from the mantelpiece and lit several red-and-green candles. The coffee table had been cleared of the magazines and papers and now held a Christmas tablecloth of white and gold and two small star-shaped candles softly glowing. Bing Crosby's honeyed voice drifted from the stereo speakers, further weaving the Christmas spell.

He knew there was no possible way she'd used all the decorations in the boxes, but was intrigued and impressed with those she'd selected. All of the decorations on the tree and those few she'd set on the mantel or in the bookshelf carried the same theme, all homemade, each lovingly created by someone they both knew.

"It's beautiful, Allison," he said, stunned by the truth of it, awed by her uncanny gift to him. Of all his Christmas treasures, she'd unerring chosen his favorites. It was as if she'd gotten into the deepest recess of his heart and pulled the knowledge from him and set it free.

He'd set out to give her a day, a Christmas to make up for those she'd missed, for the one she'd spent in the hospital. He'd wanted to take her mind off all that troubled her, to love her, to let her have a single day of respite from worry. And instead, she'd turned the tables on him and given him a present of stunning magnitude: her acknowledgment.

He tilted her head back and slowly kissed her, amazed by the depth of his love for her, fearing for himself when this lovely day was over. If he lost her now, he would be lost himself.

Hating the February afternoon icy cold sleet pelting him from the south, pressed against the back wall of the stud's home, the man calling himself Quentin squinted his eyes against the spittle of ice that had come in suddenly in that way Allison had told him Panhandle winter storms would do. He struggled to hear what was happening inside the country stud's house.

Incredibly, making him feel disoriented and off balance, all he could hear were Christmas carols being loudly played on a stereo. He didn't know who was singing, but the voice conjured up vague images of old black-and-white movies and the sight of his full-color drunken mother sprawled on the sofa.

He shook his head and concentrated on hearing still more. He didn't know why they would be inside the house playing Christmas carols. It made no sense. And things that made no sense troubled him. Gnawed at him.

Just as Allison gnawed at him.

He reached a hand to the window, fully intending to test its flexibility, but a low growl sounded behind him. Turning his head very slowly, he saw a large German shepherd peering out of the opened but thankfully screened window in the country stud's pitiful little clinic.

The same dog that had growled at him when he'd taken the pentobarbital from the shelves of the stud's clinic. But the creature had been inside a cage then, not roaming loose.

Now the animal growled softly, not menacing yet, but he suspected it might turn that way if he did anything other than simply leave. Slowly. Carefully.

The dog chuffed, then resumed the low snarl. He removed his hand from the vicinity of the window. The growls ceased. He stretched it back, the snarling resumed.

He stepped away from the wall, and the shepherd gave a sharp bark.

The dog was another problem he'd have to take care of, he thought as he hunched into the wind and quickly crossed back into the Hampton field closest to the clinic. He'd suggested they till that particular field for the week.

He was a good employee. He did more than his share. That was the way to get ahead in the world: do more than your share. His father had taught him that before he'd gone. Abandoning him. Forgetting him as completely as his mother had done in her peculiar way.

And as thoroughly as Allison had managed to do.

Why were they listening to Christmas music?

He shook his head. He would have to think about it. He would have to think about a lot of things. This wasn't a game, as Allison seemed to think. This was deadly serious.

He hunched tighter against the icy sleet and followed the shinnery, the scratchy scrub oak that comprised the north end of the Hampton field. He chuckled a little at the word. Like the town of Almost itself, the word didn't exist outside this small pocket of the world.

Allison had told him that, too. In between her longings for the country stud. His smile faded abruptly.

The following day was Sunday. No one in this flea-bitten town would be working. All would be still and quiet according to God's rules. And those that didn't obediently trot off to one of the Almost churches would be hiding inside their homes, keeping out of the storm.

Except him, of course. He would have a lot to do.

A dog was a simple matter. A little tricky maybe, but simple. Allison and her stud weren't quite as easy. But certainly not impossible.

Why, nothing was impossible for him when it came to thinking of Allison. Nothing at all.

Allison thought no Christmas day had ever been as perfect as this one day in late February. Even the weather had conspired with Chas and produced snow and sleet.

The boys were all with Carolyn, safe and warm; the animals in the clinic were inside and needing no tending until late evening. The food had been delicious, and the music and decorated tree a feast for ears and eyes.

And there was Chas. Sexy, loving, as down-to-earth as a man could get and so filled with surprises. In many ways, on this day, during the hours they'd spent together, he'd given her back a slice of her early womanhood, those days when she'd been carefree, daring, even childish.

But somehow, during the years, he'd remained exactly what he was, the country vet, the large, quiet man with the biggest heart in the world. He hadn't referred to the heated words they'd exchanged in the clinic earlier, nor had he repeated the words of love he'd spoken then.

In fact, he hadn't once said a single thing to make her feel uncomfortable or worried. No mention of the possible danger that waited outside his house for her, no reference to her fugues or time lapses.

She'd never felt so at home or so nurtured anywhere on earth.

And this, from the man who had so thoroughly devastated her that she'd truly believed back then that she could not survive without him.

He'd granted her this one day, an unmeasured, unstructured day to rest, to recapture a hold on her self, her emotions. Her life. And he'd done so, knowing her confusion about him, about the past and present, the dreadful uncertainty of the future.

Watching him as he moved about his house, covertly studying him as he talked or swayed with the music or nibbled at the treats he'd prepared, she told herself she was simply accepting the day as the gift he'd intended. But she knew, down deep inside her somewhere, was the clear feeling that he somehow owed her this.

And that this one day together, pretending love, pretending all was rosy, this one day was all they would ever have.

The phone had rung about four o'clock, and even that interruption seemed in keeping with the tenor of Christmas. Chas had answered it while keeping his smiling eyes fixed on her. After the initial chitchat endemic to the Panhandle, he chuckled a little and said, "No...she's fine. She's right here. You want to talk to her?"

Allison shook her head. She didn't care who it was, she didn't want any outside influence impinging on the perfection of the day. She needn't have worried, whoever it was had only been making certain she was safe.

"Yeah. I'm going to keep her here tonight."

Incredibly, his face tinged red and he looked away from her.

"But that reminds me," he said, "Would you do me a favor, Sammie Jo, and spread the word that if anyone sees a stranger in town they should call me immediately?"

He turned away from her somewhat and shook his head as if Sammie Jo could see him. "I should have realized the boys would tell Carolyn and Pete about last night. And Carolyn would mention it to you.... Yeah. I think he probably followed her out here from New York.... Right. A stalker type."

Allison felt a chill work down her spine. No matter how perfect the day, danger still lurked out there in the gloomy afternoon. Somewhere. From someone.

She glanced at the thick drawn curtains. Moments before, she'd been grateful they were closed, blanking out the world, keeping her safe inside. Now they seemed to be hiding dangers that might be creeping up on her. If she pulled them back now, would she see that dreadful disembodied hand, or worse...would she finally see her tormentor?

"Don't worry. She's safe...I promise.... I'll fill you in tomorrow.... Right now? We're having Christmas." He chuckled again and moved back within smiling distance.

He hung up after farewells and slipped the cordless telephone onto its cradle without looking down. He never broke his linked gaze with her. "Sammie Jo wanted to know if I had mistletoe."

"And do you?" Allison said, her heart starting to beat in that rapid, thready way she experienced every time he looked at her with just that glint in his warm brown eyes.

"I've got a lot more than mistletoe," he said, slowly making his way across the living room. He stopped inches from her, close enough that she could feel the warmth emanating from him, the want rising between them.

Her mouth was suddenly dry, her breathing ragged. She'd believed that the passion was surely spent, that all longings had been answered. She'd been wrong. One look from those depthless brown eyes and she was on fire again, the dangers outside the house forgotten, the past well laid to its uneasy rest. All that mattered was this day, this moment. This man. And her one holiday out of time with him.

His kiss was all the sweeter the second time. And his touch all the more tantalizing because knowledge and familiarity lent it a tenderness that their mutual passion had swallowed before.

But in the end, their second union carried even greater intensity than the first.

Watching him now, in the darkened living room, studying him as closely as he studied the flames in the fireplace, she wanted to cling to the magic of the day, to the intimacy that seemed to spring so effortlessly between them.

But with a sense of a woman putting away her girlhood toys, a resigned acceptance of adult needs and demands controlling her actions, she knew the magic day must come to a close, that all the passion in the world couldn't stem the need for words.

As if reading her mind, he sighed a little and closed his eyes. "Allison?"

"Yes?"

"We have to talk."

"I know," she said. But she would rather have run outside in the ice storm dressed in nothing but his shirt.

"Not about what's going on with you now. About the past."

She'd known that's what he meant, but she shook her head anyway. "No. That's gone."

Still not looking at her, he said, "The past is never gone, Allison. It can fade from memory, it can be dulled with time, but it's never gone. It's part of us. And we have a past together, however badly things might have gone awry."

Awry, she thought. A good wood. Short, descriptive, to the point. And wholly lacking in depth. A person taking the wrong road to a neighbor's house goes *awry*. A Tinkertoy tower slipping and nearly falling goes *awry*.

What happened between she and Chas—what Chas had done to them—was to *injure, destroy, ruin,* to *shatter.*

And yet, on this day fifteen years later, he'd given her magic. And of all the people in the world, who was standing beside her now when her entire life might be in jeopardy, her mind little better than Swiss cheese? Chas Jamison.

"I'm so confused," she said slowly. Honestly.

"I know," he acknowledged.

"Not just about the past, but about the present, too, Chas. And I don't just mean the memory lapses or the panic attacks. I mean what I'm feeling about you. About you and me. Or maybe it's like you said and the past isn't ever really gone. And that can be confusing, too.''

He looked over at her then, reaching over to where she was sitting to cup her face in his broad hand. ''I know you don't like to hear it, Allison, I know the words get all chewed up in feelings from the past, in the confusion going on now, but I do love you.''

He didn't stroke her face or do anything more than continue to gently hold her in the palm of his hand. ''That comes without strings, Allison. The way I believe love should. If someday you want to do something about it, that'll be up to you. And if you don't, that will also be up to you. But I think you should know, and really believe what I'm saying, because it's true and it's from the heart.''

She didn't know what to say to this declaration, any more than she'd known what to say in the clinic. But she wasn't angry with him now for saying the words. And she knew she didn't want to wound him now. She knew that some part of her cared too much for him, for what he'd done for her this day and for that past he swore wasn't gone, to want to hurt him with ancient accusations.

But she couldn't lie to him about the present, either. She didn't know *what* she felt for him at this moment. She only knew she was anything but indifferent.

She stammered some of this, wishing she knew exactly how she felt.

''Come sit with me,'' he said, scooting over a little from his place on the floor in front of the sofa and dragging a cushion from the couch for her to sit on. She slipped from her chair and sat on the cushion, nestling into the crook of his arm, laying her head on his chest.

Just being there in his arms made her feel safe and peaceful. And so very aware of him. Was that love?

But how could she give in to loving a man who had hurt

her so very badly all those years ago? Could the past be pigeonholed, neatly set aside, as in her dream when her father-clock wanted her to bury the past?

Wrapped in the warmth of his arms, lulled by the dinner, by the fire, by the love she felt radiating out from him, she told him about the dream.

Chas waited until she'd finished the entire dream before saying anything, though his hand continually either stroked or held her close to him.

"And then you woke up, trying to catch the box marked Yesterday?"

"Yes, and then the sound of the clock ticking was still going on at the window. And I saw the hand."

"But the hands on the clock—your Dad—they were on November?"

"Yes."

"And you quit smoking in November."

She felt a flicker of fear. And a mild resentment. She didn't want to remember her troubles now. Not on this day. Not while so comfortable in his arms. She hadn't told him about the dream because she'd needed reminding about the present.

But in the face of his statement, she had to wonder why she *had* told him about it. Her subconscious mind trying to reveal the truths again?

"Yes," she said tersely. Her heart beat arrhythmically, tock...tock...tick-tock.

"Allison...what was in the box marked Yesterday?" he asked.

The man who called himself Quentin aligned his devices on the cleaned dresser. He set out the remaining three ampoules of the pentobarbital he'd stolen right from the stud's own clinic and arranged the sterile disposable needles beside them.

One for the shepherd, two for the sheep. He chuckled at his own wit.

He began humming "Baa-baa Black Sheep" as he set out the remainder of his toys, a length of cotton rope, a ball gag, the rest of the fishing line and a portable clock. He set a knife alongside the other things, then picked it up again, turning it in his hands.

He ceased humming.

He met his own gaze in what was left of the mirror, a jagged shard that revealed only his upper face. His reflection couldn't smile, but he did nonetheless. He held the sharp knife blade up beside his eyes and turned it until it captured a glint of the light from the unshaded lamp. The refraction bounced from the knife to the mirror and back.

"You'll remember now, Allison," he said. "You'll remember *everything*. 'Yes sir, yes sir, three bags full.'"

Chas felt the tension rippling through Allison, knew that whatever had been in the box in her dream was of far greater importance to her than he'd suspected at first.

But she didn't answer him. Instead, she asked, "Was your marriage to Thelma a good one?"

The question rocked him; it was so far removed from anything he'd suspected she might say.

"No," he answered. It was easier to just admit the truth and be done with it than to elaborate, to try softening it with explanation.

She sighed a little, and he wished he could know what she was thinking, what she was feeling. Finally she cleared her throat a little. "Why? Why wasn't it good, Chas?"

He could tell her that Thelma had been an alcoholic. That would put the blame squarely on Thelma's shoulders, and he could appear the selfless, long-suffering husband, noble father of Billy. But it wouldn't be the whole truth. He deserved some of the blame for Thelma's fascination with vodka and rum.

"We tried to make it work, for Billy's sake," Chas managed to say eventually.

This was Allison in his arms now, a woman he claimed to love. Commitment, a possible future together—these things were based on honesty, on revelation of feelings and beliefs, and bonded by values. If he dodged the truth now, he would be creating a fissure that could only widen later, separating them, and they already had too many gaps between them as it was.

"Thelma and I married for all the right reasons, just to the wrong people," he said. "I was in love with you. She knew that. Accepted it, I thought. But not inside. Inside, where she really lived, she needed much more from me than I was able to give. And so she was desperately unhappy. She began drinking. It was a stroke that took her, the doctors said, but I think it was a basic lack of hope."

Allison didn't say anything for the longest time. But he felt a teardrop dampen his shirt and lifted his hand to her face to feel several spilling free.

"What is it?" he asked. He hadn't meant to hurt her with his honesty. He stroked her cheeks to brush away any further tears.

"Somehow it was easier thinking that you'd been happy together," she said slowly. "I don't know why the fact that you were unhappy, that she was...and that *I* was so unhappy, too...that all seems such a terrible, terrible waste."

"But there was Billy," Chas reminded her softly.

Allison gave a choked sound before she said, "Yes. Of course. And he's worth all the pain, isn't he?"

Chas didn't know quite what she meant by that question,

if she was being sarcastic or, if not, whose pain she thought Billy worth—his, certainly, and Thelma's, perhaps.

"I love Billy," he said softly. Firmly. "He's the whole world to me."

"I know. You should feel that way."

He ached to tell her the raw truth right then, even opened his mouth to do so. But she clenched her hand in his shirt suddenly, pulling it tight across his shoulders, making his collar bite into his neck. But she didn't raise her head from his chest.

"Chas…"

Every pore in him yelled at him to move now. To get up, go to the kitchen, find his way to the bathroom, call a long lost friend in Denver. Anything. On this day of wonder and revelation, he was about to hear even more. And instinctively he knew he didn't want to hear whatever she was about to reveal. Not at all.

Her dream had been right. The past should be buried; there were some things that belonged solely to the past.

Fear clutched at his chest, in the form of Allison.

"When you told me you were marrying Thelma Bean, I couldn't think what to do or say. I just ran, if you remember."

"I remember," Chas said. His heart had started to beat in swift, painful thuds. He knew something was coming. Something dark. Some terrible truth. God, it had only been hours before when he'd preached at her about the past, about just letting it go, opening it up. And only moments before when he'd demanded they talk about the past.

"Susie was in the car," she continued.

"Don't…" he said, though it was really a plea.

She ignored him, though her hand on his shirt pulled even more fiercely, as if she needed the hold on the fabric to be able to explain.

"We were supposed to be going to Lubbock, remember?"

Chas remembered that, too. There was nothing he *didn't* remember. But he was terrified of what he didn't *know*.

"I was crying. I was swerving on the road. Susie kept begging to take over the wheel. When I almost ran into the ditch, I pulled over. I let her drive."

"Oh, God, Allison. I'm so sorry," he said.

She shook her head against his chest, her hand still bunched in his shirt, still dragging at the material as if holding on to a lifeline. Her fist beat once against his chest, not painfully, but as if she were beating the knowledge into him.

"No! You don't understand."

He waited, stilled, desperately fearful of whatever it was he didn't understand.

And when her words came, they spewed in a rush, like a flash flood, filled with debris and detritus, hurt and confusion. "I...I was pregnant, Chas. And w-when the car rolled, it didn't kill just Susie. It wasn't only Susie. You asked what was in the box marked Yesterday...now you know."

Chas felt his head jerked back as if yanked by invisible hands. His eyes slammed shut, squeezed tightly against the pain, a searing-hot knife blade that cut through the very core of his being.

God, what had he done?

He remembered that day as vividly as if it were yesterday. Her coming to the clinic, nervous, angry, he'd thought. She'd looked at everything but him. And he, still smarting from her rejection of his plans, and fresh from Thelma Bean's need, had blurted out his intention to marry Thelma.

She hadn't waited for explanations, though her face had paled to a shade that should have alarmed him, would have alarmed him if he'd been anything but absorbed in his own world of hurt and self-righteous nobility.

He'd been angry that afternoon. Wounded. Smarting because he'd laid his plans for their future out before her and she'd scoffed at him. Had he told her about Thelma in some measure of revenge, of retaliation?

He hadn't known she was pregnant. She must have been so scared. So young and so very, very scared.

And then the accident.

He'd gone to the hospital, but she wouldn't see him. Refused to see him. She'd fled Almost as soon as she was able to walk and had never come home again. Until now.

And now he knew why. The knowledge was a white-hot agony burning through him.

How very much she must have hated him all these years.

He felt as if he couldn't breathe, that his lungs had been frozen with this terrible knowledge. At that moment, he was sure he would never draw breath again.

All the decency, all the rationale for the decisions made fifteen years ago, the noble choices that determined his entire history suddenly seemed questionable.

She'd been pregnant. Dear God. His *child*. His, hers. *His* child.

Threads of molten regret and an icy guilt winged through him, wiping out all the good things he might have ever done, the wonderful, silly little things that had made his life seem whole, if somewhat lonely at times.

Allison's fingers relaxed their grip of his shirt and soon, despite his stillness, in spite of his silence, began to smooth the bunched fabric into some semblance of normality.

But the motions didn't soothe him, didn't take away one iota of the maelstrom of agony churning in him. Surfacing over and over was the image of her Yesterday box.

In his bedroom, naked and waiting for him, she'd said, "I can't have any more children."

Her meaning now became more than crystal clear; it became the facets and slivers of that shattered crystal, each piece embedded in his heart, in his soul.

He wanted to cry out loud, to yell as loudly as he could, to scream out his denial, his fury, his longing and his horrible guilt to the universe, as if by wailing it out into the air he would be absolved.

But absolution wasn't possible. Nor even, judging by her soft body nearly wrapped around his, something required.

She'd carried this knowledge, this *agony* for fifteen years. Never once had she let anyone know. Not Sammie Jo, not Taylor. If she had, he'd have known. Because, despite his confused pain, he knew that if someone was paying the slightest bit of attention, there were no secrets in a small town.

Unless that someone had been young, scared and pregnant.

That was why she hadn't known about Thelma. That was why she'd thought Billy was his, had believed him capable of loving her and being with Thelma at the same time.

Chas wanted to pull her into himself, never to let her go.

But knowing so much now, he had to ask the final question. He had to know why she'd turned him down when he'd asked her to be his wife. Especially since she'd been pregnant. In a choked, nearly voiceless tone, he rasped out the question.

She was silent for so long that he tightened his grip on her. "Allison?"

"You didn't ask," she said.

"What?" he asked blankly.

"You didn't ask me, Chas."

"But—"

She sighed heavily. "I was young. I was foolish."

He felt her shake her head against his chest. He ached to be staring into her eyes but knew she'd never be revealing so much if he were.

"I don't understand," he said, telling the absolute truth. "I *did* ask you."

She sighed again. "Not really, Chas. You told me. It sounds so silly now, saying that. And childish. But that's just what it was. Not monumental, not huge. I never knew that until I came back home. All these years, I did think it was huge. A betrayal so horrific that I could never talk about it. But now I see it for what it was. My part in it, yours."

He was frowning, trying to puzzle out her meaning.

"It was just a stupid little game. I just wanted you to ask me to marry you, not to tell me." She said this sleepily. Dreamily. "I was a *kid*. Don't you see? Just a kid. I wanted the bended knee, the outstretched hand. Flowers. Everything. What did I know?"

"But that's what I felt," Chas said, stunned. Shocked. "That's everything I felt." He didn't add that he still did. He couldn't, not in the face of everything he'd learned that afternoon.

"Was it? I didn't know. And even if I did, it doesn't really matter now, does it? We can't change the past," she said. She yawned. Incredibly, stunning him, she just *yawned*. "But I didn't know it then. Then I was just…miffed."

"Miffed," he repeated. "Miffed?"

She chuckled slightly. "Piqued. Angry. Upset. I wanted to teach you a lesson."

He realized her humor hadn't been over finding the situation amusing in the slightest. It had been a purely self-deprecating, despairing chuckle, and he knew it the moment she said, "Guess the lesson backfired."

"Backfired." He felt stupid. Slow. And felt the flickers of a dark anger rising in him.

"Yeah. You married Thelma. Susie died because I couldn't even see to drive because I was hysterical. My father blamed me."

"No." Chas felt the word yanked from him. "You're wrong, Allison. He wouldn't have."

"He did. I saw it in his eyes. When I woke up in the hospital. Besides, he said so."

Chas closed his eyes again. So much hurt, so much pain. All carried for too long. No wonder she hadn't come back for her parents' funeral.

And he'd been the one to let her run out of the clinic that day, her face paler than pale, her eyes blank with shock. *Pregnant with his child.*

"She took Deadman's Curve too fast. She didn't know. I didn't warn her. We were just *kids*. Kids. The car rolled and she flew through the windshield. She hadn't buckled her seat belt. I didn't know that. I reached for her hand on the pavement. I crawled to touch it. But Susie wasn't there. Only her hand."

Chas felt as if the entire world had turned upside down and shaken him free. He was being catapulted through the universe, ungrounded, completely unable to find a hold in a world he'd always known.

How could she ever bury that particular heartache from the past? How could he now? How could he hope to ever know what to say to her *now?*

Outside, in his clinic, the dogs started barking. He frowned, almost grateful that he might have to go check on them, guilty that he felt a sense of relief.

Allison had been right when she said she was ambiva-

lent. Not indifferent, no. About the two of them, because
of what lay between them, she could never be indifferent.
Ever. And now, with this knowledge, he would never have
that simple faith in the rightness of things, a trust that things
could work easily, naturally.

Because even knowing the past, even understanding the
depths of pain, the sharpness of the despair he now felt for
the future, he still could only choose the life he had lived,
the mistakes, the woes, the gifts...and Billy.

The dogs, the shepherd cross in particular, began barking
furiously. Frantically.

Strangely Allison was relaxed in his arms, her breathing
steady and regular. Her palm lay flat against the shirt material she'd grasped with such fervor earlier. She didn't
seem alert, alarmed or even cognizant of the sounds coming
from his clinic. She seemed quiescent, relieved perhaps. Or
maybe just weary.

His heart bled for the girl she'd been, for the woman she
was now. And his mind raced from the past to the present.
He didn't dare think about the future.

Because through his own actions in the past, or whatever
was making the animals in his clinic go crazy, Allison was
in trouble. Big, old-fashioned trouble.

He'd been a party to the pain of the past, an anguish he
was only becoming aware of, but he'd be damned if he
would be any part of such suffering in the present.

"I've got to go check on the animals," he said.

She stirred. He couldn't see her face, could only feel her
soft, gentle form resting against him. He had the odd notion
that she'd half fallen asleep, as if the admission from the
past had sapped every ounce of her strength, as if the con-
fession had drained every last bit of her reserves.

"Allison?"

"Mmm?"

"I want to talk about what you told me. But I've got to go check on the animals."

"We don't have to talk about it," she said rather dreamily. "Not anymore."

His hand drew her more tightly to his chest. "We do. There's a lot to talk about, Allison. Whys. Whats. Everything. But the dogs are going crazy, and I've got to go check it out."

"Okay," she said easily. Too easily, he thought. And he thought this very *un*easily.

He slid from beneath her and pushed to his feet. She scarcely moved, only curled a little tighter onto the cushion he'd pulled from the sofa. Outside, the dogs were still barking frantically. Inside, Allison appeared asleep.

He swiftly dragged his coat on and stomped his feet into his boots. He gave her one last glance before he opened the door to the February storm and the freezing sleet. "I'll be right back," he said.

In a perfect world, she would have raised her head, flashed him that high-intensity smile and said, "I love you, Chas."

The words would have served as a shield against the bitter cold of the sleet needling his face and hands. The smile would have wrapped a warm scarf around his neck.

But the world was far from perfect. And Allison was about as far from ever saying those words again as a human being could ever get.

Chas slid a little on his porch steps, fought the icy wind as he pulled the door closed behind him and turned into the storm. Defenseless.

Chapter 11

Chas found general pandemonium inside the clinic.

All the dogs were loose and barking at each other or the one-pawed cat, thankfully still locked in her cage.

Tense, prepared for a battle or worse, he searched the three-room clinic and the holding pens with a caution hitherto unknown. And once he got the dogs settled down and back in their pens, he crossed through the breezeway leading to the barn, where the larger animals were restlessly pacing in their stalls and pens.

He didn't have that creepy being-watched sensation prickling on his skin, but he knew that someone had been in his clinic. Nothing overt, except the dogs, had been disturbed. But a hackamore outside one of the horse's stalls lay on the floor, mute evidence of an intruder.

He picked up the hackamore and looped it over the peg, absently soothing the young horse nervously pawing at the stall gate.

"And who was in here, huh, Chico? Who got you so worked up?"

The horse, who had been in and out of the clinic at least fifteen times in his young life because he had a curiosity that made a mockery of so-called horse sense and was invariably straying into danger or nibbling something he shouldn't have, calmed down somewhat, though his eye rolled at the back entrance several times, as if expecting a return of whatever had frightened him.

When the horse stopped kicking at the gate, Chas gave him a few extra oats and molasses and gave him a good scratch, looked the barn over one more time and pulled the door to, leaving on the lights.

He stopped dead on reentering the small-animal section of his clinic. The shepherd cross was back out of the cage. He found himself hunching to a fighting stance, arms loose at his sides, knees bent, eyes raking the brightly lit clinic, ready for anything that might spring at him.

Nothing did.

The shepherd wagged her tail slightly and chuffed at him, as if applauding his humorous actions. She sat down, tail still sweeping the floor. She didn't just look pleased with herself, she grinned at him.

He slowly straightened. "Well, you little devil. You got out of that cage all by yourself, didn't you?"

Her tail wagged with more vigor, as if acknowledging the truth of his surmise.

"And did you let the others out?"

She chuffed at him, a hiccup of a bark. Truthful dog.

Chas found himself grinning. "An escape artist, hmm?"

She chuffed again.

He couldn't help but contrast the behavior of the unrepentant dog with that of the cowed animal that had been curled in on herself in that cage for at least two weeks.

Her real healing had begun the moment Allison had talked to her, cried over her.

"She stole your heart, too?" he asked, stepping farther into the room.

Though the shepherd's ears twitched when he moved, she didn't back away from him or flatten to the ground as though afraid he would strike her.

"I'll make a deal with you," he said, crossing to the cabinet where he stored the dog and cat food.

Her eyes followed his every move, her head swiveling to keep him in sight at all times. Her tail lay still on the concrete floor.

"I'll leave you out tonight. But you have to promise to let the others stay in their cages, okay?"

She chuffed and he grinned.

"I'll take that as a yes."

He filled the other animals' dishes and replenished their water. And he carefully locked the doors to their cages.

The shepherd backed up when he approached her cage and stood stiffly away from him as he opened the cage door and stocked her dishes, as well. He left the door standing wide open and held out his hand to her.

She whined a little, but didn't come to him. Earlier, still thinking someone might be in the clinic, he'd just grabbed the animals by the scruffs of their necks and hauled them firmly into their cages. Now, she was registering a protest, knowing he could subdue her easily, but tacitly announcing her decision not to comply with the cage routine.

And he knew that in the inexplicable way of dogs, she'd accepted him, but had bonded with Allison.

He knew how the shepherd felt. He wanted to warn the shepherd how hopeless that bonding might prove.

He returned the remaining food to the cabinet, shut the door a bit more carefully than normal and turned back around to, face her. "You keep an eye on things tonight, okay?"

She barked once.

"And you'll call me if someone tries getting in here?"

She wagged her tail.

As he closed the door to the clinic and locked it carefully, he told himself he was being a total idiot, feeling lift in spirits just because a stray mutt was showing a little gumption.

But as he reached the door to his house, he understood why the dog's behavior had made him feel better; her display of ingenuity, her pleasure in it and her stubbornness later all spelled a healing.

And where one wounded spirit could be healed, so then might another.

Allison felt Chas pull her up and into his arms. She pressed against the cold air wafting off him, the way a fevered person will turn into a cold compress.

Some dim part of her was aware that if she had to, she could rouse fully, become alert again, but resting so easily in his arms, in his house, enfolded into a perfect day and spent by revealing the past, she allowed the lethargy to eke away her strength. She needed his cosseting, his attention, and she needed to think. To really think clearly for the first time in months.

It had taken coming home after all these years to see the past for what it was, a series of really terrible misunderstandings, of human frailty caught up in tragic fate. And it had taken a perfect day with Chas to let her know that by locking those misunderstandings and hurts away in the same dark box as the tragedies in her life, she'd created hurts and pains that had remained scarred for years and years.

Hadn't that psychologist she'd interviewed said something of the sort? His face swam into memory, a clean-shaved, rather effete man. She could almost hear his voice. Humming something.

Her heart jolted in fear when the memory shifted and she saw another image of him, dark-haired, no glasses. Effete mouth turned cruel with contempt.

She shook her head. They weren't the same man. Her mind was playing tricks.

"Allison?" she heard Chas ask as if from a great distance.

She struggled to understand the memories colliding in her mind, unknowingly squirming in Chas's arms.

"Dorchester," she said suddenly, feeling a jolt of adrenaline shoot through her. She stiffened in Chas's arms, almost causing him to drop her.

He caught her more tightly and stumbled a little as her sudden shift sent him sideways. "What?"

"Michael Dorchester."

"What about him?"

"That's the name of the psychologist I interviewed for *Timeline* on a piece we were doing about...about love. No. Yes. Something like that. I almost remember."

She struggled a little more, wanting to be put down, wanting to *think*. To remember.

Maybe revealing the past had turned a key in her mind, one that allowed the recent past, the very murky recent past, to surface somewhat.

Chas let her slide to the floor but kept his hands on her arms, steadying her. He didn't speak at all, as if waiting for her to continue.

She had a quick flash of memory, letting her glimpse an image of Dorchester sitting in Studio B, calm, polished, blond haired, wire-rimmed glasses in place, fiddling with his mike. And she had another image of him, dark-haired, no glasses, standing over her, demanding something of her. Something she didn't want to give him.

"But he had blond hair," she said.

"Who?" Chas asked.

She told him about the two contrasting visions. "But it was the same man, I'd swear, no matter how little it makes sense."

"A disguise?" he suggested simply.

And she knew he was right. About all of it. She didn't know how she knew, but every single instinct in her demanded she pay attention. "A disguise," she repeated slowly.

She'd been focusing on the problem all wrong, she realized. She'd been trying to understand what was going on in her head. She'd been groping for some rational explanation, when the easiest one had been right before her all the time. She couldn't hope to understand the reasons for what had been done to her because they were *irrational* to begin with.

A stalker with a twist. With a terrible, bizarre twist.

And with that surety came more knowledge, as if a floodgate had been opened in her mind. The trigger had been in telling about the past. About Susie. About her pregnancy and the loss of it.

Because she had told someone about it before. She'd told Michael Dorchester. Under hypnosis.

"Th-that's why he used the...the hand," she said suddenly. "He knew about it. He knew how it would affect me. He *knew*."

"Because you told him."

"Because I told him," she agreed slowly, disbelief creeping over her. Disbelief because she'd never told anyone that macabre and terrifying story before. Until she'd told Chas today.

And yet she must have told someone. This Dorchester. This mousy little blond-haired man with wire-frame glasses. This terrifying raven-haired man with blazing eyes that told the story of his madness.

And who would know how to hypnotize someone easily? A psychologist.

"God. He asked me to dinner. I didn't even think about it for a second. I just said no. I was lighting a cigarette at the time. He said he could help me quit those evil things. I barely paid him any attention. He gave me his card. He said he could do it using hypnosis. He had a surefire cure."

"And once he had you under, he just—"

"Raped my mind." Then, at Chas's wince, she added, "Well, what else can I call it?"

What else did the man know about her? Obviously he knew about Almost. He knew about Susie. He had to know all her inner fears and longings.

"But why did he do it? Because I didn't accept his pathetic invitation to dinner? Is he so sick that a single rejection tipped him over an edge?"

She could see the answer to that question in Chas's eyes, feel in the suddenly fearful grip on her arms. But he said, "We don't know anything about him, Allison. For all we know, he's done this sort of thing before."

"Well, we can find out a few things," she said firmly.

"How?"

"I'm a reporter, remember? That's what I do."

And she felt like one for the first time in months. She jerked the phone up from its cradle and punched the number to the *Timeline* research desk from memory. She smiled broadly at him. He frowned in puzzlement.

"I remembered the number," she said. "Hello, Jenny? This is Allison Leary."

Within minutes, she had the information she wanted, but not at all the results she'd expected. She hung up the phone in a mild state of shock.

"What?" Chas asked. "What did she tell you?"

"Dr. Michael Dorchester died two months ago."

"What?"

"In a car wreck."

Chas frowned.

"In the same car wreck that landed reporter Allison Leary in the hospital," she said dully.

She thought of that list of questions she'd made earlier in Taylor's kitchen while the boys groused about their cereal. The questions seemed so small now. The mystery so enormous.

When the phone rang, Allison jumped at least a foot into the air and she felt Chas's hands clench too tightly on her arms, showing that he was equally on edge.

He answered with a short, quick bark of his name. His face softened nearly immediately. "Hi, Carolyn," he said. "Sammie Jo's right—Allison's here with me." He chuckled falsely and winked at Allison. "The old-fashioned kind. No presents, but lots of decorations."

He handed the phone to Allison. "She wants to talk to you," he said.

Allison didn't want to talk to anyone. She wanted to continue sorting through the strange memories in her head, placing them in alternate piles: things she *knew* had happened, and those she was confused about.

"Hello?"

Carolyn swiftly recounted what the boys had told her and what Sammie Jo had called about later. "We've had at least ten phone calls, but no one's seen any strangers hanging around Almost. Charlie Hampton's still a little spooked about what happened here a few months ago, when the triplets found—and lost—that dead drug dealer outside his barn, and he keeps a weather eye out for anyone new. He'll alert his field hands tomorrow to keep their eyes peeled, too.''

"I really appreciate all this," Allison said, and was surprised to find tears filming her eyes.

"You're family," Carolyn said. When Allison didn't say anything, she added, "I learned when I came here that in Almost, *family* is synonymous with being protected. I suppose you've been gone long enough that you'd forgotten that?"

Standing in Chas's warm living room, talking to a sister-in-law she'd never met before the wedding, feeling the nearly palpable caring in this woman's voice, Allison realized she'd never known that about Almost. She'd never understood it as she was beginning to do.

"We won't let anything happen to you," Carolyn said confidently. Calmly. *Protectively.* "Oh, and I'm to tell you that the boys will be bringing their tapes tomorrow for your expert advice on editing."

Allison managed to choke out a promise to peruse the tapes, and, luckily for her peace of mind, Carolyn rang off after saying she would drop around in the morning, if the weather cleared, adding that the boys were eager to feed—and play, she said laughingly—with the animals in the clinic.

She numbly handed the phone to Chas.

"She's a great gal," Chas said as he deposited the receiver into the cradle.

She smiled, albeit a bit tremulously. "I never knew," she said.

"You never knew what?" he asked.

"That people could just love. She's never met me. The only thing I ever did for her was to send something for their wedding, and silver cups or spoons for the girls when they were born. Nothing more. Not even a sympathy card when Craig was killed."

Chas didn't say anything.

"And here she is calling me family. And letting me know that I'm important to her."

Chas still didn't say anything, but his face held such exquisite pain that she had to look away.

"Oh, Chas…I feel like I'm eighteen again and don't understand anything. I'm not sure I even know how to accept such things as Carolyn is offering."

"Sure, you do, Allison," he said finally. "All you have to do is close your eyes and hold out your arms."

She did as he suggested. The dark was soft and loving.

And his kiss tender and firm.

And his body firmer still.

The man calling himself Quentin packed his "toys" into the small duffel bag he'd washed the night before to partially rid it of the copper-scented bloodstains that had marred its nylon interior.

The day had dawned bright and shimmery. Outside his dingy trailer, the world was a gleaming, glittering white, with thick hoarfrost clinging to every branch and fence post. The ground his team of invisible farmworkers had tilled so carefully lay beneath a blanket of sparkling white diamonds.

He smiled to himself. For everyone else, it was a day of rest. Sunday. And everyone in Almost attended one of the Almost churches, Baptist mainly.

Allison had told him that. Dreamily. Softly. Letting him have every morsel of information. Eyes closed, beautiful face in repose, she'd tried resisting his relentless push for knowledge at first, a perfect example of a strong-minded woman. But slowly, inevitably she'd given in to his demands for more. And more. Until she'd told him everything in her mind, heart and soul.

And then, amazingly, she'd just erased him from her memory. Gone.

She was supposed to love him. That was her destiny. His. She would tell him everything, then love him for the telling, for the accepting of this knowledge.

Instead, she'd woken up the last morning without remembering him at all. Gone. All gone. The days of tending to her needs, the times of drying her tears, brushing her soft blond hair, touching her sweet, soft skin...she'd erased it all. Forgotten him as completely as if he'd never existed.

Today, however, she would be made to remember. While all the other pious little hicks hid in the safety of their churches, he would force her to remember him. And he'd force her to be sorry she'd ever forgotten him.

She'd remember him, all right. It would be the very last thing she *did* remember.

Tock...tock...tock...tick-tock!

Allison sat up in bed without consciously doing so.

The pounding continued.

Disoriented, turning to the window, expecting to see a disembodied hand, she heard a muffled but frantic voice calling, "Doc! Doc! It's Billy!" It came from the direction of Chas's front door.

Even as she reached out to touch Chas's sleeping form, he rolled over and up, his eyes wide open, his entire attention focused on the world outside his dreams.

He was out of bed and running down the short hallway to the living room before the pounding on the door resumed. She imagined she could feel the icy blast of cold air when she heard him wrench the door open.

She'd recognized one of the triplet's nearly hysterical voice as the instigator of the summons. As Chas pulled the door open, she whipped her legs from the bed, grabbed up some garment from the floor and threw it over her head, tucking her arms into the sleeves. She raced down the hall in time to see a coatless Chas shoving his bare feet into his cowboy boots and half hopping out the front door while zipping up his pants. He'd dragged a sweater over his head and thrust his arms in the sleeves as he galloped across the stretch of ground between the house and the clinic.

She realized she was standing stock-still, watching his ungainly run through the wide-open door.

She flew back down to the bedroom to frantically search for her pants and, finding them flung atop Chas's dresser, yanked them up while desperately searching for the left shoe. That proved to be tucked under the corner of the bed, and she hobbled down the hall, dragging the shoe onto her foot before grabbing her coat and darting out the front door, slamming it behind her.

She skidded on the icy porch, nearly falling, and slammed into the front support, which saved her from spilling face-first onto the frozen ground.

She could hear the sharp, agonized screams of a horse and the furious barking of a dog. Overriding these panicked sounds, she could all too easily hear the frantic cries of all three of her nephews as a dissonant and frightening harmony to Chas's deeper, equally frenzied yelling.

She leaped over the steps and slipped on the icy ground. She fell to one hand, wrenching it backward painfully as she heard Chas issue an agonized "No!"

She scrambled on all fours to propel herself forward. Her fingernails found purchase in the ice, and she hurled herself toward the clinic, desperate to be there, an urgency spurring her numb limbs.

She burst through the front door of the clinic, propelled by sheer will and slick surfaces to discover the primary examining room of the clinic in contrasting order and chaos. The animals in the cages, cats and dogs alike, were sounding their alarm and fear. One cage stood open, the cage that had held the shepherd cross. The rest of the clinic seemed perfectly normal.

For some reason, this alarmed her far more than seeing it in total disarray might have done, for she had *expected* that. Seeing everything in order rang a severely discordant bell in her psyche.

She took all this in during a single breath as she grabbed at the doorway to stop herself skidding into the room, then used the opened door to propel herself to the other side, racing toward the sounds of greater trouble.

She shot through the doorway leading to the stable with no thought whatsoever, only the awareness that one of her "family" was in danger.

The door flew back with a resounding echo that made at least two heads whip in her direction, shoulders ducking as though from a blow. Desperate fear shone from eyes that could have been hers.

"Aunt Allison!" said one of them and raced to throw his arms around her, gripping fiercely. *Josh.* Sobs racked his thin frame.

"Do something!" Jason cried.

Like a series of still photographs, the situation in the barn revealed itself. A jet black horse with a white blaze down its forehead, screaming in fear and defiance, was rearing up and pawing the air. A young boy with dark hair lay too still upon the hay-strewed floor. And trying to reach his son, Chas was pinned against the back entrance to the barn, a streak of blood trickling down his pallid face, apparently already struck once by the razor-sharp hooves. She saw him frantically jiggle the handle on the barn doors, but they didn't budge.

Instinctively Allison sought the third of her nephews and found him huddled in a fetal position against a closed and presumably empty stall. The shepherd cross was pressed against him, whining, never taking her eyes from the raging horse.

Allison whirled, shoving Josh away from her and running from the room.

"Aunt Allison!" came Jason's wail of protest. The depth of his betrayal followed her out the door, tearing at her heart, slowing her for an agonizing second, then dogging her heels as she tore through the front rooms of the clinic and out the door, but she had no time to explain her actions.

The sun momentarily blinded her as she scrambled beneath the portal of the clinic's entrance and slithered to the low steps. She fell to one knee, cracking it hard against the concrete stairs, and with a grunting, pleading inhalation of frigid air, she clawed her way to a crouched run.

She lurched around the back of the clinic, to the far side of the barn, knives of pain digging into her left side, her thoughts on Billy's still form, on his father, waving his hands to ward off the slashing hooves of the young horse. To save his son. At the very real possibility of the loss of his own life.

Chas.

A thousand images of him threatened to undermine her focus on reaching the back doors of that barn. The way his eyes crinkled at the edges, the laugh lines around his mouth. The length of his fingers. The way his heart thudded against his broad chest. The delicacy of his touch against her sensitive skin.

"No!" she gasped out, rolling through the slats of the corral, then skidding around the distant corner of the barn, lunging to the doors.

Someone—*Dorchester* or his doppelgänger—had shoved a two-by-four through the doubled handles, securing the door as firmly as if with a doubled chain and locks.

Her hands were frozen and had no grip at first, but she tore at the four-foot length of board and finally yanked it free, spinning it away from her with a yell of primal rage, wrenching open the door, terrified of what she would find.

Petrified.

Chas spilled out of the door and staggered against her, knocking her flat to the ground. He tripped over her, falling himself, which saved both their lives, for the horse, seeing the smallest chance of escape, leaped toward the door with a scream of rage and panic, a living, breathing instrument of pure destruction.

Even as Chas landed upon her, knocking the wind from her lungs, she saw the horse's underbelly sailing over them, saw the powerful weapons of his shod hooves, felt the heat of his frenzied leap.

"Billy!" Jason called from inside the barn.

She had a moment to ponder the mystery of being able to discern the differences between the boys. Why now, when all was in chaos, could she distinguish the nearly identical children?

Chas groaned and rolled off her with an oath and, without bothering to push to his feet, clawed through the ice to the barn to reach his son.

"No, no, no..." she heard him repeating, his voice anguished, the denial a prayer against the worst fate could deal.

She couldn't move. Gripped in the fever of fear, of disbelief, she didn't want to raise her head and see what he might discover. She couldn't bear that tragedy, couldn't bear watching it happen to him.

"Please, please, please..." she mouthed, seeking help from that which she'd denied so many years before. All she could do was to utter the single word, a host of need and want inherent in the one desperate cry.

Her heart broke and a sob escaped her when she heard Chas's great raspy voice tear on a sob.

"Billy...Billy... Oh, dear God, Billy..."

She forced herself to move. No matter how much she would have preferred to disappear, to melt into the icy ground, she had to move now. Chas's entire world was shattering before his eyes. In his helpless hands.

She had to stretch out a hand to try to retrieve him from that dark precipice of undying agony.

So much was clear to her now. So much, and too late, now that total disaster had struck.

She clambered through the thick snow and crawled to Chas's side.

He was sprawled on the barn floor, legs akimbo, holding his limp son in his big arms, rocking forward, his mouth open, a silent sobbing racking him, his forehead bleeding, his eyes not on his still son but on the ceiling of the barn.

Allison froze beside him, feeling every nuance of his grief, his pain, his total and complete loss.

And in that moment of absolute empathy, realized that she loved him. Too late she understood that all perfect days have perfectly opposite sides. Too late she knew that words left unspoken, hearts left unburdened, often remain silent, burdened.

In a blinding, painful clarity, she understood that if she'd said the words to him before, he would have had some measure of hope to cling to, something to hold himself together. But she hadn't said them.

And now, confronted with the depth of his pain, the still body of his son in his arms, she couldn't. Much as she ached to give them to him.

All she could do was to crawl forward one more step and wrap her arms around his shaking, trembling shoulders and hold him fiercely, her heart as broken as his.

He didn't shake her free or lean into her. She knew he was totally unaware of her, as indifferent to her as to the icy air.

Yesterday had perfect, a day out of time, a miracle.

Today the sun shone brightly and Chas was rocking the still form of his son in his arms, utter despair impaling his soul.

The triplets edged forward, tears running down their faces.

"Is he okay?"

"Doc?"

"Is he d-dead?"

Chapter 12

Allison looked down at Billy, willing him to move, projecting every desire she'd ever had into the need to have him just lift a single finger. All the dreams she'd had in the past fifteen years were focused in this one wish, this one prayer.

For Chas.

"Doofus. He's not dead! Lookit, his finger's moving."

"Yeah! See? He's moving!"

Chas's head snapped down, his eyes suddenly ablaze with raw hope, with a longing so intense that Allison felt burned by the latent heat radiating from him.

"D-daddy?"

A huge, monumental sob burst from Chas's lungs, and he pitched over his son, as if pulled there. He ran a terribly shaking hand over the boy's face, skimming unbroken skin, touching yet not, seeking injury but not pressing, only reassuring himself that his son was alive.

"Billy...oh, thank God, Billy..."

Allison had let go of Chas the moment Jason had said Billy was moving, and now she allowed relief and exhaustion to carry her to the rock-hard floor of the barn. She sat down stiffly, not feeling the cold concrete, unaware of her bruised back and bleeding fingers, but all too aware of the myriad emotions roiling inside her. Her hands dropped between her legs, and her head lolled forward.

The shepherd cross whined a little and nestled against her, lending her warmth, some measure of comfort. Numbly Allison put her arms around the dog and leaned her cheek against the dog's soft head.

All these years, she'd carried a notion that she'd lived through the worst of pains, the hardest of agonies. She'd blamed herself, blamed Chas. She'd drawn that pain deep inside her, blocking any pathway to love, to light.

Watching Chas as he'd held his still son in his arms, she'd realized that her pain, the agony that had always seized her, was no greater nor any less than any other human being's.

But now she saw clearly that there were worse things than suffering pain herself; there was watching a person she cared about tormented by extreme agony and being utterly helpless to remove it.

She felt she grew up in those few seconds between her nephew's excited revelation and the moment when Billy opened his eyes and looked up to meet his father's tear-filled gaze.

And in that startling epiphany, she understood that life wasn't about the pivotal, stressful moments, the times one easily remembered; it was about the times one forgot, the easy, comfortable moments that slipped unheralded and un-noticed, not the first step, or the first tooth, not even the Christmas days given out of season, but the moments of having a child sitting in a lap, giggling over a book, the laughter on a beloved aunt's gaunt face. Life wasn't about deadlines and panic, but about a sister's hug, a nephew's embrace, a lover's antics. It was about a hurt shepherd cross offering comfort. And it was about understanding a gift and taking it with love.

But most of all, life wasn't about something that happened fifteen years ago; it was about a living boy in a loving man's arms.

"Th-there was a man in here, Dad," Billy said. "He was messing with Chico. I yelled."

Allison's skin prickled as Billy's words impinged on her consciousness. Fear for Billy, empathy for Chas had driven the significance of the deadly two-by-four wedged in the barn doors from her mind.

She raised her head to look at Chas and saw his jaw clench and a muscle in his cheek twitch, a kinetic energy working through him, an anger a thousand times stronger than any she'd felt in the past.

Someone—they both knew who, whoever the mysterious *who* might prove to be—had nearly murdered Billy. Chas's only son. And perhaps, in some small measure, by strange transference, the child she'd never had.

On Chas's chiseled face, she could read a determination to enact vengeance. The urge for reprisal, for retaliation, for complete and utter eradication, carved itself onto his features, lending them a hard, severe look, an expression that sat ill on his broad face, but a look that brooked no argument.

"Wow, like you s-saw somebody?" Josh asked, having crawled out of his curled-up position by one of the stall doors. "What did he look like?"

"B-black hair. Scary eyes," Billy mumbled. He continued to stare up at his father. "He looked at me before he ran out of the barn. It was really weird, Dad. He looked mad, but not at me, you know what I mean? He looked like he was hurt or something. I dunno, like he didn't want Chico to really kick me or anything.''

"Did Chico kick you?" Jason asked.

"Like, did the guy limp or have a yucky scar on his face?"

"Are you going after him, Doc?"

Allison had never loved her nephews as much as she did at that moment, as the normality of three prepubescent boys' questions infused a bit of color and life into Chas's rock-hard face.

Or maybe it was because his son moved in his arms, total faith on his young face. Fear, yes, but faith in much greater measure, in the rightness of the world, in his father to set that world to rights.

"Is Chico okay?" Billy asked, struggling to sit upright.

A choked sound erupted from Chas's throat, and he pulled his son tightly to his chest. "Damn the horse," said the man who had devoted his life to saving animals. "You're okay. That's all that matters."

And watching them, Allison knew that he was right. That *was* all that mattered.

But she also knew that if she stayed near these people she loved—and she knew now that she did love them—another would be hurt. Because of her.

And that was something she couldn't allow to happen.

One of the triplets dashed to the open barn doors. "There's footprints in the snow! Over there, in Mr. Hampton's field. We could follow them!"

"No!" Allison cried, lunging forward to grab at him. She collided with Chas, who had moved much more swiftly than even her quick jump forward. He pushed Billy into her arms and grabbed Jason back from the door.

"Everybody stay here! Call Sammie Jo, tell her to get

Carolyn to drive Billy to the hospital in Levelland. And call the troopers over from Lubbock.''

With that, he burst out the door, the picture of fury, action and determination.

''Chas, wait!''

He slowed, but only turned halfway around. His glowering concentration nearly froze her words, her need to stop him. ''You can't go after him,'' she said.

He didn't say anything, but resumed his stride forward.

''Chas!''

He held up a hand as if blocking her words.

''Chas, damn it! You're not armed. You're not even dressed!''

He whirled around at this. ''I'm going to tear the bastard apart with my bare hands,'' he all but yelled at her. ''You think I'm just going to stand by and let him nearly kill my son and get away with it? Especially after what he's been doing to you?''

He whipped back toward the far circle of the corral, completely ignoring the still skittish lathered horse. He jumped on the first railing and vaulted the remaining barrier and stomped into the ice-covered Hampton field without looking back.

Somehow Allison knew he wouldn't give up until he found their attacker. And she found herself uttering her second heartfelt prayer of the day.

She wanted to go with him, to follow him. This same man he tracked was also the one who had been stalking her. Billy had been harmed because of *her*.

But she couldn't leave Billy. Chas had left his son in her care. In her arms. Unconsciously she tightened her hold on the boy, looking down at his strained features. He was watching his dad crossing the ice-covered field, coatless and hunched against the cold, but somehow appearing all the more formidable because of this lack of protection.

"What's he going to do?" Josh asked.

"Yeah, he doesn't have a gun or nothing."

"Doc told us to call Sammie Jo."

"Call Uncle Pete. He was with the FBI. He'll know what to do!"

"Yeah!"

The triplets dashed off, racing into the main clinic, where the dogs were still barking, except for the shepherd cross huddled against Allison.

Hearing the dogs bark, Allison realized that only minutes had passed. When Billy's inert form had been on the ground, it seemed lifetimes had gone by.

"Is Dad going to be okay?" Billy asked. His man's voice was gone now, leaving only a scared boy behind.

She pulled him a little tighter to her chest and felt something shift deep inside her, a melting of something long frozen in her heart. "He'll be fine," she said, petitioning all the gods not to let her be lying to this fine young boy.

His eyes shifted from his father's diminishing form to look up her. His dark eyes seemed troubled. "He isn't my real dad, you know. I mean, not like a biological father."

Allison could only stare at him. She didn't, *couldn't* understand what he was saying to her.

"But he loves me like I was his real son. This proves it, doesn't it? I mean him going after the guy who let Chico out and locked us in?"

The boy's question demanded she speak, that she force herself to swallow her stunned confusion and reassure him. "He loves you more than anything," she said. "He told me so."

Billy smiled shakily and nodded. "I guess I knew that. I mean, I do know." Tears rose to pool in his eyes. Then spilled free with his next words, mute testimony to his fear and shock. And his extreme vulnerability.

He released a sob and turned into her, his cold hand clutching her coat, unaware that he'd loosed another, far colder hand to clench her heart.

"And I l-love him, too. He's the best dad in the whole world."

"Yes," she agreed slowly, not entirely sure where the words were coming from. "Yes, I think he must be."

The man who called himself Dorchester in New York, Michaels in Anton and Quentin in Almost exhaled a sobbing breath. His hands shook as he set the nylon bag on the dresser inside his narrow trailer. He met the tortured gaze of his reflection.

The boy wasn't supposed to have been in the clinic. He'd never meant to harm the child. Children were sacred. Off limits.

His reflection didn't look knowing, hard and sure. In the single shard of remaining mirror, this other part of himself only appeared frightened, as scared as he'd felt as a child, as he felt right now, wide-eyed and ready to be sick.

He'd run, sealing the door behind him with the two-by-four. He'd nearly turned back to remove it. *What was he doing?* But he'd run anyway. Leaving the boy locked inside with the drug-maddened horse.

He drew a deep, ragged breath.

It was all Allison's fault. She'd forced him to turn the horse loose. She'd forced him to hurt the boy. *He,* who would never hurt a child, who had devoted his entire life to the care and well-being of those who needed help.

And children always needed the most help.

And they were the only ones who deserved it.

And where was Allison when the boy had walked in the barn? Under the haystack, fast asleep.

The eyes in the mirror hardened.

Now she owed him on two accounts, first for forgetting him. Second, for forcing him to harm a child.

Oh, how he hated her.

And to think he'd once loved her.

She was enough to drive a man crazy.

He didn't bother to collect anything beyond the items in the nylon bag and the keys to the battered pickup. The rest wouldn't matter. They couldn't be traced to him. And even if they were, how could Dr. Michael Dorchester, dead and cremated in New York, be associated with a crime in Almost, Texas?

He swung out of the trailer, squinting at the sharp brightness of the day. He slid a little in his sprint to the still warm pickup truck.

He didn't think anyone had seen him, but he couldn't take the risk. There was only one way he was safe, and that was to go to the farmer whose fields he'd been tilling. The old man would be his alibi. *What, Quentin? Why, he was with me this morning, talking about some newfangled crop he'd heard tell of over in New Mexico, thought Jerusalem artichokes might just work round here.* And the old man would laugh heartily at the notion, though if he were smart, he'd try the crop.

While he was chatting up the farmer, he would just casually mention that he saw someone running across the field. A fellow with blond hair and glasses. A city slicker.

Battered though the pickup was, it still turned over on the first try and lurched away from the small trailer, furrowing the clean white stretch of road.

The man who called himself Quentin looked up at the clear blue sky, the deep, deep blue and smiled a little. In less than a half an hour, the desert sun would have baked away his tracks. And those of the pickup. There would be no evidence left at all.

He felt so much better he began to hum as he maneuvered the road. He stopped when he realized it was a Christmas carol.

Sane people didn't sing Christmas carols in February.

Chas realized he was fighting a losing battle when he was about halfway across the first ten acres of the field. The sun was all too swiftly aiding the psychopath's escape by erasing his footprints.

And the guy had been clever, running in an irregular zigzag pattern that was hard to follow even with clear prints.

But Chas continued anyway, rage propelling his steps, his own anguished words to Allison, the fear in his son's pale face, reverberating in his head, in his heart.

If he didn't continue, if he didn't find this man and stop him cold, he would never be able to look at himself in a mirror again. He would never be able to meet his son's gaze and feel like a father.

And he would never be able to assure Allison that all would be well, that he would be able to keep her safe.

But some fifteen minutes later, when Pete Jackson pulled up in his Jeep Cherokee, having driven down the narrow farm lane at the edge of the field, Chas had lost all sign of the man's prints.

Pete got out of the cab and tossed him a jacket. Chas looked at it for a moment, then eased it onto his arms.

"Carolyn's taking Allison and Billy to Levelland. The kids are with Sammie Jo."

Chas nodded and stared out at the now damp but very brown field. Here and there, he thought he could make out a footprint or two, and maybe far beyond them, the recent tracks left by a vehicle, but there wasn't anything in sight as cover, no houses, no trees. Nothing out this way but the workers' shacks and then nothing until Charlie Hampton's place.

"Chico's still in the corral," Pete said quietly.

Chas turned to look at this man who had burst into their lives about a year or more before. "How's Billy?"

"He'll be fine. Just a bump on the head. How's yours?"

Chas lifted a hand to his cold forehead. He'd forgotten the horse had grazed him with a flailing hoof. The blood had stopped flowing and was dried against his brow. "I'll be all right."

"We'll find whoever did this, Doc."

Chas nodded, looking back at the broad expanse of field. Miles of open farmland.

"We can drive on a ways if you want," Pete said.

Chas knew the former FBI agent thought the search futile at this point but was too kind to say so.

"We will find him," Pete said again.

Chas couldn't look at the man he'd liked and trusted from the first day he'd showed up on Carolyn's ranch. He didn't want Pete to see how close he was to letting his pent-up rage fly loose. And he didn't want Pete to know that if—when—he found the man who'd tormented Allison, who had very nearly killed his son, he wouldn't be worrying about handing the man over to the cops. He was just going to end it, right then and there.

All the vows he'd ever taken for preserving lives, animal or human, meant nothing at that moment. He, who had built his life around vows and promises, understood that they had no more substance than the melting snow. Less.

"Come on," Pete said. "Let's get you to the hospital.

Sammie Jo's been calling everyone in town since last night, telling them to watch out for a stranger. We'll find him.''

Chas climbed in the cab of the Cherokee and buckled his belt. He stared across the brown field as if he could make the stranger appear by sheer will alone.

But the field remained as empty and barren as his heart.

In the waiting room of the hospital in Levelland, Allison accepted the cup of hot coffee from Carolyn's steady hands. Her own shook noticeably.

"Pete'll find Doc," Carolyn said. She smiled. "He's pretty good at that sort of thing."

"He didn't have a coat on."

Carolyn blinked at this. "No? Well, it's already warming up out there."

"What if he did find Dorchester?" she asked.

"Who is Dorchester?"

Allison stared at her for a long moment, stunned that her sister-in-law didn't know. She closed her eyes then and sighed. There was so much *she* didn't know. Carolyn took the cup of coffee from her hands, then enfolded Allison's fingers within her warm grasp.

"I don't know who he is really," Allison said heavily. "In fact, I don't know anything anymore."

"You don't have to tell me."

Allison opened her eyes and met those of this stranger who claimed her as family, who held her hands lovingly. Who had raced to the hospital with her and Billy, who had held the boy's hand while the doctors examined him. And suddenly she wasn't looking at a stranger anymore. She was meeting the eyes of another sister. Another person who *loved* her.

When had she allowed her life to become devoid of love? Could it really have been fifteen years ago on a lonely stretch of highway? A sleeping beauty, pricked by pain and loss, woken not by the prince but by a madman.

She began her story with the only partially remembered interview with Michael Dorchester and finished it with Billy's concussion. She left out the past tragedies, both real and imagined. She left out the way Chas had taken her to heaven and brought her home again. And she left out her confused and myriad emotions about him, about Billy's revelation to her that Chas wasn't his biological father.

When she wound to a close, Carolyn tightened the pressure on her fingers. "You know, there used to be a legend around here. Two of them, in fact. One was that there was something in the water that the Leary women drank that turned them all beautiful."

Allison smiled faintly. She remembered hearing that one when she was little. She thought it was true of Carolyn, though she was technically a Jackson now.

"The other one was that all the Leary women were unlucky, that something terrible would happen to them and those they loved before they could find true love."

Allison's smile slipped. She thought of her mother, her untimely death. She thought of her cousin Susie. Of Taylor's first husband, Doug. And she thought of her brother, Craig, and this lovely woman who had been his wife. Another Leary woman.

And she thought of Chas, who'd told her twice now that he loved her. Of his son, who lay in the hospital room beyond them, sleeping under the watchful eyes of the nursing staff.

Maybe it was her turn. Her heart thudded in her chest, and she felt lightheaded with the shimmery hope. Maybe, just maybe she'd be able to let go of the past long enough to embrace a future.

The nurse slipped out of Billy's room and signaled them. "He's awake," she said softly.

Carolyn nodded at her. "You go on. I think Chas would want you to."

Allison rose unsteadily, wondering how her sister-in-law knew.

As if reading her mind, Carolyn smiled softly. "Billy's been wanting a new mom for a long time now."

Allison's mind flashed on the painful past, a past that didn't seem anywhere as horrific as it had been only the morning before. She thought of Chas kissing his fingers to the air, muttering in his exaggerated French accent. She thought of the naked pain on his face as he'd held Billy.

She didn't smile back at Carolyn; she only squeezed the hands that had warmed hers and turned them loose.

Billy was partially raised in his bed that seemed far too large for him. Now that she knew he wasn't Chas's biological son, she could see the subtle signs of a different set of genes in him. The darker hair. The darker eyes. The lips shaped like Thelma's had been. The narrow face.

But when he turned and smiled at her, his hand half lifting, his grin open and welcoming, she knew that whoever his father may have been, he was definitely Chas's son.

"Dad...?" he asked before she was halfway into the room.

She shook her head. "But Pete's gone to fetch him and bring him here."

He released a big sigh of relief and smiled again, this time nervously, she thought. His fingers plucked at the blanket sheathing him, and he looked down at little peaks and valleys he created.

"How are—?" she began.

At the same time he asked, "Allison?"

His eyes lifted to hers, and he mumbled an apology for interrupting her.

"That's okay. What were you going to ask?"

His eyes shot back down to his nervous blanket plucking. Three more mountains formed before he spoke up.

"I know that you and Dad were, like, friends before he married Mom."

Allison felt as if her jaw was unhinged.

"Mom told me. A long time ago."

If he'd held a gun to her head, she couldn't have spoken then.

"The thing is...she told me how she knew this and she went to Dad anyway and begged for him to help her. Cause she knew he would. And I guess he did. You know, like say he would marry her. Because of me. Because she was pregnant with me, you know."

He flattened all the mountains and started again. Her heart bled for him, and she ached to reach out and smooth the hank of hair hanging down on his forehead away from his face. And she wished she'd had one quarter of his tremendous maturity and courage all those years ago. She wished she had it now.

"The thing is, see, I think Dad's still in love with you."

Chas burst into the hospital like one of his own abruptly released animals, his eyes cutting right and left, seeking those people he knew, looking for immediate information about his son.

Carolyn grabbed his arm.

"Where is he?" he asked, spinning around to face her.

"Allison's with him," she said. If she'd tossed a glass of ice water in his face, nothing could have made him still as rapidly as hearing this.

She nodded at him as he assimilated this bit of information. "He fine. He likes her, Doc."

"He's okay?"

"A concussion. A bruised forearm. No breaks. He's hardheaded. Which is more than I can say for you."

Chas felt his head was mush at the moment.

"Where are they?" he asked.

She cocked her head down the hallway he hadn't been plunging into. "Room 335."

He started to move in that direction, but she didn't release her hold on his arm. "Doc?"

He turned, trying to quell the frown rising in him at her detaining him.

"Allison's a Leary. Probably more so than the rest. She's all of them, all wrapped up into one. She's got all their stubbornness. All their pride. All their love. All their pioneering spirit."

"What are you saying, Carolyn?"

"I'm saying that Allison loves you, but it'll take an act of Congress before she'll ever let you know it. I don't even know if she knows it yet."

Chas stared at this lovely woman for a long moment, then bent to kiss her cheek. He looked up to see her husband slowly walking up to join them. "You're a very lucky man, Pete," he said.

Pete smiled and put his arm around his statuesque wife at the same time she released her hold on Chas's arm. "You have no idea."

"Sometimes you just gotta make your own luck, Doc," Carolyn said, and smiled up at her husband.

Both their words followed him down the short hallway, slowing his footsteps.

By the time he reached the door, he no longer felt like a papa bear on a mission to find his cub.

And he was glad, for he heard his son's voice. And Allison's.

He stood outside the doorway, listening shamelessly, closing his eyes as he had outside Taylor's house the night of her wedding, hearing those two beloved voices mingling.

"...kind of like a puppy following after a bigger dog," Allison was saying. "Like the boys follow you around."

Billy chuckled, and a huge knot of fear loosened in Chas's chest. "Yeah? But that's pretty cool. I mean, like, you're famous and everything now."

"Fame isn't all it's cracked up to be, Billy."

"No? How come?"

"Oh, a big city can be a pretty lonely place sometimes."

"Why don't you just stay here, then?"

Chas found himself holding his breath, nodding at the empty air around him.

"And what would I do for a living, hmm?"

"Marry Dad," Billy answered promptly. "Like, wouldn't that be perfect? I wasn't kidding a while ago when I said that I thought he still loved you. Like Mom said. Well, it's true. I think he still does. I saw the way he looks at you and stuff."

So much for hiding things from your children, Chas thought, but he leaned forward to hear Allison's response.

"He said he does."

"So, like, what's the problem?"

Oh, Billy, Chas thought, I hope to God you never know.

"It's me, isn't it?" Billy asked.

"What?" Allison asked, sounding as stunned as Chas felt outside the room.

"Well, if Mom hadn't gone to him and talked him into marrying her, he'd have married *you*."

Out of the mouths of babes, Chas thought, his heart breaking.

"No," Allison said swiftly.

Chas felt his blood draining.

She cleared her throat. "That's not the way it happened at all, Billy."

Chas held his breath.

"You see, I *did* know about your dad and Thelma. Your dad wanted a child so badly, you see. Wanted *you*, I mean, that he asked Thelma to marry him. Maybe your Mom didn't know the whole story. He told me, but I didn't w-want kids back then. S-so he married your mom, so he could have *you*. And he's never regretted it one single day. He told me so."

"Really?"

"I have to tell the truth to millions of Americans every week—you think I'm going to come all the way back home and tell you a lie?"

Chas pushed his way into the room.

Billy lit up and waved at him. "Dad! You're okay!"

Chas realized it hadn't mattered one iota to Billy if he caught the man or not; his safety had been all that his son had thought of. And what was more important to his son than that? Being there for him was paramount; possibly losing his life in a stupid encounter with a psychopath wouldn't do Billy—or Allison—any good at all.

Allison had frozen, her back still to him.

He shook his head, understanding so much, so unable to reveal any of it. He all but flew to his son's side and scooped him into his arms for a huge hug. God, he loved this kid so much. Allison hadn't been lying about that part, though he would owe her for the rest of his life for her other lies.

Feeling Billy's spindly teenage arms around his shoulders, he fought the sting of relief tears, and didn't care who saw them.

After a few moments, he released Billy to turn to Allison, but she'd gone. "Just a sec, okay, Bill?"

"Sure, Dad," his son said, a knowing look on his young face.

Chas dashed from the room in time to see Allison and Carolyn walking out the hospital front doors. Down at the other end of the hallway, Pete raised his hands out from his chest in the universal "who knows?" gesture, then made car-driving motions and pointed in the general direction of Almost.

She wasn't just leaving hospital. Every instinct in him screamed that she was leaving Almost. Leaving to keep everyone safe. Leaving him. Again.

He turned back to his son. "Billy, I don't know what all you and Allison talked about—"

"She's really great, Dad. You know, I think she loves you."

Chas stared at his son as if he'd never seen him before. "Pretty sneaky, Billy. Pulling the same trick on both of us?"

Billy looked startled, "You heard?"

"I was outside in the hallway."

Instead of looking guilty or sheepish, Billy just grinned at him. Chas realized his son had taken Allison's statement about the past at total face value. Some shadow he'd never realized had lurked in his son's eyes was gone now.

"Well, you were right when you told her that I loved her…but I didn't hear her telling you any such thing."

"Oh, like you're always saying, some things people don't have to say out loud, you know?" Billy said, his mouth curved into a mischievous smile, his eyes alight with fun. Then he seemed to catch some whiff of his father's fear. "What's wrong, Dad?"

"Did she tell you about the man in the barn this morning?"

Billy tensed up even further. His eyes widened as he sat forward. "No. Who was he? What did he want?"

Chas drew a short breath, then told his son the raw truth. "He's a stalker, Billy. He's been after Allison for months. I hope you don't think—"

"Did she leave, Dad?"

"She's on her way back to Almost."

"You better go after her. I'll be cool here. I got TV, and nobody's gonna bug me in the hospital."

Maybe Allison hadn't been lying after all, he thought; this was one terrific kid. And he *would,* even knowing the terrible truths, do it all over again just to have him.

"I'll be back as soon as I can," Chas said, dragging his son up for another bear hug. "I'm gonna ask Pete to stay here with you."

"Cool."

Chas headed for the door, but his son's "Hey, Dad!" stopped him at the threshold. "You better wash that blood off your forehead. It's like you always told me, ladies don't like grungy guys."

Chapter 13

All but flying down the farm-to-market road leading to Almost, pushing Pete's Cherokee to its limits, Chas could only think of one thing: getting to Allison in time.

He realized his main thrust wasn't to rescue her or protect her; it was to *stop* her from leaving Almost.

He growled in frustration as he saw the clock on the dashboard. She didn't have that great a lead on him, but he knew how Carolyn drove, as fast and surely as a race-car driver.

He was hunched over the steering wheel like a crazed man, as if his leaning forward could actually propel the Jeep to greater speed. He glanced around the interior, as if seeking an elusive power booster, something, *anything,* to allow him to catch up with her, and his eyes fell on Pete's cellular phone tucked between the front seats.

A slow smile creased his aching face.

He'd tried telling Allison that she didn't have to go

through anything alone. And he'd been trying to accomplish his goals by doing the same thing.

He picked up the phone and tapped in Sammie Jo's number. "You remember that promise you forced from me, about making sure Allison stayed in Almost? I'm going to need your help on that, Sammie Jo."

And he swiftly outlined what he needed her to do for him.

"And I think you've only got about fifteen minutes," he warned.

Sammie Jo assured him that fifteen minutes was a lifetime in Almost.

No matter what arguments she'd used, Allison had been unable to dissuade Carolyn from accompanying her into Taylor's house. She'd begun with the nearly surefire "I'm fine, thanks. See ya."

Carolyn had chuckled a little, but gotten out of the car.

She'd tried reminding Carolyn that her daughters and the triplets must be worried.

Carolyn had picked up the telephone and called Aunt Sammie Jo.

"They're watching a movie," she said when she hung up. "And they asked me to remind you to watch the video they shot for their documentary on Almost."

She pulled a videotape from her large handbag and plugged it into the VCR and clicked the television onto the right channel. On-screen came the most atrocious footage Allison had ever seen. It was jerky, dizzying in its wild angles and inexperienced photography.

"Oh, look, there's Cactus kissing Aunt Sammie Jo," Carolyn murmured. "Why, those boys. Look at the theme. It's a whole tape of people kissing. Taylor and Steve in the background. Pete."

Allison stood, mesmerized by the strangely alluring video. Then she saw herself and Chas on Taylor's back porch. He was drawing her into his arms, a slow smile fading from his face. She remembered the way his hands had slipped into her hair, tilting her head upward for his kiss.

She remembered how frightened she'd been that day. How conflicted.

Now, with her memories largely intact, and the past laid open to him—to herself—she felt like such a different woman from the one on the video. She wasn't the frightened girl anymore, nor was she the hard-bitten, love-blocked reporter. She was something else entirely.

Watching herself kissing Chas on-screen, feeling those warm, soft lips even now, she understood what she was. She was a woman in love.

And she resolutely turned from the television. She was also a woman who wasn't going to stick around to bring more danger to those she loved. Not to Billy, not to the triplets. Not to Chas.

"Who's that?" Carolyn asked.

Allison glanced back over her shoulder at the screen and froze in place. "That's him!"

"Who?"

"Dorchester or whoever he is."

Her heart scudded painfully in her chest, as if trying to burst free. The boys had been wanting her to look at this footage for days. If only she had. Maybe Billy wouldn't have been hurt, maybe Chas's forehead wouldn't have been slashed by a flaying hoof.

"That's the man that hypnotized me. Oh, dear God, he *kidnapped* me." A flood of memories far more dizzying than the video washed through her mind.

"But I don't understand. How could the boys have caught him on tape when no one else ever saw him?"

As the camera panned jerkily, Allison pointed at the screen. "That's why. He's been with the field hands. Just one of them. No one ever even notices the farmworkers. I told him that. When I was under. I told him *everything*."

A sick dread rippled through her. All her secrets, all her hopes, he'd stolen them all from her, giving nothing in return but the cessation of her addiction to cigarettes. Not quite a fair trade-off, she thought with a wry, dark bid at humor.

She tried one last, desperate ploy for Carolyn's departure. She didn't want the argument she knew her sister-in-law would give her. She didn't have time for it, not if she was going to be able to lure this Dorchester away from Almost.

"I left some things at Chas's house. Would you get them for me? Oh, and the animals will need feeding."

"Homer Chalmers is doing that," Carolyn said blandly, removing her coat and turning up the heat in the house. "And we can get your things later. Or Doc can bring them over."

"What about Pete?"

"What about him? He's at the hospital with Chas and Billy." This last earned her a sideways glance.

She gave up. "I'm leaving, Carolyn. I have to."

"Okay," Carolyn said. "Running's good."

"What?"

"It's action of a sort. Not the best kind, maybe, but whatever works for you."

"What are you saying?" Allison asked.

"Me? Nothing. I'm only agreeing with you."

"I can't let anyone else get hurt because of me."

"What about Doc?"

"I'm talking about real physical danger."

"And a heartache that's lasted fifteen years isn't physical danger?" Carolyn asked calmly.

"You don't understand." Even as the words slipped from her mouth, she felt they were childish. Petulant.

"You're wrong, Allison. I do. A couple of years ago, a couple of local thugs tried running me off the ranch so they could use the place as a drug-storage facility. They threatened us, they chased us. They tried to kill us."

"You had Pete."

"I *found* Pete then. But not by running. By staying and fighting for what was mine, what I wanted. What I loved. I even had to fight Pete to stay."

"But I don't even know who I'm really fighting," Allison explained. "And the longer I stay here, the more the people I love are in danger."

Carolyn walked up and grasped Allison by the shoulders. She looked down in the younger woman's eyes, meeting them squarely. "Then let the people who love *you* help you. Running isn't the answer, Allison. It never is in the long haul."

"You don't know the whole story."

"Yes, I do," Carolyn countered as calmly as ever. "Sammie Jo told me a long time ago."

"No, she never knew—"

"That you were pregnant and lost the baby when Susie was killed in the car wreck. She knew. Everybody knew, Allison. This whole town is family of some kind. Everybody knows. Except Doc, maybe. I don't think anyone would have wanted to hurt him because everybody knew he was doing a kindness for Thelma and Billy. But everybody's heart bled for you. Every one of them would have laid down his or her life to make things all right for you."

"But—"

"And still would. Doc most of all."

The telephone rang, making Allison start, but Carolyn only turned loose of her to pick up the receiver from the end table. After her initial hello, she was silent for several seconds, then said, "I think that's a good idea.... No, but I will.... All set, then." She replaced the receiver.

"What's all set?"

"That was Sammie Jo. We're all going over to Doc's."

"What? Why?"

"Homer called her a few minutes ago, and it seems the shepherd cross that Doc's been tending has been raising quite a fuss."

Fear clutched at Allison's chest. "And...?"

"And he can't get in the front door of the clinic. So everyone's going there."

"But—"

"Oh, Allison, stop your fussing. You're worse than Alva Lu Harrigan. Are you going to wear that shirt? The only reason I ask is that most of the town's likely to show up there."

Knowing now exactly how Alice had felt at the Mad Hatter's tea party, Allison looked down only to discover she was wearing one of Chas's shirts. Inside out.

The man known as Quentin expected the entire town to be buzzing with the day's mishap. He anticipated every phone in Almost to be working overtime. He even laid a small bet with himself that Allison would be surrounded by several of the relatives who so betrayed her fifteen years ago, or more likely, the country stud.

But never in his wildest imagination had he so much as considered that the townspeople would turn out as if Allison's troubles were the next county fair. She'd never told him that. She'd blocked that from him. How?

And then he knew. She hadn't known it herself.

From his hiding place inside good old Doc's closet, he'd been all set to grab the pair of them and force Allison to remember him while the country stud watched. He even smiled a little now, remembering the plan.

His smile slipped. It hadn't been Allison and her stud who entered the house. It was some old biddy with a casserole dish. Followed by some old man with a cane and a cowboy hat big enough to fit on one of his cows. Some younger people had followed them, each of the women carrying a dish of some kind.

The old farmer he'd been blistering his hands for wrestled a large cooler in through the door and called out, "Sodas are here!"

Children filed in, teenagers, young adults, middle-aged couples who oohed and aahed at the sight of a Christmas tree in Doc's living room.

One of the party-goers started the stereo playing after some discussion about Doc being such a softy as to have kept all those old albums all these years. And soon Christmas music wrapped the conversation in bizarre novelty.

From his crack behind the closet door, he watched as several of the smaller children lay flat on the floor drawing pictures they carefully folded into imperfect squares only to place them beneath the softly glowing tree.

Nothing made sense. And fear warred with his rage. This wasn't right. Nothing about it was right. It wasn't just that Christmas music was playing in the waning hours of the February evening, nor that townspeople were arriving at house when the host was noticeably absent. They were all accepting of it. As if it were *normal*.

He wanted to scream out at them to look around, to listen. *You're all insane,* he wanted to yell from the safety of the closet.

And still the people arrived. Laughing, talking, arguing, looking happy or disgruntled, but none of them appearing confused. Some liked the tree; others didn't. Some remembered Allison, while others had to be reminded of who she was, what she had been. One wore a Santa Claus hat, yet another was dressed all in funereal black.

He'd spent every waking hour of his life trying to understand people. He'd believed he knew how they worked, how they ticked. He knew what buttons to push to get them to speak, what triggers to use to make them stop.

But this strangely homey scene was frightening on a deep, profoundly disturbing level. Not one of these people pouring into the house seemed to find the situation at all odd or unique.

With all of them there, however, he would have to wait. He quietly pushed his way back to the recess of the closet filled with empty suitcases, fishing boots and a couple of doggy toys that he discovered squeaked when touched. Luckily the music and conversation were so loud that no one else noticed.

Except one little girl of about four who ran for his hiding place on chubby little legs.

Unerringly she went for the closet. He held the doorknob securely as she stretched up on tiptoe to tug at it. When she finally toddled away, bored with the open door that wouldn't open farther, he heaved a shaky sigh of relief and settled back among the dirt and clutter of the country stud's closet.

He wished he had thought to carry a mirror in the nylon bag of tricks. He always felt better when he could see himself. He felt stronger. More in control. And he knew if he could look into his reflection's cold eyes, these tears rolling down his cheeks would miraculously dry.

Chas arrived at his home and ended up having to leave Pete's Cherokee out in the street since his entire long driveway was filled with cars. Lights blazed from every room of his house and he could hear the warm sounds of laughter and Christmas music wafting out into the cold dusk.

He hurried to the house, his heart nearly bursting with the affection he felt for these people who had all poured out on this Sunday February afternoon to help him help Allison.

He walked through his front door into a veritable warm ocean of love.

"Is Allison here?" he asked the first person he saw, which happened to be Alva Lu Harrigan, dressed more as though going to a funeral than a rescue.

"That girl was always late to everything. And into mischief? Sammie Jo tells me she's in some kind of trouble again. There, what did I tell you?"

She wandered away from him, her attention snared by a child trying to reach one of the tree's decoration. "Now, you! Stop that, you hear me?"

Chas smiled at her retreating form. A crabby mother hen, clucking every step of the way, she'd nonetheless undoubtedly been one of the first to arrive to help Allison.

"How's Billy, Doc?"

"Terrible thing about your boy, Doc."

"This what you had in mind, Charles?" Sammie Jo asked, laying her frail hand on his elbow.

He grinned down at her. "This is exactly what I wanted."

"Carolyn's bringing her over from Taylor's."

"Any sign of the stranger?"

"Charlie Hampton said one of his field hands saw a city-slicker type running across one of the fields."

"Is Charlie here?"

"He is that, but you're not going to talk to him until you come in the kitchen and let me see to that cut on your forehead."

Chas chuckled. "Billy said it looked grungy."

Sammie Jo led him to the kitchen, shooed someone off a chair, and made Chas sit in it. "Can't reach you way up there. Lucky for you Allison's no shrimp like her old aunt."

Chas didn't say anything to that. He closed his eyes as Sammie Jo washed the dried blood from his brow and tried not to think of Allison's reach, Allison's anything. Naturally that was all he *could* think about.

"Hey there, Homer. Tell Charles about that stranger Charlie Hampton's field hand saw. You were out there this morning."

Homer, nearly eighty years old, chuckled and coughed. "This fella name of Quentin dropped round this morning to try talking Charlie into planting Jerusalem artichokes— don't that beat all? Whaddya do with 'em, I asked him, he said they put 'em on salads. That's all. Just salad. I told him—"

"Homer! Tell Charles about the stranger he saw."

"Oh, right. Anyways, this Quentin fella says he spied a city boy with blond hair and glasses a-running across the back forty of Charlie's place earlier today. Reckon it was about the time your son was being laid flat by Charlie's horse. The boy okay?"

"He's fine," Chas said, frowning over the information Homer had given him. Billy had said the man's hair was black. Allison had remembered it being *both* black and

blond. Black when he didn't wear glasses, blond when he
did.

"Quit frowning, Charles. You're making my job more
difficult." He winced as she dabbed at the cut. "You
shoulda had them take a couple of stitches when you
were—"

A sudden swell in the noise emanating from the living
room was immediately followed by a quick roar, nearly a
cheer.

"Allison's here!"

Allison was certain every square inch of Chas's home
was holding a human body. Palpable love stretched out to
greet her, and hands reached for hers, for her hair, her
shoulders. The triplets wrapped themselves around her
waist.

"Did you see the video?"

"We're here to help you catch the bad guy!"

"I wish Steve Kessler, Texas Ranger, was here!"

Christmas music blared from the stereo, an entire chorus
singing "Oh, Little Town of Bethlehem."

Tears stung Allison's eyes, and she blinked rapidly to
drive them away.

Nearly as one, the crowd looked from her toward the
kitchen.

Chas stood in the doorway, filling it.

She didn't know what to say to him. This entire congre-
gation had to be his doing. To protect her. To surround her
in his world of love.

She loved him. She knew this with the clear certainty of
the sun rising or setting, with the complete surety that a
moon and stars appeared on cloudless nights.

But was love enough to bridge the past? Even his son
had been affected by it, hurt by it. And although she'd

finally released the pent-up emotions clinging to those terrible days in the past, nothing could change what really happened. She was permanently, physically scarred by it. Didn't Chas deserve more than that? Didn't he deserve a child of his own loins? He who loved so deeply and so easily, didn't he deserve everything?

She didn't know what showed on her face, but she was left in no doubt of what he was feeling. His love for her blazed from his warm, warm brown eyes. And a stark vulnerability held him still, while a muscle jumped and spasmed in his tight jaw.

Carolyn pushed past her with the boys' video in her hand. She crossed to Chas's VCR and popped in the tape. "Come look at this, everybody," she said. "This is the man who hurt Billy, who's been stalking our Allison."

Allison was struck by the nearly eerie contrast of the chorale singing "Deck the Halls," while Almost townspeople crowded in to view a stalker that had been among them.

"Why, that's young Quentin," Charlie Hampton burst out. "He's been working my soil. He can't be the one. He saw a man running..." he trailed off. "Lied to me. Flatout lied."

"Anyone else see him around?" Carolyn asked.

Several heads nodded. Now that they thought about it in context of his being a field hand, sure, they'd seen him.

Sammie Jo had sold him a loaf of bread and a hunk of cheese just yesterday.

Martha Jo had served him coffee at the Almost Café, he and the other field hands.

Jackson Bean had seen him driving that old red pickup truck.

Delbert Franklin hadn't worn his hearing aids and asked what everybody was talking about.

Charlie Hampton said, "I let him stay in the hired hand's trailer, the one on the back forty."

As one, all eyes turned to Chas. This was his "lady" who'd been harmed by the man, his son who had been hurt by him. It was up to him to make all the decisions regarding the man's capture.

He nodded slowly, and no one there had any doubts that he was aching to go with the four men silently donning their coats to go check out the trailer. But when he looked over at Allison, they all understood why he wasn't leaving with them.

He was sticking right by her side. Every minute, until the stalker was all sewed up tight.

Someone helped Allison remove her coat, a task slightly hampered by the folded shirt she held so tightly in her hand.

The front door opened, and the four men filed out, faces grim, expressions varying from anger to determination.

"You be careful out there, Dallan," Mickey Peterson called out, and her admonition was echoed by other wives.

The last of the men out the door gave a whoop, and the front door slammed open as something huge charged the room. Several shrieks punctuated the lunge, and Allison automatically ducked, but not soon enough.

Hit squarely in the back, she was shoved face-first into the crowd of family and friends by the full weight of an assailant. An assailant who began frantically licking her face, whining desperately at her.

The crowd started laughing and scolding and pulled the happy dog from Allison and helped her to her feet.

"Looks like you've got yourself a dog, Allison," Jackson Bean said.

Allison shook her head.

"What's her name, Aunt Allison?"

"Yeah, whaddya gonna call her?"

"I'd call her 'Leaper,' because she sure can jump."

Allison looked down at the dog standing at her side, gazing up at her with utter adoration. Her tail was whipping Alva Lu Harrigan's leg, much to that lady's disgust.

"So you think you're mine, do you?"

The dog chuffed and grinned up at her.

Allison sighed, not having the foggiest notion how she felt. Was it possible to have too much love?

"Well, then, the boys are right. You'd best have a name."

The dog's tail wagged more furiously, and she wriggled a little.

Just looking at the dog, Allison felt immeasurably connected. The way she felt in Chas's arms, when gazing into his eyes. Maybe, just maybe love had a chance.

"Chance," she said aloud. "Will that do?" she asked, knowing that she'd seize any chance now. She glanced over at Chas and saw that, in his wholly empathetic way, he'd discerned part of her reasons for the unusual name. His eyes seemed to blaze even brighter.

"You'd better come with me, then, Chance, because I have to put this away," she said, waving the shirt in the general direction of Chas's bedroom.

As if on her wavelength completely, the dog jumped forward, happily leading the way through the opening people were allowing them, her tail beating against knees and, in the case of the smaller children, giggling faces.

Chance raced around the bedroom sniffing at everything as Allison deposited the shirt on Chas's dresser. She was relieved to be alone for a second. She stared at herself in the mirror, assessing the flushed glowing face of her reflection.

She looked as she was, a woman in the deepest of loves. Behind her, near the closet, Chance suddenly let out a shrill bark, followed by another and another. In a volley of frantic growls and barking, the dog lunged at the closet door.

Even as Allison turned to see what the trouble was, Dorchester burst from the closet, kicking viciously at the dog, sending Chance sprawling beneath the high bed.

Before she could draw breath to scream, he'd leaped across the room and grabbed her in a half nelson, cruelly dragging her against him, backing away from the opened door leading to the hallway still crowded with people.

"Chas!" one of the triplets yelled.

A woman screamed. A baby began to cry. The Boston Pops played "Jingle Bells."

"Remember me now, Allison?"

She couldn't talk, could scarcely breathe. His forearm pressed against her throat, cutting off her windpipe. She gagged a little at the pain, at the pressure.

Chas burst into the room and teetered over the threshold as he took in Allison's predicament.

"Stay back, stud!"

Chas held his hands before him in a conciliatory openness.

"What is it?" Delbert Franklin asked. "Won't somebody tell me what's going on?"

Homer Chalmers pushed Chas on into the room and stepped inside himself. Allison felt his ancient eyes swiftly assess the situation. "You don't wanna hurt that little gal, boy," he said.

"You stay back, Grandpa," Dorchester said. Perhaps as a warning, he wrestled Allison roughly, making Chas jerk as if it were his body pinned and not hers.

Homer didn't move. "You ain't my kin, so you got no business calling me Grandpa."

Amazingly the man holding her chuckled a little. "Now, there's a really scary threat."

"Is it the stalker?" Allison heard Alva Lu ask someone. "What's he doing to her?"

"Quick, Martha Jo, Johnny's gun is the glove compartment of the pickup."

"Is he crazy or what?"

The man holding her jerked her back against him. "Are you people *insane?*" he screamed. "It's not Christmas! And Allison doesn't belong to you! She belongs to *me!*"

His voice stretched so hard and tight with his roar that it screeched on his final note. He wrenched her around so that he could see her in the mirror. See himself, Allison realized.

It wasn't until that moment that she knew that he had a knife blade pressing against her temple. Everything had hurt, all had been frightening, but until then she'd thought her greatest danger lay in his arm squeezing the breath from her. She gave a small whimper.

From her angle, she could see Chas clearly reflected in the mirror, saw every nuance of his anger, his fear for her. And she saw Homer Chalmers calmly reaching behind him for something someone was handing him from the hallway.

"Let her go," Chas said. "You can't possibly get away with hurting her. There's too many people here. You can't kill us all. One of us...me...will stop you."

"Shut up!" Dorchester snapped. His eyes darted from Chas to Allison to his own tortured gaze. But amazingly, as he met his own reflection's wild eyes, he seemed to steady, to calm down. He drew a deep breath, then another.

While he was doing this, Homer quickly yanked his hand back behind him, and Chas took two gliding steps farther into the room.

Dorchester's eyes shot to Chas. "Stop right there, stud.

You're never going to touch her again. I'll make sure of that. I know what you did to her in the past. I know. She told me. She never told you, but she told me.''

''She told me everything,'' Chas said.

A flicker of doubt crossed Dorchester's face, but he hid it immediately. ''She didn't,'' he stated firmly. ''You see, stud, I know her innermost thoughts. Everything she wants.''

''I know she doesn't want what you're doing now,'' Chas said. His voice was far calmer than his face.

''She will. Allison. Are you listening, Allison?''

She tried to nod, unable to vocalize.

Sickening her, he continued to hold her against him while playing with her hair. She heard Chas utter a choked groan.

''Then I want you to sleep, Allison. Sleep for me now, Allison.''

''No!'' Chas yelled, and started to lunge.

Dorchester raised his knife arm menacingly, pressing the point of the knife painfully against her temple. A thin trickle of blood snaked down her cheek. ''One more move, stud, and she'll be asleep forever.''

Allison felt a flicker of hope. When Dorchester had been exhorting her to sleep, she had felt a curious tingle in her arms and realized that she was susceptible to a posthypnotic suggestion. He could make her go into a trance. Right here, in the midst of danger, he could make her fall asleep.

But only if she allowed him to do so. When he'd so thoroughly abused her mind before, she hadn't known what was happening to her, had no tools to fight him with. Now she did. She knew what he was, and she understood everything about herself and the loving people behind her.

''Allison,'' he said commandingly. Compellingly. ''Test case.''

Her arms tingled and her vision wavered. A phrase. He'd used a specific phrase. That's what she'd been, his test case. His experiment. The tingling sensation passed, and Allison realized that she had won her battle against his will.

She closed her eyes anyway, hating the sound of Chas's agonized moan.

"You hurt her, you bastard, and I swear I will tear you from limb to limb all by myself," Chas growled, then he called her name aloud.

It took every ounce of will she had not to respond to the despair in his voice.

"Raise your hand, Allison."

She did so, hoping he wouldn't notice how badly it was shaking.

"Very good. You can lower it now."

She did this, as well, balling her hands into fists, waiting for an opportunity.

"Now, tell this country stud what you really think of him. Tell him all about the past." He loosened his grip around her neck, rocked her forward. "Open your eyes, Allison. Look at him when you tell him how you really feel."

She opened her eyes and found Chas's tortured gaze. Trying to mask any expression on her face, she spoke directly to this man she loved beyond reason or thought, and beyond anything in the dark past.

"I love you, Chas. I always have. I always will."

Dorchester was so stunned by her statement that he rocked back slightly, but just far enough away from her that she could now use her arms to flail at him. She slammed her fisted hand into his groin and felt a flash fire of dark satisfaction as he let loose an explosive cry and released her.

She whirled away from him even as Chas lunged and

Homer Chalmers grabbed her and pushed her back behind him. And Chance, that brave and wonderful dog, joined the fray.

The fight was mercifully brief. Chas outweighed the madman by some forty pounds and had anger, fear and adrenaline spurring him onward. Dorchester went down like a bag of cotton seed. And went out like a light at one solid punch from the man who could lift a three-hundred-pound heifer from the back of a trailer.

''What did he think?'' Homer asked the room at large, ''That we was just going stand around and let him kill our Allison?''

Chapter 14

Allison stifled a yawn and then chuckled.

"What?" Carolyn asked from her position on the sofa, nestled in Pete's embrace.

"I was picturing the write-up Alva Lu will put in the Almost Historical Society notes. 'The February Christmas party ran very late at the home of the local veterinarian, Dr. Charles Jamison.'"

The last of the guests, mostly family, grinned tiredly.

"Where's Doc?" Carolyn asked.

"He's in with Billy," Allison said. She turned to Cactus Jack and Sammie Jo. "That was really great of you to go fetch him."

"It was a wonder the hospital let him out," Sammie Jo said.

"You didn't give them a whole lot of choice, honey," Cactus explained. "She threatened to beat the whole lot of them with her wig if they didn't turn him over to her."

"I guess I still don't get what that guy was after," Jason

said. "I mean, he just wanted to *know* stuff about you, Aunt Allison?"

She shrugged. By the time the state troopers had come to take Dorchester away, he'd only rambled on about his great love for her and how she'd betrayed him. "I don't know," she said. "He was crazy, honey."

"Like a bedbug," Sammie Jo said, patting her husband's leg.

"Think I'll get me another piece of pie," Cactus said, pushing to his feet.

"I'll join you," Pete said, doing the same.

And within seconds, everyone in the room had moved to the kitchen, leaving Allison alone in the glow of the fire and the Christmas tree. She heard them laugh, her family, and smiled, at peace with the world for the first time in fifteen years.

She smoothed out the letter she still held in her lap, the letter Sammie Jo had given her after the troopers had hauled Dorchester away.

"I want you to read this, honey. It's your letter, but I didn't know if I was ever going to get an opportunity to give it to you. Your daddy wrote it and gave it to me, telling me I was only supposed to hand deliver it to you, so if you had any questions you could ask me about 'em. It's yours now," Sammie Jo had said.

Allison had had to stop twice in the act of unfolding the single sheet of paper, her hands had been shaking so badly.

My little Allison, I know you are thinking some pretty harsh things about me, about all of us most likely. But some of those things aren't true and you've got to hear those things right from me. First of all, I never did blame you for what happened in the car that day. I was so damned upset about Susie and so scared for you, the words just came out all wrong. And I was so guilty about being glad it wasn't you down in that morgue. You've got a lot of me in you, Allison. Good stuff, I hope, but some of my stubbornness, too. You don't have to always look for the bad side of things, honey. Everything comes with two sides. You can look for the good just as well. And there's a lot of good things out there. I just want you to know that I love you and I always have. And I'm as proud of you as a parent could ever be. You'll come back home someday and you'll read this letter, and you'll know that in my heart, you were never gone.

                                                        Love, Daddy.

She raised the letter to her lips, tears falling softly. "I love you, too, Daddy," she whispered. "I always did."

Some slight sound made her lift her head to find Chas standing just inside the room, his face hidden by shadows.

"Are you okay?" he asked, not stepping forward.

She nodded. "I'm fine now."

He didn't answer. She saw him make a rather convulsive movement with his hands.

"Did you mean what you said in there, Allison? When he was hypnotizing you?"

"He didn't hypnotize me," she said. "I blocked it."

"I know that," he said roughly. "Did you mean it, though?"

It was too soon to talk about this, she thought, and then realized how close it had been to always being too late. Most of her life she'd spent ducking love, ducking the joys and pains that came with it, and all because she hadn't spoken so long ago, hadn't said what was on her mind when Chas had laid out his enthusiastic forecast for their future together. The letter from her father crumpled in her hand.

"Yes, Chas, I meant it. Every word."

He slowly walked forward, until he towered above her just inches away from her. Then he slowly lowered to one knee and drew her suddenly trembling hand into both of his.

"Allison Leary, will you please, please marry me and be my dearest love for the rest of my life?"

And she understood so very clearly at that precise moment that the past, any doubts she'd had before, could not be allowed to have any weight when balanced with the sheen of moisture in his eyes, the depth of his love for her.

"Oh yes, Chas. Nothing on earth would make me happier."

Chance the dog sat up and chuffed her approval.

And before she was drawn into Chas's loving arms, Allison caught a glimpse of her family all gathered in the kitchen doorway smiling at the two of them.

She knew then there was no such as thing as too much love.

Epilogue

Two years later...

Allison rested her cheek against Chas's bare chest and ran her hands along the muscled planes of his warm body. She smiled when she felt him absently petting her hair much as he might have done to Chance had the faithful dog not been outside guarding the clinic.

The glow of the lights from the Christmas tree turned his long legs to rich roseate color.

His heartbeat was still a little fast, belying his casual caresses, and her smile broadened. She knew from her reading, from hearing friends talk, that intimacy between married couples generally ebbed after the so-called honeymoon period. Not with her and Chas. If anything, it grew deeper, richer and infinitely more rewarding with each encounter. She wondered if it had to do with the lost years, that perhaps each of them had a burning need to smooth away the time they had missed.

She wasn't surprised when his stroking stilled; his uncanny knack for reading her every thought even stronger than it was back in the days of her youth or when she'd returned home after all that time gone.

"Allison?"

"Hmm?"

"Do you have any regrets?"

Her smile faded abruptly. "No," she said. The single word was definitive. Everything in her life, good and bad, had led her to this moment with Chas, to his strong and good love, to her total acceptance of that miracle. But he probably knew she was lying. There was one regret.

"I love you," he murmured, pressing his lips to her crown. "I always have. I always will."

In that mysterious way they shared, she knew he wanted to say more, had something that needed telling, so she hugged him back but waited for him to disclose whatever it might be.

"It's quiet around here now that Billy's off to college."

She thought about the gangly boy who had seemingly overnight transformed into the tall young man majoring in biology in preparation for medical school. Not Chas's by blood, but by every stamp of his innate character. And now her own in addition.

Like Chas, she missed the boy with an ache as much physical as emotional. "He'll be home at Easter." As always, the simple use of the word 'home' struck her forcibly, making her hold Chas a little tighter.

At first, in those early days of marriage, he'd worried that she'd become bored with her new 'simpler' life. But he'd finally come to accept that she'd never been happier in her life. And she knew the same was true of him.

Except for today, when something was clearly bothering him.

"Sammie Jo was saying the other day that with the triplets growing up and Carolyn's Shawna and Jenny turning into young ladies right before her eyes…that she was going to miss having little ones around."

Allison stiffened. This was the subject she and Chas never really talked about. The regret. She'd told him about the baby, of course, on a tearful night long ago. And he'd fought back his own tears as he'd held her, then made love to her as if trying to erase the memory, a memory not even her nightmare with Dorchester had eliminated.

She tried pulling out of Chas's embrace, but he held her fast against his warm body.

"Don't go," he said.

"Chas—"

"I know. We've always known that we can't have any more children together."

Despite the pain the topic brought, she had the fleeting thought that she loved him all the more for the casual way he'd said *we* can't have any more children, when it certainly wasn't true—he could.

She couldn't relax in his arms now. She felt something akin to one of the panic attacks that had seized her so painfully two years ago. And he didn't let her escape and run now, just as he hadn't then.

"But that doesn't mean we can't raise a child together."

The whole world seemed to still. All she could hear was a roaring in her ears and the thundering of his heartbeat against her cheek. And felt the hope. A staggering, terrifying hope.

"We did a pretty fine job with Billy."

"You did," she managed to croak out.

"And who was it who coached him through his finals? Who talked him into trying out for that play? Who helped him with his tux for the senior prom? Who listened to his girlfriend troubles and saved the day?''

Allison's eyes filled with tears, though she couldn't have said what the tears represented.

"I want us to adopt a baby, Allison. I'll understand if you don't want to rush into it right away, but I'd like us to talk about it.''

When she pulled away from him this time, he let her go. She rose and brushed her now moderately long hair back from her face. She couldn't think what to say to him. Couldn't think how to say anything. He deserved his own child. He'd sacrificed everything to raise Billy, his happiness, his life with her. And had never once wished otherwise.

"Allison?''

In the single, agonized vocalization of her name, she heard his deep longing, his love for her, his acknowledgment of her pain and doubts. And his understanding.

"Yes,'' she said.

He didn't speak then, and she knew that he was trying to assimilate her answer.

"I'm saying yes.''

Still he was silent and finally, having blinked back most of the tears, she turned to him and lifted her hands to cup his dear face. "I love you, Chas. Like you, I always have and I *always* will.''

"Allison—''

"Shhh,'' she whispered, angling her little finger over to press gently against his lips. "You are the best father I've ever seen. And I would love to raise a child with you.'' She couldn't hold back the tears now, the emotions were too strong for any semblance of control. She loved him so much.

"Are you sure?" he asked.

"As sure as I am of our love," she answered brokenly.

He wiped the tears from her face, not bothering to hide the sheen in his own eyes as he met her gaze gravely. "Then I can tell Sammie Jo her scheme worked?"

Allison gave a watery chuckle. "Her schemes almost always do."

He grinned crookedly and pulled her close for a long, lingering kiss that once and for all put all debts and wrongs from the past firmly to rest.

"What can you expect when they come from a town named Almost?" he asked.

"Everything," she answered, kissing him back fully, loving the way his hands lowered to run over the swell of her breasts, loving *him*.

"Everything it is then," he murmured, pulling her atop him, sliding his hands down her back, massaging her, nuzzling her, enticing her to renewed passion.

"Half the town must be talking about it already then," she said, digging her fingers into his hair and gasping a little as she rose to sheath him with her own silken heat.

"Oh, they're already planning the christening party," he said before capturing a taut nipple and plying it with his tongue.

Allison inhaled sharply, arching back even as she leaned into him. "I suppose they've already picked out the name."

"Sure," he said, pausing only long enough to draw her down upon him, groaning as he slid deeply within her. With a visible effort, he continued, "They're calling it 'Doc-and-Allison's-youngun.' All one word."

Allison chuckled and cradled him to her breasts, relishing his strong hands on her back, then forgetting what made her chuckle as he drove slowly and steadily into her. And soon, she couldn't remember anything at all except her overwhelming love for the man who had been her husband now for two blissful years.

Much later, once again nestled in his arms, the Christmas tree lights again sending a glow over their sated bodies, Allison chuckled. ''I guess we'll have to explain to our son or daughter why we set up the Christmas tree in February.''

''Why? Doesn't everyone?''

* * * * *

Don't miss MARRIED BY DAWN,
the next wonderful story by Marilyn Tracy.
Look for this memorable romance in
Silhouette Intimate Moments's
special two-in-one collection,
BRIDES OF THE NIGHT,
IM883, available in October 1998.

Follow That Baby!

Don't miss Silhouette's newest cross-line promotion

Five stellar authors, five evocative stories, five fabulous Silhouette series— pregnant mom on the run!

October 1998: THE RANCHER AND
THE AMNESIAC BRIDE
by top-notch talent **Joan Elliott Pickart**
(Special Edition)

November 1998: THE DADDY AND
THE BABY DOCTOR
by Romance favorite **Kristin Morgan** (Romance)

December 1998: THE SHERIFF AND
THE IMPOSTOR BRIDE
by award-winning author **Elizabeth Bevarly** (Desire)

January 1999: THE MILLIONAIRE AND
THE PREGNANT PAUPER
by rising star **Christie Ridgway** (Yours Truly)

February 1999: THE MERCENARY AND
THE NEW MOM by *USA Today* bestselling author
Merline Lovelace (Intimate Moments)

Only in—

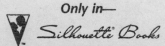
Silhouette Books

Available at your favorite retail outlet.

The World's Most Eligible Bachelors are about to be named! And Silhouette Books brings them to you in an all-new, original series....

World's Most Eligible Bachelors

Twelve of the sexiest, most sought-after men share every intimate detail of their lives in twelve never-before-published novels by the genre's top authors.

Don't miss these unforgettable stories by:

Dixie Browning

Marie Ferrarella

Jackie Merritt

Tracy Sinclair

BJ James

Rachel Lee   Suzanne Carey

Gina Wilkins

VICTORIA PADE

Susan Mallery   **MAGGIE SHAYNE**   *Anne McAllister*

Look for one new book each month in the
World's Most Eligible Bachelors series beginning
September 1998 from Silhouette Books.

Silhouette ®

Available at your favorite retail outlet.

SILHOUETTE·INTIMATE·MOMENTS®
commemorates its

15 years of rugged, irresistible heroes!

15 years of warm, wonderful heroines!

15 years of exciting, emotion-filled romance!

In May, June and July 1998 join the celebration as Intimate Moments brings you new stories from some of your favorite authors—authors like:

Marie Ferrarella
Maggie Shayne
Sharon Sala
Beverly Barton
Rachel Lee
Merline Lovelace
and many more!

Don't miss this special event! Look for our distinctive anniversary covers during all three celebration months. Only from Silhouette Intimate Moments, committed to bringing you the best in romance fiction, today, tomorrow—always.

Available at your favorite retail outlet.

INTIMATE MOMENTS®
™ *Silhouette*®